THE W

Harvill *Secker*

LONDON

1 3 5 7 9 10 8 6 4 2

Harvill Secker, an imprint of Vintage,
20 Vauxhall Bridge Road,
London SW1V 2SA

Harvill Secker is part of the Penguin Random House group of companies
whose addresses can be found at global.penguinrandomhouse.com

 Penguin
Random House
UK

First published by Viking, USA in 2018

A CIP catalogue record for this book is available from the British Library

penguin.co.uk/vintage

ISBN 9781787301191 (hardback)
ISBN 9781787301207 (trade paperback)

Printed and bound in Great Britain by Clays Ltd, Elcograf S.p.A.

Penguin Random House is committed to a sustainable future for our
business, our readers and our planet. This book is made from Forest
Stewardship Council® certified paper.

MIX
Paper from
responsible sources
FSC
www.fsc.org   FSC® C018179

For Selina, Izzy, Megan, and Marissa

ONE

Last night Rebekah tried to murder me again. It had been a while since I'd had that dream, not since we left Asherley, a place I called home for one winter and the bitterest part of spring, the dream only ever recurring when Max was gone and I'd find myself alone with Dani.

As always, the dream begins with Asherley in the distance, shining from afar in a bright clearing. There is no greenhouse, nor boathouse, just a stand of red canoes stabbed into the pebbly beach. In fact, the Asherley of my dream looks more like it might have back in its whaling days, when from the highest turret you could still spot tall ships dotting Gardiners Bay.

Overpowered by the urge to be inside the house again, I pass easily through the thicket of forest that surrounds the property. I want so badly to wander its wood-paneled halls, to feel its plush red carpets beneath my bare feet, to move my fingers in the play of sun through the stained-glass windows, but an invisible force keeps me out. I'm relegated to the bay, where I float like a sad specter, made to watch those who still haunt Asherley act out the same strange pantomime.

I can see Max, my Max, relaxing on an Adirondack, one in a line like white teeth dotting the silvery-green lawn. He's reading a newspaper, framed by the majestic spread of Asherley behind him, its walls of gray stones, its crowd of terra-cotta peaks, its dentils studded with carved rosettes, anchored by the heavy brow of its deep stone porch. Every lamp in every room of the house is lit. A fire roars in every fireplace. The circle of windows at the top of the high turret burns like a sentinel over the bay, as though the house were about to put on a great show for me.

I call for Max but he can't hear me. I want to go to him, to touch his face, to smell his hair, to fit my shoulder under his arm, our sides pressed together. My throat feels strangled with that longing.

On cue, she strides out the back door, carefully balancing a tray of lemonade. She's wearing a white lace dress with a red sash, her blond hair glinting in the sun, her face so eerily symmetrical she'd almost be odd-looking except for the singular perfection of each and every one of her features. Here is Rebekah making her way down to Max, changing her gait to accommodate the steep slope of the back lawn. Now Dani bolts from the house behind her, laughing, her chubby legs charging straight for the water and for me. She's three, maybe four, her hair, far too long for a child, is the same white blond as her mother's. I often wish I could have met Dani when she was this young and unformed. Things might have been very different between us.

My body instinctively thrusts forward to catch the girl, to prevent her from running too far into the bay and drowning.

Rebekah yells, "Be careful, sweetheart," which Max repeats. She puts the tray down. From behind, she wraps her arms around Max's shoulders and warmly kisses his neck. He places a reassuring hand on her forearm. They both watch as Dani splashes in the shallow water, screaming and laughing, calling, "Look at me, I can swim."

Then, as she always does in the dream, Rebekah becomes the only one who spots me bobbing in the bay, too near her daughter for her liking. She straightens up and walks towards the water, stalking me like a lion not wanting to disturb its prey. Still in her dress, she wades into the water, moving past a frolicking, oblivious Dani, until we are finally face-to-face. Her eyes narrow, forming that familiar dimple over her left brow.

I try to flee but my legs are useless.

"Who are you?" she asks. "You don't belong here."

Rebekah's mouth is close enough to kiss, a woman I'd seen in hundreds of photos, whose every contour I'd memorized, whose every expression I'd studied and sometimes un-consciously mimicked in my darker days, when my obsession was most acute and I had no idea how to live at Asherley, how to be a wife to Max, or a friend to Dani.

"I do belong here. She needs me," I say, pointing to Dani, my impudence surprising even me. I try to move but my feet are rooted in the sand below, arms floating beside me like weeds.

"She doesn't need you," Rebekah says, placing her hands on my shoulders in a reassuring manner. "She needs her mother."

Then she rears back slightly. Using all of her weight, Rebekah shoves me under the waves with a sudden violence, flooding my vision with air bubbles. I fight for the surface, to scream for Max to help me, but she's stronger than me, her hands a vise on my shoulders, her arms steely and rigid. In my dream, she's not angry. Rebekah kills me slowly and methodically, not with hate or fear. She's being practical. I am channeling vital resources away from her, rerouting Dani's feelings, altering Max's fate. My murder is conducted with dispassion and efficiency. And though I don't want to die, I can't imagine going on like this either, careful of my every move, looking over my shoulder, afraid to touch anything, break anything, love anything, worried his past will surface again and ruin what I've worked so hard for, what we've worked so hard for. Her task complete, my body painlessly dissolves into the waves and I disappear. I am dead and made of nothing. I am gone.

I woke up gasping for air, my hand at my throat. I kept reminding myself that everything is okay, we are okay, that we are alive and she is dead, cursing the fact that the dream had followed us here, our last stop, I hoped, for a good long while.

My back ached when I stretched that morning, unfamiliar beds the only downside to our decision to travel for the rest of the year to shake loose the recent tragedies. We found it helped to establish a routine. I would get up first and make us breakfast, for we only stayed in places with kitchens, a home-made meal the best way to start our wide-open days. We tried not to think too much about the past, about Asherley. It was gone, along with all of its secrets. We were building new memories, creating new stories, ones we might find ourselves telling new friends one day, finishing each other's sentences, saying, *No, you go, you tell it. No, you—you tell it better.*

Mostly our days were languid; sometimes I'd plan a museum tour or we'd take a long drive past ruins. Our nights were spent reading rather than watching TV, sharing the couch even if armchairs were available, our toes gently touching. There were few conflicts, though I was no longer naive enough to believe two people as different as we were, who'd spent as much time together as we had, would never bicker. But the truth was we were still getting to know each other.

4

Waiting for the omelet to thicken, I poked my head into the bedroom, resisting the urge to caress that thatch of dark hair that I had come to love in a quiet, calm way, a marked difference from how I loved just a short while ago. Hard to believe it had been less than a year since I'd met Max Winter, a man whose love seized me by the shoulders and shook me out of a state of dormancy, and who ushered in another emotion I had yet to meet in my young life: jealousy, the kind that grows like kudzu, vining around the heart, squeezing all the air out, fusing with my thoughts and dreams, so that by the time I understood what was happening to me it was almost too late.

I carefully closed the bedroom door, padded across the cool tile floors of the living area, with its dark armoires and overstuffed armchairs, and threw open the musty blackout curtains. I stepped barefoot onto the hot stone terrace, the sun so bright it hurt my eyes. In the distance, warm air steamed off the sea. From below, I could hear the Spanish-speaking shopkeepers already arguing over sidewalk space, and I was gut-punched by long-ago memories of a mother who sang to me in her mother's language and a father with sunburned shoulders, pulling fish out of the sea, their silver bodies violently jackknifing on the scarred deck of the boat we once lived on, our sleeping quarters the size of the smallest pantry you could find at Asherley. I could have fainted from an old grief. Here they were again, coming at me from afar, watery mirages of the people who once loved me, and I them, their long shadows cast by a low morning sun.

TWO

There wasn't anything in my past to suggest that I was the type of woman who would fall in love with a man like Max Winter, not in the course of a year, let alone in just under a month, but fall in love I did—an incredible thing to happen to someone like me. I say this not to be modest or self-deprecating, but I truly was unremarkable. In the books that I grew up reading and in the movies I loved to watch, the young women who had had these whirlwind affairs were beautiful or had something odd about them that upended their perfection, making them more beautiful for it. A gap in their front teeth, perhaps, or strangely set eyes, fun and dangerous women in whose wake men collapsed like felled trees. Or they were entirely oblivious to their beauty, women who came into themselves after a powerful man bestowed upon them the financial security or sexual satisfaction that had so far eluded them. Though you might have mistaken me for this type of woman, I was not that either. I was and am still unremarkable. My features are even, my body trim, hair, eyes, and skin compatible with each other in ways that make sense. Even my character, self-sufficient and serious-minded, watchful and earnest, doesn't draw attention to itself. Men do not clamor after me. And before Max I had never been jealous of women like that. They made the men in those scenarios seem ridiculous. I'd watch them at the club's poolside bar with their sunburned scalps, their cigar smoke and signet rings, their sunglasses barely camouflaging the direction of their gazes. They looked and behaved like toddlers in a grocery store, dazzled by abundance. Meanwhile, the wives of these rich men, watching their men watch other young women, vibrated with the nervous energy of animals that sensed a looming natural disaster. So when I was swept off my feet, as they say, by an older wealthy American who made me feel as though I'd never need to eat again, I thought, after initial reluctance, that I might as well surrender to the lark, as long as I knew not to get used to it.

I had wanted what my parents had had, a calm and private union, unknowable to others. My parents were disillusioned Americans who chose to live and work on a small fishing trawler where there was no separation of tasks, just days spent quietly and diligently in each other's company, taking turns tending to me. I was born on that boat in choppy water, and by luck of both latitude and longitude I was given American papers, too, mailed to us, since my parents never wanted to return to the States. My fiercest memory is of my mother bobbing me on her hip in shallow water, teaching me to swim. The feel of my mother's wet skin against mine formed a deep sense memory, often triggered when I'd see other mothers holding their babies on the beaches of Grand Cayman, where we moved when it was time for me to go to school. They chose it because it was quiet and small and under no threat of political tumult, its poverty, of which we were a part, mostly hidden amidst the prettily painted homes outside George Town. From kindergarten to the twelfth grade, I attended a strict Christian grammar school in George Town, cooled by straw fans and shuttered windows, where we were taught, British-style, by rote and a smack on the hand with a ruler.

When I was six my mother died of cancer. She wasn't sick for long, maybe three months, my father often skipping a day on the water to go to the hospital and hold her hand. I'd meet them there after school. If her pain was manageable, I could see her. Other times I'd have to wait in a small gray room down the hall that became, to me, the physical manifestation of sadness.

Not long after she died, arthritis set into my father's wrists, making it impossible for him to pull heavy nets. He didn't complain. He wrapped his wrists in tape and took a job at a local charter company ferrying rich people out on fishing excursions. He loved the work, but struggled to take orders from his boss, an imperious Australian named Laureen Ennis, one of the richest women in the Caribbean. She was entirely self-made, someone who should have been a role model to me, were her character not so repulsive, her manner so coarse. Stranger still, despite her considerable wealth, she spent almost no money to look rich. Her nails were chipped and dirty, her clothes rotating sets of stretched-out gym wear. She went too long between dye jobs so often sported inches of white roots. But it was her voice that was the most grating, so loud you couldn't tell if she or the recipient of her braying lecture was going deaf. At supper, my father occasionally mimicked her, his deep voice lending it a guttural roughness that made me laugh.

"Your fahtha is a lazy arse. Eets not moy fault he hezzint saved enough to retire propleh. Oym an idiot for baying sore ginerous. Oy aughta foyer you both."

Almost immediately after high school, I went to work for Laureen, too, the option of a higher education less and less

8

likely the older and more infirm my father became. Laureen had charter companies all over the Caribbean. My duties at first were secretarial, keeping track of boat schedules and who was captaining what vessel. I also recorded the catches, photographing the more spectacular ones for the walls of Laureen's office at the end of the pier. My father knew exactly where to find the big fish, even if it sometimes meant spending the night on the water, an extra charge I had to press clients for when they docked. Those who returned with an ice-packed yellowfin tuna, or a four-foot blue marlin, didn't mind paying. When these clients felt generous, I'd carry their fish to the kitchen myself, some still alive and as heavy as children, for the chefs to cut up, cook, and serve. They'd wrap the bones and guts in paper for me to dispose of in the sea.

Eventually I learned to drive the boats so my father didn't have to steer and throw lines, exacerbating his arthritis. It galled Laureen to lose me in the office, galled her to pay me for a job she said my father should be able to do alone.

Then five years ago, sixty miles off Gun Bay, my father had a massive heart attack while helping a client pull in a large wahoo tugging at a line. I scrambled down to the deck and held him for a moment, his eyes glassy, left foot kicking the shoe off the right. One of the men barked at me.

"What are you doing down here? Get us to the goddamn hospital!"

I'd piloted the boat, an eighty-two-foot Viking, only once before, so I prayed that the large cruise ships weren't crowding the city docks. While one of the men (a doctor, I found out) worked frantically on my father, the rest hovered in a semicircle, blocking my view. The doctor only stopped

9

resuscitating him long enough to help carry him to the waiting ambulance.

I sat alone in that small gray room while a different stranger delivered to me the same news about another parent. Laureen paid the hospital bill, the ambulance bill, the emergency docking bill, the funeral bill, and she refunded the doctor's bachelor party, a debt that became like weather between us, rarely mentioned, always felt. She gave off airs of largesse as she moved me from our modest rental in Bodden Town to a staff townhouse near the marina, where pay was docked for a cramped room with a single bed, and where kitchen and bath facilities were shared with a rotating cast of young internationals who worked on the island, spoke at various decibels in various languages, and whose fucking and fighting would, every four to six weeks, cause a sudden reshuffling of the living arrangements. I felt like a nagging column on Laureen's ever-expanding debt ledger, giving her greater license to limit my days off and schedule overnight trips that often left me operating the boats alone, in all-male company, ignoring those periodic knocks on my cabin door, tests to see how far my services might go.

For months I grieved, tightly and privately, keeping my pain to myself until I could be alone. Then one day, I decided I could no longer be a grown woman weeping in a single bed. I buried the rest of my anguish and got on with my life, astonished that that was all it took, a simple decision, which I suppose, in retrospect, revealed something unsettling about my character. Despite what passed for shyness, I could be ruthless like that, make a decision and then act, filing and organizing emotions as efficiently as I did a boat schedule in high season. Emotions were things for which I did not have the time or the luxury.

I was in the office one day trimming the edges of a nice write-up about Laureen to pin on the office wall when the brass bells signaled Max Winter's entrance into the overly air-conditioned hut. As automatically as breathing, Laureen stripped off her stained hoodie and stood to greet him, her ample, sun-spotted chest leading the way. Her wide arms assumed a hug, but Max instantly sliced through those intentions with a stiff extended arm, an awkward moment I pretended not to see.

"Well, if it isn't Mr. Winter, or should I say *Senator* Winter? It's been such a long, long time."

"I'm just a state senator, so no need for titles," he said, looking over her shoulder to give me a perfunctory nod.

I didn't remember Max Winter from previous years, which wasn't unusual. Laureen had a whole cache of clients she took personal care of: bankers, sports stars, celebrities and the like, people who didn't like the obviousness of St. Barts or the sleepiness of St. Martin, people for whom banking was a full-time job and the Caymans was where they could both work and play. She hoarded them, bragging about the exorbitant tips she'd declined because they'd formed friendships, or so she said, trusting her enough to drop lascivious details about affairs and divorces, though I knew she'd merely overheard them talking from the bridge.

"Anyway, it is so good to see you again, Mr. Winter. The club didn't alert me that you were returning. I would have been more than happy to handle your needs there so you wouldn't have to come all the way down to my ratty old office. Get Mr. Winter a coffee," she barked at me.

"Oh no," he said to me. "Please don't go to any trouble."

"By the way," Laureen added sotto voce, "my deepest condolences to you and your lovely daughter. I read about that awful business. Has it been a year already?"

I pricked up my ears, eager to know more about this "awful business."

"Eighteen months," he said. "And thank you, I appreciate your kind words. But I am wondering about a boat. For tomorrow. Something manageable that I can handle alone."

"Oh, I wouldn't hear of that. I'm more than happy to take you out tomor—"

"No. Please. Though I do appreciate the offer. You must be busy this time of year."

"Nonsense. January is between high seasons."

I spoke up. "The Commodore is available. One person can handle it easily. I just need to clean it out and put gas in it."

"Thank you. I know that boat," Max said. "I'll come by around eight. Does that give you enough time to prep it?"

"Plenty."

His nose was slightly crooked, the only lived-in thing about his handsome face. I imagined he'd played sports and had an accident with a baseball or football. Maybe an interesting story involving a fistfight at a private school. The thought instantly endeared him to me.

"Mr. Winter, I'm telling you, that little boat won't do. Let *me* take you out on the *Lassie*—"

He gave me a steady look, which I held until my face burned.

"I'd like to take the little one. I'll come for her in the morning."

"At least let me bring her around to the club dock, Mr. Winter, all nice and gleaming."

"I'd prefer to leave from here, if you don't mind," he said.

There was an edge to his voice now. He intended to be alone on that boat, and this now worried me, given Laureen's hushed condolences and his general air of sadness.

"I don't mind anything. Will you need snorkeling equipment? Will your daughter be with you?"

"No. Dani's with her aunt in Paris for the month. She's at that age where she prefers her company, anyone's company really, over mine," he said, looking at me.

"Let us pack a picnic for you, then. Call up the kitchen," she commanded me, "and let them know Mr. Winter wants—"

"I'll grab some food from the takeaway. I didn't catch your name."

This time he was talking to me. I was about to respond when Laureen beat me to it, her accent mangling the emphasis so that it sounded less exotic than it was.

"Pretty," he said, studying my face as if to solve something about its relationship to my name. "Suits you. Are you new?"

"I've been working here about eight years now."

"Why have I never seen you before?"

He seemed genuinely bothered by this oversight on my, or Laureen's, part.

"Maybe because I've never seen *you*," I said, a little impudently, my face warming.

"This one's not one of my more friendly staff, that's for sure," Laureen said. "If I didn't shove her out the door she'd be content to sit in the air-conditioning all day checking her Facebook."

I rolled my eyes at Max. She knew I had no interest in such things.

"Yes, well, all right. I'll see you both in the morning," he said and thanked us each by name.

The bells clanged behind him.

"Now there's a man who has suffered," she said, a hand on her chest, eyes lingering on the door. "Poor man's wife dies in a car accident just before he wins an election. Then he's got to raise that kid on his own." She shuddered. "I don't like the idea of him alone on the water. Did he seem depressed to you?"

I wanted to say *Of course he's depressed, his wife's dead*, but she was already telling me the Winters were longtime members of the club, where they owned a few of the private bunga-lows, the biggest reserved for their personal use.

"And they live on a private island that's been in the fam-ily for hundreds of years. An old king gave it to them. And the house, it's like a castle straight out of a Disney movie. Presidents have slept there. Republican ones, that is. He's probably the only Republican I could hold my nose and vote for. He's not one of those right-wing nutters. More of the old-school variety; high brows, low taxes, that sort of thing."

She turned to face me. "Aren't you a dark surprise? I've never seen you flirt before. You embarrassed yourself by a lot. He might be single now, but you do realize he's the sort who will end up with a movie star. That's about the only act that could follow the first Mrs. Winter. Rebekah was something else to look at, I'm telling you. You know, she once offered me a hundred-dollar bill to stay here because she was waiting for an important phone call and was worried she wouldn't get a signal on the ocean. It never came, the call, but it was me she trusted to sit right where you're sitting and wait for that call all day, and I did. Of course I didn't want to accept the money but she insisted. She had a lot of class, that one. The daughter, though? Total piece of work. The biggest snot-nosed brat ever. D'you know a couple years back, that one had half the police on the island plus a helicopter looking for her? She thought she'd go partying with a group of athletes from some college in Florida. Not even thirteen years old, she was. Those poor boys, all in tears when they found that out, swearing up and down no one laid a hand on her, but not for lack of *her* trying, they said. She could have ruined their lives just like that," she said with a snap of her fingers. "But at the last minute she said the boys were telling the truth. She'd just wanted to make them suffer a little. Girls like that, they don't get happy endings." She meandered to the back office holding her ledger to her chest, flip-flops slapping at her dirty, cracked heels. "Nope. They end up dead or in jail, leaving everybody to wonder which fate they deserved more."

THREE

For the rest of my shift, I thought of nothing but Max Winter's visit. While hosing off his boat and prepping it for the morning, I thought of how he'd held my gaze and the warm smile he'd given me, a small enough gesture people trade a hundred times in a day, yet this one's effect lingered. He'd paid attention to me. He'd said he liked my name. He'd wondered why he'd never seen me before, as though I were someone to be remembered. He'd said, directly to me, that he would come for the boat in the morning and bowed when he'd said my name, using the proper emphasis.

It was a short walk from the marina to staff housing, but there was a stretch of West Bay that had no sidewalk, and I often took the beach route to avoid walking next to traffic along the unlit highway. The sand made for a more challenging hike but it was better than being in a car's blind spot. Besides, on certain nights the walk cleared my head, and that night I needed it.

When I reached the townhouse the sound of another wild party wafting from our living room stopped me cold. The townhouse was one of three Laureen owned, stacked side by side like tombstones at the end of a bleak cul-de-sac on the other side of the highway. I stood listening to the insistent bass pulsing from the house while slowly deflating. I had nothing left, no reserves to cut through what would be a forest of drunken people crowding the stark rooms, draping over each other on the greasy couch, every tabletop a wasteland of empty bottles and overflowing ashtrays. I looked back across the highway towards the blinking lights of the marina, feeling like misery itself had tapped me on the shoulder and offered me its arm. What else was there to do but trudge back to the pier and the cot in Laureen's office?

I didn't bother with the beach route back. I was so tired I almost wanted a truck to swerve to miss a chicken and hit me. And to make a bad night worse, I spotted a lone male figure approaching, staring into his phone, the screen lending his face a glowing malevolence. When you're a woman walking alone along a highway at night, it's a toss-up over what's scarier: a drunk driver who can't see you or a man in your path who can.

My instincts always assumed the worst. But when the man suddenly stepped out in front of an oncoming car, another instinct kicked in and I screamed, "Look out!" A screech of brakes, and the man's phone spun in the air as he plunged backwards into a bush. I scrambled towards him, retrieving the phone. When he finished brushing dust off his pants and stood upright, I found myself looking at the face of the man who had occupied my thoughts all day and with such intensity that for a moment I worried I might have manifested him.

"Thank you—*it's you!*" Max Winter said, accepting his phone. "Good God, my phone must have blinded me."

"Are you all right?"

"I am, yes. I think you might have saved my life."

Cars sped by us, illuminating his face every few seconds, his expression hard to read. I thought of Laureen's concern about his taking the boat out alone. *Was* he depressed?

"Are you sure you're all right?" I stepped closer, boldly placing a hand on his forearm. "Let me help you."

"I promise you I'm fine. I'm more embarrassed than bruised," he said. He glanced at his phone before pocketing it.

"What are you doing out on the highway anyway? You should be using that," I said, pointing to the walkway raised over the road, off-limits to staff at night.

"I got a text from my daughter. It's the middle of the night where she is so I couldn't ignore it. We got to texting back and forth, and yeah, the rest is history. Where are *you* heading so late?"

I hesitated. I didn't want him to know I lived the way I did. Lots of people had roommates and I was only twenty-six. But suddenly my life felt dingy and squalid and I wanted to give him the impression that I was older, more sophisticated.

"I forgot something at work. I was just going back to get it."

"Well, lucky me you did. Let me walk you. The least I can do in return is to make sure you're safe." I began to protest when he added, "Please don't worry, you won't be spotted."

He knew, then, that staff wasn't allowed to socialize with club clients, not even for a benign stroll like this. If Laureen saw us I'd be fired on the spot.

Placing a hand on the small of my back, he led me across the road, then down the path along the south side next to the hydrangeas, my earlier route. He knew exactly how to get to the beach from there, and he seemed aware we'd be able to walk in near-total darkness all the way to the edge of the marina. We stood at what he intuited was my drop-off point, the foot of the long dock dividing Laureen's property from the country club's, which, by day, had the ambience of a small hospital where wealthy people might go to convalesce. But at night, from this vantage point, the club seemed a warmer and more intimate place, relaxed and cozy.

Max checked his watch, then looked around like a spy. "Okay, run. I'll wait right here."

"You don't have to do that," I insisted. "I can get home by myself."

"Regrettably, my dear, because I was raised by a chauvinist pig *and* her sexist husband, I do have to walk you home."

His joke made me laugh, but I still had to make a choice: either introduce him to the shabby chaos of staff housing or tell him I was planning to sleep on a cot at work because of it.

"The thing is, there's a party going on at my place and I really need to sleep. So I'm staying out here tonight."

He looked out at the clapboard office at the end of the pier.

"I mean, does it lock? Is there even a blanket?"

"Yes, and a pretty good pillow," I said. "So it's not a big deal. And what a view!" My arm swept across the dark beach.

"It's better than the one I have."

"So no need to feel sorry for me, Mr. Winter. Besides, I have an early morning, what with this last-minute demanding client who wants his boat to be ready to go first thing."

"Wow. What an asshole."

"He's a senator or something," I said, rolling my eyes. "But only a *state* senator."

He laughed a little too loud.

"Mr. Winter, keep it down," I whispered, craning around for witnesses.

"Please, call me Max," he said. "Nothing else."

"Max."

He tilted his head, his focus on a point between my eyes, just above my brow. It felt intimate, this look, like a prelude to something, not quite a kiss, but something that overwhelmed me even unexpressed.

"Well, good night, then," I said.

"Yes, of course, good night. But I'm going to wait right here to make sure you reach the office safely. I'll leave when you flick the light on and off. Deal?"

"Deal."

"And I will see you again in roughly nine hours." He checked his watch. "Actually eight. Even better."

I nodded by way of saying good night again and turned to leave.

Making my way down to the end of the pier, I was aware of his eyes on me. I willed myself not to turn around to check whether he maintained his vigil, worried he'd mistake it for coyness, an invitation. It was only when I unlocked the office, flicked the light switch on and off, then collapsed on the cot that I fully exhaled, kicking my legs a couple times like a schoolgirl with a crush.

Of course I didn't sleep. There was, in fact, no blanket, and the pillow was the orthopedic cushion from the office chair, but I didn't care. I welcomed the adrenaline rush that accompanied these brand-new feelings. Maybe Laureen was right. Maybe I was, indeed, a dark surprise.

FOUR

I stirred awake with the sun, stretched, and tied my hair into a knotted fist on top of my head, securing it with an elastic band. Then I smoothed down the wrinkles of my uniform shirt and turned on the computer. Before the screen came fully alive, I spotted Laureen making her way down the pier two hours earlier than her usual start time, and an hour earlier than mine. The way she stomped—the entire office bobbing with her steps—meant I had screwed something up. Panicked, I scanned the office. I had started the coffee. The day's schedule was scribbled on the whiteboard. I had prepped Max's boat the day before. I just had to bring it around to the pier. At the last second, I plucked the cushion off the cot and tossed it onto the chair. Laureen's angry knock reminded me I had forgotten to unlock the door. When I opened it, she blew past me, her perfume chokingly strong, her eyes darting around the office. She plopped herself down in front of the computer.

"Total shit show," she muttered. "The fucking Singularis sunk near Eleven Mile off Barbuda. Bunch of shivering Brits waiting for a charter back to St. Barts. Fucking one's the Queen's cousin or something."

She found the number she was looking for and immediately laid into whoever answered the call, presumably the pilot. "Bruce, you fucking moron. How many times have I said don't go off route? . . . I don't care if he's next in fucking line to the fucking throne. Is he gonna pay for this? No! . . .

21

Well, you'll have to wait. Janie will call when the charter gets there. I'll see you in St. Barts . . . 'Cause I gotta meet the Prefect, that's why . . . Yeah, it's *that* bad. I was told to bring luggage. And a lawyer. You might wanna do the same, asshole." She slammed the phone down.

"It's a lot of oil, apparently," she said, rubbing her face with her hands. Her pilot didn't know about the shoals, and now her biggest yacht was polluting a rare bird reserve upon which the United Nations had just put a protective stamp.

"I'm so sorry," I said, thinking of the birds. She'd be fine. Her insurance would pay for what God couldn't replace.

"Right," she said, slapping the desk and standing. "Let's go."

Cold resistance filled my veins. "But the marina. We've got clients. They'll be coming by soon."

"Piss on the clients. I need you to help me pack."

Quickly I glossed over the client problem with bigger ones that might arise were I to abandon the post, though I was careful to leave out Max's reservation. The fuel ship arrived today. Two wedding parties were checking into the club. And of course someone had to sign out the watersports equipment, a side business Laureen had regretted as soon as she launched it because it took up too much of my time.

"Right. Bloody hell. I just want to pull out all my hair by the roots."

After Laureen reluctantly agreed I should stay, I trotted behind her to her car as she breathlessly rattled off all the other tasks I'd have to handle if she was kept away for more than a week (maybe two!). As she listed them I nodded and nodded, seemingly making a bargain with myself to say yes to everything she asked for in exchange for a blessed week (maybe two!) of her absence, a most excellent trade-off.

She started her car and rolled down the window to bark her final orders.

"I almost forgot! Max Winter's coming for that boat this morning."

"Oh, that's right," I said, laying a gentle hand on my clavicle.

"He's accustomed to special touches. Make sure the bar is stocked. He likes plenty of ice in the coolers and lots of beach towels. Get the club to supply sparkling water, lemons *and* limes, and don't forget a sharp knife. And make sure they charge his bungalow for all this shit, not me. Ask John-John to check if the backup radio's working. He's in charge while I'm away."

"Yes, got it," I replied. John-John was her longest, most loyal employee.

"And fix your goddamn hair."

I propped my bun back in place on top of my head and she squealed away, black smoke spewing in her wake.

By then the sky was fully awake, a wide blue expanse, the light so bright it took a second for me to figure out from which direction the sun was coming. Under my hand visor, I saw early club members crowding grotesque piles of food set up al fresco for breakfast. Cracked red crab legs jutted out at all angles from two overflowing platters, and fruit cups lay in a vivid pattern waiting to be plucked by women watching their weight and children who never finished them. It was the smell of bacon mingling with the salty wind that did me in. I became faint with hunger, unable to remember my last meal. I walked defiantly over to the hotel tack shop, a place usually off-limits to staff, but Laureen was the only real hawk about it and she was gone. *Gone!* I was a prisoner let out of her cage, so ecstatic that a bottle of warm water, a granola

23

bar, and a desiccated orange, the last in the basket, was all I wanted in life.

"Run along," the cashier whispered, waving away my money. "You know you're not supposed to be here."

I blew her a kiss and dashed away. I'd finished the stale bar by the time I got back to the office, where Max Winter was already waiting for me, calmly reading a pamphlet.

"There you are," he said, smiling, sitting next to a large basket covered with a white napkin.

"Good morning, Mr. Winter," I said, the joy in my voice a little alarming. It had felt like an eternity since we'd said good night to each other not fifty feet from where he was now standing, looking tanned and relaxed, a completely different person than yesterday.

"Call me Max."

"Max," I said.

His eyes drifted to my hands.

"I hope you haven't ruined your appetite," he said, taking the plastic wrapping, the shriveled orange, and the bottle of water from me, carefully placing them on the desk. "I brought you breakfast. I figured room service didn't come down here."

He was standing close to me now, eyeing the large knot of hair on my head, which I could feel had tipped on its side again.

"Let me . . . there," he said, gently centering my bun.

"Thank you," I said, blushing. "I can get the radio signal out of Miami now."

"Oh, good. What are they saying about the weather?"

"Clear morning, rain in the afternoon."

"So it's best if I *not* pilot the boat alone."

24

He reached into his basket and handed me a soggy fried egg sandwich.

"Thank you . . . Max."

It was the best soggy fried egg sandwich I had ever eaten, the right amount of salty, the toast pliant with butter, the lettuce wilted to perfection, a red tomato wedge giving it a tart bite. Same with the fruit cups, chilled but not to the point of hurting my teeth, and served with silverware. He poured hot coffee from a thermos into the fancy china cups the club only used for dinner service. There was no doubt Max Winter was flirting with me. I wasn't the type to imagine such things. And yes, I was flirting, too, there was no use pretending otherwise. That thing in me that was let out of its cage had begun to stretch its legs.

As we ate he told me he'd been coming to the Caymans every year for about twenty years, except for last year—the reason, I assumed, having to do with the death of his wife. But he didn't elaborate and I didn't press. He asked me how I ended up here, his assumption being that I wasn't born here. I told him I was American but that lots of folks who look and sound like me were born and raised here. The island was a cultural mishmash, its uniting industry international banking.

"Ah, capitalism. The great equalizer."

"For some," I added, feeling clever.

He handed me a linen napkin and removed my empty plate, and I felt tended to in a way that confused me, warmed me, made me want to cry. It would be a lie to say in the past twenty-four hours I hadn't imagined what might be possible between someone like him and someone like me, that Max's ministrations didn't tug at that dark part of me that fantasized about

25

being rescued from an uncertain future, perhaps in exchange for rescuing him from a sad past. Being plain and forgettable didn't exempt me from his stupid, intractable fairy tale.

"How old are you?" he asked, placing the dirty breakfast dishes in the basket. My face flashed hot with the idea that our minds might have been fixating on the very same potential obstacle at the very same time.

I told him, quickly adding, "But I feel ten years older. Especially when I sleep on that cot."

He laughed. "Even if you were ten years older, you'd still be quite young."

I asked him how old he was.

"Old enough to be your father, I guess. Your young father."

His eyes lingered on me as I did the math, seemingly searching out my reaction, as though to ask, *Do you mind? Am I too old?*

Truth was I didn't mind. He was about as old as I thought he'd be. Yet I had always assumed, being fatherless only a few years, that I'd be immune to those unconscious paternal tugs that seemed to draw young, aimless women (mostly beautiful) to older (mostly wealthy) men. I saw that dynamic play out all the time at the club. The more pronounced the age difference, the more it seemed to stunt both parties' growth, the women with their babyish voices, the men, with their tufts of white chest hair and fat tanned shoulders, growling at them. Often all that remained between these mismatched pairings was a permanent sense of disappointment in each other, one for getting older and one for never having been young in the first place.

"So. Where's my boat?" He peered through the blinds into the marina.

"Oh, right!" I leapt to my feet and fetched the keys from the locked cupboard in the back room. "I'll bring it up to the dock. It's fully stocked with all the things Laureen told me you liked. The big key's the ignition. Little one is for storage under the seating in the stern, where the fishing poles—"

"Actually," he said, pressing them back into my hand, "I won't be able to do the driving today. It turns out I do have some work to do. So I'll need a captain after all. And I'd like to put in a request for you."

Before I could disappoint him, John-John entered the office, breathless with the news about the oil spill. At fifty-five, he was still spry. As we caught each other up, my eyes darted over to Max, who seemed to be figuring out how this news affected his day, our day.

When John-John's attention drifted to the picnic evidence, I quickly introduced him to Max. They remembered each other from previous years.

"So as you've probably figured out, Mr. Winter," I said, "I can't help you today. We're all that's holding down the fort until we can pull in some backup."

Max looked sternly at John-John, giving the impression of a customer trying to stay calm. "So are you saying this young woman can't pilot my boat? I booked this yesterday. Should I call Laureen?"

I stared at my shoes as John-John reassured him.

"That's not necessary. Of course I'm not saying that, Mr. Winter." To me he hissed, "You'll have to go." He said he'd man the office the rest of the morning until he took a wedding party out for their lunchtime cruise. If there were drop-ins, too bad, he said, they'd just have to go somewhere else. "We can't do the impossible," he said, shrugging. And one of us would be back in time to lock up at night.

Max went to the kitchen to order a cold lunch while I ran to my quarters, navigating around the remnants of the previous night's party. I took a fast shower, threw a clean uniform over a bathing suit, and let my hair loose.

By the time we returned, John-John had brought around the boat. Max and I hopped aboard. I started up the engine. I could see him behind his sunglasses smirking a little as I slowly steered the boat out of the marina. In full command of the vessel, I let out the throttle once we passed the last buoy.

FIVE

What can I say about the four weeks that followed that wouldn't sound ripped from a paperback romance? That's how long Laureen was away, and to this day I count those weeks as the luckiest and happiest of my life. Except for two quick trips Max made to New York, we saw each other nearly every day after that first foray, when I took him for a half-day cruise around Grand Cayman, he insisting I point out landmarks related to my childhood. There's where I went to school, that building with the white bell tower; we lived there in Bodden Town, before I had to move to staff lodging when my father passed away; here's Spotts Beach, where my mother taught me how to swim.

Strangely, talking about my parents didn't tip the mood to maudlin or sad, even when Max gently pressed for more about what happened to them. I knew too much about the nature of grief to think mine was gone for good, but that morning I was momentarily relieved of a heaviness that had dogged me for years, a gift which I wholly attributed to Max Winter.

I threw down anchor off the coast of Rum Point, where we ate our lunch in the helm out of the sun. I began to try to see the island through the eyes of a grateful tourist rather than a disappointed inhabitant who felt jailed rather than liberated by all that blinding water. Buildings that looked shabby up close glowed white with promise from a distance.

Even the red-roofed shops dotting the harbor looked like a pretty foreign canton, and not a cheesy tourist trap.

"Born on a boat, lives on an island, now an orphan, working for a witch. You're a Grimms' fairy tale set in the Caribbean."

I laughed. It was an odd compliment, considering how those stories generally ended. I hadn't talked about myself that much in years, not even to my more inquisitive roommates.

"What about you? Tell me about you, your home. Laureen says it's stroyt atava Deezney movay."

"Yes, Asherley," he said, busying himself with attaching a long lens to an elaborate camera. "You do a great impression of her. What else does Laureen say about me?"

I hesitated. I didn't want him to think we gossiped about him. "Well . . . she said you're an important man who's been through a difficult time."

His face softened. "Seems we have something in common, both of us orphans."

"But you have your daughter."

He smiled. "Yes. Dani. She's full of life, that one. I try, but she's a complicated little thing. Very brave. Or maybe just reckless." He focused his camera on two seabirds climbing and diving into the surf.

"She's a teenager," I said. "Aren't they supposed to be reckless?"

He dropped his camera and turned to look at me squarely. "You don't seem the type that has ever been reckless, with anything or anyone."

Despite the essential truth of his observation, it was one of those compliments, again, that I puzzled over. Did he mean discerning and mature, or dull and stable? To counter the possibility of the latter interpretation, I replied, too quickly, "Well, I wish I could be reckless sometimes, do whatever I want, say whatever I'm thinking, go anywhere I please, with anyone I want, and never come back here if I don't want to. To be honest with you, recklessness is a luxury to someone like me."

"Please don't say that." He said it as though he'd asked this of me before, to no avail. "I like you just like this. Dependable. Hands on the wheel. Keeping everything afloat, so to speak."

To punctuate this plea he snapped a picture of me before I had a chance to protest, or even pose in some flattering way, which I found mildly alarming.

"You're looking at me like I stole your spirit. I shouldn't have done that without asking."

I stepped forward and placed my hand on his camera. "It's okay. I'd like to see it."

He flipped back to the shot. I veiled the tiny screen and we crowded in to look. Lit from behind, my hair a whirl of dark waves caught in the wind, I barely recognized myself. It was an arresting photo; I couldn't hide my pleasure.

If anyone were to have passed us that day on the boat, what would they have seen? A regular couple enjoying a bounty of good decisions they'd made in life, to be together, to afford to come here, to take out a boat, to pack good food to eat on a cloudless day? Up close would they have noticed my nervousness? How I hoped my driving seemed fluid and expert. How every time my eyes darted around to find Max they seemed to catch him looking at me. Or perhaps they would have thought this is the father and that is the daughter, and she's manning the boat on her own for the first time, and his smile indicates more a paternal pride than an older man wooing a young woman.

31

His phone rang. Turned out he did have work to do that day, banking, the kind I imagined was usually conducted in windowless rooms, at long tables surrounded by men in suits. Yet there he was, leaning casually on the handrail, legs crossed, squinting at me while he openly discussed his business, using terminology that had little to do with money but everything to do with wealth, which, my father taught me, were two very different things. One bought you shoes, he said, the other power; one attention, the other secrecy, which was the most important commodity of all, because that's how rich people stayed that way.

His mood was lighter after getting a bit of business out of the way and he began, unbidden by me, to finally talk about his life; his daughter; his sister, Louisa, with whom he was close ("We bicker like old married people, but we're partners in crime"). He even cued up a recent photo he'd taken of Asherley in the distance, probably the only vantage point from which one could take in the entirety of the house. The photo was recent, from a few weeks ago, so the grounds were covered in snow.

"It's called Queen Anne, this style of architecture. Quite different than the classic center-hall designs you see up and down the Gold Coast."

I nodded as though I had any clue what constituted Queen Anne architecture or where one might find the Gold Coast. To me Asherley simply looked like a remote winter palace, its turrets topped with a dozen red snow-capped spires, its windows deep-set like old eyes.

"It's very beautiful. How old is it?"

"The house itself is around two hundred years old. My great-great-grandfather Ashton Winter built it for his bride,

Beverley Daneluk. Of the Massachusetts Daneluks," he added jauntily, as if to emphasize the hoity-toityness of the match. "That's where Dani's name comes from."

Max explained how the house took years to build, the labor mostly provided by bound boys, indentured servants who lived and worked the land to pay off family debt.

"Ha, like me with Laureen," I said, only half kidding. I prodded him for more. He confirmed what Laureen had said, how Charles I had granted the island to his family. For three of the four hundred years they'd lived there, the Winters were farmers, until his grandfather and father worked on Wall Street and he eventually went into politics.

"A lot of the original structures are scattered here and there. Stone ruins from the first house, foundations from a barn built in the 1700s, parts of the bound boys' quarters. People come and tour the island every once in a while, conservationists and the like," he said. "And except for some updates, the house had been pretty much untouched until Rebekah decided to make renovating Asherley her life's work."

It was the first time he'd spoken his late wife's name. Did I imagine his shoulders sinking a bit, sadness creeping in around his features? Or was that happening to me? I tried to change the subject to something benign, asking him why he'd gone into politics, but she lingered there, too.

"Oh, that was Rebekah's idea. She was canny like that," he said. "Always thinking of next steps, always thinking of things that might benefit the family, or Asherley, pushing me to make more of myself. No one knows more about local politics than you, she said, and owning Asherley means you want to have a say in the decisions made in the county. And she was right."

Then he showed me a picture of Dani, who looked much older than fifteen, and posed in such a knowing way that I struggled (and failed) to find something to comment on beside her looks.

"She's very beautiful," I said. *She was beautiful, the house was beautiful. Jesus.*

"She's a number of other things, too, including expensive," he said, putting his phone away. "Now I sound like one of those assholes from the club."

"Hardly," I said. I could have listened to more, but the gap in the conversation prompted him to check his watch.

"Time flies fast in your lovely company. You could do me a great favor by dropping me in town. I have a meeting in less than an hour. I'll cab back."

The only thing I minded was that we were closer to George Town than the club, which meant less time in his company. I pulled up anchor and turned the boat around. At the city dock, he didn't say goodbye, he said, "See you tomorrow," to which I replied, "Okay," and waved, not asking when or how I would see him, so long as I did.

I sped back to the club, feeling depleted by his absence, the motor kicking up walls of water behind me. My mind retraced our morning, how he lit up talking about Dani, dimmed with Rebekah. I thought about the laughter, the food, the conversation, how it flowed easily from subject to subject, and how we each seemed to intuit when to press and when to back off, a dance whose steps we already knew.

I docked the boat sloppily, deciding to clean it at the end of my shift to take advantage of the empty office. John-John was probably still out with the wedding party. I fired up the computer to satisfy my awakened appetite for more about Asherley, about Max and Dani, but mostly Rebekah. When I entered her name and clicked "Images," the screen flooded with her face.

I knew she'd be beautiful, but she demanded more attention than I was prepared to give. Her wide eyes meant your own had to travel back and forth between them to take them in, their vaguely blue-green color varying from picture to picture. And her hair seemed undamaged by the chemicals required to achieve that blond hue. She had about her a carnality that was hard to ignore, especially the way her lips (often wearing the same shade of brick red) remained slightly parted whether she was smiling or not. The slight variations of her expression, that mouth, the white-blond hair, the flashing eyes, the pale shoulders and long, lean arms, duplicated over and over again with every click, gave the impression that there was a virtual Rebekah factory out there somewhere, still churning out perfect models even after her death.

At first I couldn't bring myself to open the news links about her death or look at photos of the blackened car wreck and the flattened acres. But they were the first stories that popped up, her death covered numerous times by the *New York Post*, the stories detailing how Rebekah's car had careened into an ancient oak on a particularly treacherous part of the road that led to the causeway connecting Winter's Island to Long Island. It had been an unusually hot summer. The ensuing fire took out several acres of old-growth forest before smoke was spotted from the mainland, the sirens rousing Max from his sleep. By then the car was engulfed, Rebekah's body so badly burned they could only be certain it was her by the diamonds from her melted wedding ring. Days later another story featured a picture of Max and Dani, both wearing dark glasses, entering an old church outside Sag Harbor. Then another story about how Max almost dropped out of the senate race, but even a break from campaigning didn't prevent his landslide victory that November.

I was fascinated by Dani's Instagram account, which boasted thirty-one thousand followers, an epic number, it seemed to me, for a fifteen-year-old girl. It looked as though she enjoyed free rein to post whatever she wanted, the recent ones from Paris an unsettling collage of girlish antics, moody tourist pictures, and sexy poses, all pursed lips, arched back, and airbrushed skin. Sometimes she was alone and sometimes she posed with a friend, with whom she seemed to imply a coyly sexual relationship. Even in her photos with Max there was a flirty, possessive quality to her embraces. Scanning much farther down her feed, I hit the mother lode, dozens and dozens of pictures of Rebekah with Dani, their likeness jarring. They had identical hair, similar style, their closeness unmistakable. With their arms draped around each other in loving ownership, they implied that theirs was an exclusive club, no other members allowed, not even Max, it seemed.

How often does Max find himself doing this, looking at pictures of his dead wife? When his pain became too much did he have a laptop resting open nearby? Had he bookmarked the tragic stories, or does he look for his favorite photos, hoping to be reminded of happier times? Perhaps his favorite was the one of Rebekah in that red-checked sundress from *Town & Country*. Or maybe he revisited the *Vanity Fair* spread of them together over the years, Max handsome in forgettable tuxedos, Rebekah in various gowns, the most striking a harsh chartreuse that would look ugly on anyone else.

Or were his favorites the ones in *The New York Times Magazine*, taken by a famous photographer when Max launched his state senate campaign, the caption "Our Future First Lady?" There was a snarky reference to her Russian roots, and how in her twenties she contemplated anglicizing the spelling of her name "to better fit into her adopted country." The story described the Winters as being "low-profile for such a high-powered couple". Rebekah said if Max won she would use her role to highlight causes close to her heart, like land stewardship and conservation, having fallen in love with the island's untouched forest and Asherley itself. The family hoped to keep the island pristine and undeveloped, despite its being worth more than a hundred million dollars. Rebekah described her biggest accomplishment, besides her daughter, as restoring Asherley to its former glory, a project that took her the better part of a decade.

I scanned through more pictures of the ten bedrooms, guessing theirs was the one described as "the most ethereal perch on Long Island." There was the great hall, with its gleaming paneled walls, the second-floor gallery lined with famous oil paintings of Max's ancestors, the prominence of the portrait artists growing along with the Winters' wealth. Though the kitchen looked more rustic than I had expected, with its pale green painted cupboards and black-and-white-checkered floor, it highlighted Rebekah's talent for updating the house while preserving its original aesthetic. The barn looked old, but was, in fact, a state-of-the-art facility for prized Thoroughbred horses, one of Rebekah's passions. But the home's centerpiece was a star-shaped greenhouse, its spires asymmetrical and dramatic, designed by a famous architect whom Rebekah persuaded to come out of retirement. Its jagged modernity clashed with the traditional design of Asherley and generated equal parts praise and criticism, one *Times* article calling it "utterly monstrous," which prompted Rebekah to scold him in an op-ed titled "Why Some Monsters Are Beautiful."

My trance was broken by the loud music coming from John-John's yacht chugging by, the passengers already drunk by dusk. After giving him a blithe wave, I sped up my search, scanning an *Architectural Digest* piece about the renovations. There she was posing in a gown in front of old kitchen appliances that were actually clever modern replicas. Whatever seemed old about Asherley was usually, in fact, a modern reproduction. The last picture in this spread was of Max and Dani, her looking too grown-up in a sky-blue minidress, Max with his arm around his daughter's tiny waist, their heads touching in the way of couples, her long blond hair a golden drape between them.

I slumped into the chair feeling sick, as if I'd rocketed back from another continent whose language and customs were entirely unfamiliar to me. This was followed by an overwhelming sense of shame, not from the snooping but from allowing myself the fantasy, however brief, that Max Winter might have found me attractive company today, me, a nobody from nothing, going nowhere. I laughed out loud at my own idiocy, at the notion that this wealthy, attractive man, this widowed senator, once married to a woman like Rebekah, who produced a child like Dani, who grew up on his own island in a castle with a name, might think of me as anything more than the hired pilot of his rented boat. He brought me that food out of courtesy. He took that (one) picture of me not to treasure it later but to fill an awkward gap in our conversation. This is what Laureen had meant when she said only another larger-than-life woman could fill Rebekah's shoes, could occupy the space she had taken up in their lives, in the world even. I was not only jealous of her, I was furious with myself for harboring, even for a day, such naive ideas about what Max Winter was doing with me. Images of Rebekah were now seared into my retinas. I could no longer see him without seeing her *with* him.

But I had done this to myself. I had invited her in. In my darkest days, I sometimes had to remind myself that it started here, in that moment, and that it wasn't Rebekah who came after me. I was the one who went looking for her.

SIX

During that strange and potent month, it did not take long for us to become easy, constant companions, something Max seemed utterly blasé about, but I attributed my own comfort to putting an abrupt end to my investigations into his and Rebekah's life. I had to. It was making me sick. I was like a potential addict who, after sampling heroin once, realized its easy, deadly appeal and vowed never to do it again. I decided to simply enjoy "it" while "it" lasted, whatever "it" was. I knew I was incomparable to Rebekah Winter in every way, and I decided jealousy was arrogance in disguise. As if I could compete with her. Even dead she was more fascinating than my own living presence. And Max, he was so "other" to me that my place in his life could only be fleeting, even while I was standing next to him at the helm of a boat or enjoying a furtive meal on the other side of the island. (In my defense we had not so much as kissed by that point, so I had no idea how much sex would irrevocably shift my understanding of what was, indeed, growing between us.) Also absent in those early days was any significant time spent around other people, which meant our courtship grew inside a vacuum. With no witnesses to comment on its existence, I was left uncertain sometimes whether any of it was real. One day Max was not in my life, the next he was with me almost daily, never at the club, only at the dock if he was taking out a boat that needed a captain (me, of course), which he'd done a dozen more times since our first trip, often enough to arouse John–John's concern, not necessarily regarding any impropriety on my part but rather with my seeming inability to help Max catch any good fish.

Much of what I had to do for Laureen involved nightly visits to her "palazzo," as she called her house, to take in mail and water plants. Max insisted on accompanying me. Our initial visit happened the very night after our first cruise. At the end of my long shift I was heading to the staff parking lot on the other side of the highway to use the company truck. Max spotted me from his rental car and rolled down his window, slowing his speed to match my pace.

"You need a ride somewhere, lady?"

That was after my deep dive into his and Rebekah's life, so it was jarring to see him in person. But there he was, real, and right beside me, talking to me, asking to be in my company. Again.

"I don't get into cars with strangers," I said. "Besides, I'm just going to the parking lot."

"I'll drive you there."

"It would take you longer to drive me than for me to just cross the highway."

A line of frustrated drivers began honking behind him.

"I have candy."

"Oh well, in that case . . ."

I got in. He smelled nice, like clean water. He asked me where I was taking the truck and I told him I had an errand on the other side of the island.

"Let me take you. I won't charge you much. Mileage at most."

"It's actually pretty far."

"Even better."

Instead of making the U-turn into the parking lot, he continued down Esterly Tibbetts. The trip to Laureen's on Sea View Road could sometimes take forty-five minutes, depending on traffic. Warning him of that didn't deter him, and so the white marble of Laureen's gaudy house became the backdrop against which we would conduct the majority of our heady affair.

That became our near-daily routine. I texted him when I was off work and about to trek to the staff parking lot. I'd meet him next to Laureen's truck, which never left the lot. Any night we weren't enjoying takeout on the iron bistro table in her sunroom, we ate at the same small fish shack on the other side of George Town, where no one from the touristic part of the island was likely to spot us.

That's where we found ourselves nearing the end of our second week together. I remember the sunset was particularly pretty that night. My eyes were drawn to an armada of small cruise ships, like a dark ellipsis along the horizon.

"You went away just now," he said, following my gaze. "What are you thinking? That you'd like to be on one of those boats?"

"No. Not at all. I am happy right here. Happier, I think, than I have a right to be." My face flushed. I worried I would say too much, and yet I couldn't stop myself. "In fact, I wish there was a way you could press rewind, not to change the past, but to experience a moment exactly as it was—just once more—even if it meant it could never become a memory."

"What would be among your reruns?"

I wanted to say *This moment, right now, with you.* "Oh, I don't know. Swimming with my mother. The day before the last one I spent with my father. I suppose a day or two this week." I shrugged. "It's been quite fun. For me anyway."

He smiled, reached across the table, and placed a warm hand on my slightly colder one. It was the first time we'd touched.

"Thank you for saying that. Very few young people have craved my company lately. I'd forgotten what it's like to even be mildly popular."

He was talking about Dani, who had called a few times while we were together. Their chats were warm but short. She seemed to be checking in rather than initiating meaningful conversation. He'd startled me the other day on the boat when he replied to a question of hers that included casual mention of me. "Yes. As a matter of fact, I'm with her now," he had said, practically yelling over the noise of the sea.

The waiter arrived. Max ordered our usual: two fish specials, two glasses of white wine. Feeling unqualified to elaborate on the trials and tribulations of raising a truculent teenager, I asked him instead what memories he'd relive once more then never remember again.

He thought for a moment. "I would like to mirror your lovely sentiment and say the time we brought Dani home. But I want to remember that day again and again. So I would game the system. What I might do is choose to relive my very worst moments, if only to be allowed to erase them forever. A small price to pay, in my experience."

"Which ones?"

He turned to face me fully, his mood shifting. "Well, for starters, the day Rebekah died. And quite honestly, almost every day after that." He took a final gulp of wine and signaled for another. I regretted guiding the conversation here. What did I think a widower would choose as his worst memories? He seemed to sense my embarrassment, and rather than pull back, he closed in on his statement, sealing it off with a taunt.

"You're looking at me all doe-eyed and surprised. You think it's cruel to want to rebury my wife so I never have to think about it again. Selfish, even. But it's true. I wish I could forget it all."

The subject of Rebekah's death had dented his voice and shifted his features. *This is what it does to him to think about her.* I hated the way he looked at me in that moment, as though I were to blame for reviving her memory. She might as well have been sitting at the table with us, slowly drumming her fingers until I took a hint and left them alone.

"I think I understand—"

He snorted. "What do you understand? You're just a child who's lived on a pretty little island all her life."

I began to tear up, confirming that I liked him too much already, and that in the face of potential rejection or humiliation, I would choose to be unkind. I couldn't lash out at his grief over Rebekah, but fewer things angered me more than the assumption that I lacked depth because I was young, or that I couldn't possibly struggle in a place that was, to him, a paradise. So I snapped back, not caring what it might do to the mood of the evening, or us. *I will wreck this before it wrecks me.*

"I understand a lot more than you give me credit for, Max. You don't have a monopoly on grief, or strife," I said. "And if I'm such a child, why are you spending all this time with me? Why do you pick me up every night to go on these stupid errands, and then bring me here for a meal when you could be doing so many other more interesting things with much more important people, older people, older *women*, with better clothes and lives and money, who don't have to sneak around like I do? And Lord knows it can't be for the sex, because you don't seem to even want to touch me."

A middle-aged woman at a nearby table glanced in our direction, rolling her eyes after she assessed the scene. Of course I was overreacting. How else to disguise my shame at how much I already knew about Rebekah and his love for her? How could I not compare myself to her? How could I not think: Why are you with someone like me when you were once married to someone like her? If this is how it ends, with me in a petulant snit and him driving off in a rage, so be it.

We said nothing to each other for a moment. I felt the tiny vessel that contained our burgeoning relationship crack open and spill out. Nothing this new or fragile, built on furtiveness and lies, could survive fights such as these. I pulled at my napkin to cover my blotchy face, sending my silverware clanging to the ground and Max after it. Now I am one of those clumsy baby-women, I thought, who reverts to little-girl antics when they feel angry or scared. How often had I seen these displays at the club?

Max gently placed the fork and knife back on the table in front of me and cleared his throat. "Listen to me very carefully," he said, leaning forward to yank the corner of my chair to face him so that our knees touched. He took both my hands in his and pulled me closer, peering into my downturned face. "These past two weeks have been, for me, more than just diverting. I cannot remember a time I've enjoyed anyone's company as much as I've enjoyed yours, so much so that I have stopped myself more times than I can count from

45

kissing you hard on that very smart mouth of yours. Will you forgive me for being such an ass tonight?"

I nodded, a tear dropping onto my forearm. "I'm sorry I got mad, too."

"No, no, I liked that," he said. "More of that, please."

"We're still friends, then?"

"Sadly, yes," he said, and signaled for the bill. "But I plan to do something about that."

We walked to the car in silence. I knew what was going to happen when we got there. Before he opened my passenger door, he swiftly, gently pressed my back against the car and kissed me on the mouth. It took me a second to catch up to him, to help settle the kiss into a rhythm, which was easy for us to find. He lifted me slightly and pressed me back again, and released something like a murmuration of tiny birds through my body, fluttering beneath my skin into all the places his hands and mouth traveled.

After a minute of this, he dropped me back down on my feet.

"That was okay for me to do?"

I nodded.

"You did basically just say I should kiss you."

"I did."

"I have been wanting to almost from the moment I met you. I just . . . you're much younger than me. And I didn't want to embarrass myself, or misinterpret your attention."

"You haven't."

"Because I like you very much."

"I like you very much, too."

My phone rang, shattering the moment. It was Laureen. I wanted to smash the phone into the gravel.

"I have to get this." I walked a few steps away from him, where the light music and chatter coming from the fish shack wouldn't reveal my whereabouts or give her the impression that any kind of fun was being had.

"Please don't tell me you're already asleep," Laureen said, instead of hello. "It's only nine goddamn thirty."

"No, Laureen, I'm actually just heading back from your place. What's the news on the tow?"

"Never mind the tow. How come whenever I call the office you're never there? It's always John-John answering the phone."

"I've had a few charters this week, and I try to leave by six to water your garden before dark."

"I want you to stick by the office from now on and let John-John take out guests who need piloting. Or get that lazy arse whatshisname, one of your roommates, to do it. The British idiot. You know I prefer having a young woman at the front desk, even if it's just you."

"Sure, but—"

"By the way, John-John told me you've taken Max Winter out a few times and he didn't come back with anything. Well, no *fish*."

"Yes, well, he wasn't all that interested in fishing," I said, walking right into it.

"I gathered that much. Watch yourself, missy. John-John's not a gossip. For him to bring it up means you're being real obvious."

She tossed off a few more instructions regarding her house and reminded me she'd be back soon and that I was to meet her at the airport. She hung up without saying goodbye.

Max was texting a few feet away, the blue light from his phone reflecting on his smile. I assumed he was texting with

47

Dani. She didn't seem to keep normal hours. Or maybe that's the way it was in Paris.

I took a step towards him, stopping shy of his reach.

"Is your boss on to us?"

The kiss had shifted the atmosphere between us so dramatically I wasn't sure how to reenter it.

"You laugh," I said, "but I could lose my job."

He put his phone in his pocket and leaned back against the car. "What would you do if Laureen fired you?"

"I don't know. I suppose a part of me would be happy. I've thought of getting a job in a hotel. Maybe in management. I could also go to the Brac. I know people there."

None of this was true. But I was ashamed of my precariousness, how beholden I was to Laureen, to the debt I owed her. We drove back in silence, no mention of the kiss. Max dropped me at the foot of the cul-de-sac.

"I'll see you tomorrow."

I was tired and emboldened by the wine.

"I hope I do, Max. But you have to tell me when I will see you, and under what circumstances. I don't want to be demanding, but I have to take greater precautions now. You have privileges here. I only have risks."

"Fair enough." He took a deep breath, looking out beyond the windshield for a moment. "Tomorrow I have work to do in town, two morning meetings and lunch with an old friend I had the misfortune of running into. When I get back to the club I'll want to take a boat out in the late afternoon, sometime after four. I'll order food. Then later I'd like to see . . . what's it called? The bioluminescence field. I heard it's very pretty at night. Do you think that can all be arranged at Laureen's Charters?"

"I think so."

"Good. Now go and get some rest." He picked up my hand and kissed the back of it once, twice. "And please be sure to pack a bag. I might want to spend the night out on the water."

Even now, thinking about our past two weeks on the island can cause my face to redden, partly because I'm recalling the delicious vertigo of love taking hold, but also because my behavior became that of a woman deranged. The next morning I charged into the office and rather than asking, I told John-John that I was taking Max Winter out on an overnight cruise.

"But if anyone wants a boat and crew, even if it was Mr. Winter, Laureen said that I was to pilot, not you."

"Too bad."

He gaped at me. "I don't want to have to call her."

"Then don't. I beg you, John-John. It's not necessary. I'll cover you for the rest of your goddamn days in exchange for this one tiny favor."

I wince at the image of this wild-eyed young woman desperately clearing the path leading to her own destruction. Yet there was no reasoning with me. He threw up his hands and walked out of the office to unlock the rental kiosk, while I calmly prepped a forty-five-foot Formula, a small, attractive yacht I could handle on my own—its anchor not too heavy, its quarters roomy and comfortable—even if the weather changed overnight.

At four-thirty, Max arrived at the end of the dock dressed in jeans and a gray T-shirt, mouth stern beneath dark glasses, the thick strap of a leather overnight bag slung across his chest. He was trailed by two kitchen workers, each carrying a cooler filled with food and drinks. No one, least of all John–John, was fooled into thinking this was anything but preparations for a romantic overnight trip for two. As I said, I had lost all reason. Moving from half to full throttle once we hit open water, I had a premonition that I would be returning to a different reality, a more difficult one, likely, but in that moment nothing mattered. I let the salt air slap hard at my bare arms, my hair whip painfully at my cheeks. I removed my uniform and was wearing a silky white tank top, no bra, the only mildly alluring thing I owned. While I steered us out to the sea, Max came up behind me to take advantage of my inability to do anything about his hands on my breasts, or his mouth on my neck. Within minutes of losing sight of land, we were in the sleeping quarters impatiently consummating our relationship, blotting out any notion that this was some chaste friendship, that his intentions towards me were benignly paternal or mine at all innocent. I was no virgin (though I am, by nature, modest), but by the expert way Max moved beneath and above me, how he murmured to me with confident knowledge things about my own dark appetites that even I had never articulated, I knew he had completely ruined me for any man after him, were there to be one.

"Jesus," I whispered, collapsing next to him, coated in a layer of sweat and shamelessness, an arm flung over my eyes to obscure how conquered I felt. "I almost hate you for that."

He burst out laughing into the low cabin ceiling before curling next to me wearing a self-satisfied grin.

Every night that final week (after fleeing John–John's scolding glare), the boat became our private oasis. I dropped anchor near the glowing water, where we'd eat, swim, have sex, and then do it all over again. I was, by all measures, deliriously happy, mentally carving every moment into small chapters, the time he said that, the time we did this, the time we went there, so that when he was finally gone from my life, our brief time together would feel to me as though it had been much, much longer than it was.

What did we talk about? Everything and nothing. Local lore, the particulars of the boats we'd take out. He was fascinated by my upbringing and wanted to know how my father parented me alone after my mother died, now that he found himself in a similar position.

"How did he discipline you?" he asked.

"I think I was born obedient," I said, not too proudly. "Can't really rebel when your livelihoods depend on each other."

"Lucky father," he said. "I think Dani's bent in a way you aren't. Has been since birth. She's seen all kinds of specialists, dabbled in all manner of therapy. She'd be diagnosed with something, but the drugs would do nothing. Then we were told she had some kind of personality disorder, but she'd display few of the characteristics. Things were just getting right with her world, then Rebekah died."

We had talked almost nothing about Rebekah since the night at the fish shack. But there it was again, the name that charged the air and changed the mood.

"That must have been devastating. For both of you."

"Yes," he said. "She loved her mother very much, even though she was a very difficult woman for Dani to please."

Oddly, Dani always seemed more abstract to me than Rebekah, but the idea of having a mother like that suddenly struck me as a particular kind of burden, something

I could understand, even if I couldn't relate. Never did it occur to me that I would one day meet Dani and come to know her, and that the question of her well-being, her sanity, would be of paramount concern to me, to my happiness, to my very life.

SEVEN

I heard her and felt her before I saw her that day, Laureen back early from St. Barts, screaming my name and stomping down the dock, the whole office shuddering with her approach.

"You better be heeere. We have a lot to taaalk about," she sing-songed.

I scrambled to tidy up the desk, straighten out my ponytail, and hand-press my uniform. When she slapped open the door, I widened my eyes while pointing to the phone receiver I had shoved under my chin, already knowing from her expression she was aware of what I'd been up to. Thinking back to how much of my future she had held in her hands that day, I can still justify making that ridiculous fake phone call.

"Yes, yes, we can accommodate that reservation," I said, like a cheerful idiot. "Come right down and I'll be happy to help you. I'll be here all day. Okay. Bye."

I hung up on nobody.

"Laureen! You're back early!"

"Yes, I'm back. Move," she said, motioning me out from behind the desk.

"I would have picked you up if—"

"Tell me something," she said, flipping the pages of the daily schedule to line up with the nightly ledger. "When you take Mr. Winter out on his overnight fishing trips, how much do you charge him?" She traced her thick index fingers down the two columns.

"The full amount. It's all there and up to date. The club's been keeping a tally of his food and drinks."

It was over. The spell I'd been under for the better part of a month evaporated. Oddly, while bracing for my imminent dismissal, I wasn't angry with John-John or myself. In fact, a feeling of peace washed over me. It had all been worth it.

Satisfied I had charged for (most of) the services rendered, Laureen straightened up. "Take a seat," she said, her chin indicating a chair in the waiting area where Max and I had enjoyed breakfast that very first morning. It felt like such a long time ago now.

"Wait," I said. "Before you say anything, I want you to know that what I did never interfered with running the business. I also made sure your plants were taken care of—"

"Shut up. Please. For a second."

She came around from behind the desk and stood directly in front of me. She took a deep breath. "I actually don't need to hear any excuses from you, or reasons, or apologies," she said, modulating her voice with a dose of what sounded like kindness. "I just need you to go to your quarters and pack your things."

I stood and took a step towards the door.

"I'm not finished. I need you to pack up your things and head straight to the airport because Janie's got the plane waiting to take you to St. Barts."

"What? Why?"

"I need you to manage the charters there while I get this fucking disaster under control. I have to meet my lawyer in George Town tomorrow. I'm being sued *and* I'm suing that idiot captain, because it turns out I have hired a bunch of morons I haven't spent nearly enough time smacking around."

"But I don't think I'm qualified."

"I don't need qualified. I need someone I can trust, even though I *know* you haven't been very trustworthy of late."

"How long?"

"As long as it takes to wash away the stink of a ten-million-dollar yacht stuffed with C-list royals wiping out a rare bird sanctuary."

"I thought you came to fire me."

She looked tired all of a sudden. "I really should. Now go. I can't pay to hold that plane for longer than an hour. We'll talk more after you land."

I was frozen in place, trying to form an argument that this office, this job, even this island meant everything to me. But none of it was true. Were it not for Max, this would be about the best thing that could ever happen in my life. My reticence had only to do with him, and the promise of another week together, at most. The fact that I was weighing temporary bliss against work that could sustain me, pay my debt, help build a life for myself was something, to this day, I can barely admit.

"What if I don't want to live in St. Barts? Don't I have a choice in all this?"

She looked at me as though I'd lost my mind. "Certainly you have a choice. Here it is, kiddo. You can stay on Grand Cayman and find a job somewhere else. And since you appear to have broken every goddamn rule at *this* club, a reference will be a challenge. Or you can go to St. Barts now, receive a raise, earn your own way, live in your own apartment near the marina, and take on a lot more responsibility. *That* is your choice. And if you're not a complete moron, you'll make the right one."

I turned and fled, Laureen yelling after me, "I'll send a taxi to your place in twenty minutes. Oh, and you're bloody welcome!"

I ran down the dock, past the gauntlet of sickly sweet lunch smells. I didn't want to go away, not now, but what choice did I have? I still owed her several thousand dollars. I had no other job prospects on the island and only enough saved to tide me over for a month.

A terrific nausea set in by the time I reached the road. Morning traffic whizzed by me on the highway. I had to tell Max. I had to see him once more before I left. Maybe it was best this way, a quick rip of the Band-Aid and it would be over. Crying in an apartment without roommates might also accelerate the grieving. No muffling or stifling; no shoving it down. I could plow through my days in St. Barts, managing the schedule, giving out orders, not caring what the staff there thought of me, not worrying about being nice or liked by anyone. I could channel all this anger into a stoic competency I'd seen in other women who worked hard and lived alone. They didn't seem unhappy, sipping their white wine on their condo patios, peering into another beautiful sunset, a challenging paperback splayed across their crepey thighs. That wouldn't be such a bad life.

I made a run at a gap in the traffic. Instead of heading left to staff quarters, I went right to the private bungalows, heedless of strict club rules or how distressed hotel workers glared at my marina uniform.

Hours earlier, before we parted in the predawn hours with plans to head out after dusk again that day, I'd overheard Max telling Dani he'd be returning to Asherley soon, that the legislature reconvened in February and he'd have to be

56

in Albany a lot more since it was an election year. We hadn't discussed what "soon" meant, or whether we'd see each other again after he left. I acted nonchalant that morning, pretending I wasn't torn up inside about his looming departure, counting the hours until I could spot him coming down the dock, a basket of food in his hand. I had to kiss him one more time, to thank him, to say goodbye.

His car was parked in the drive, thank God. I banged the brass mermaid knocker and pressed my ear to the thick door. Nothing. I banged again. Maybe he was golfing. Someone would have already alerted club security, so I couldn't linger. I ducked behind his bungalow, took a shortcut through the eighteenth hole to the brush that backed onto the road across from my townhouse, dialing his number as I jogged. It headed straight to voicemail. I sent a brief text, which dangled unread.

Several cars clotted the driveway of the townhouse, stragglers from last night's party. In the filthy kitchen, two roommates sat groggily spooning cereal into their mouths for lunch.

"Hey, stranger," one said. "Didn't think you lived here any— *okaaay*."

I stormed past them and the shirtless guy passed out on the couch, slamming my bedroom door behind me. Pulling the dusty rucksack from beneath the bed, I thought how I might never have to sleep in this miserable room again, and yet why did I feel like I was being ripped from the only home I had ever known and sent into a punishing exile? For what? For behaving like a wanton local who deceived herself into thinking a rich tourist, passing time while moving his fortune from one account into another, might have loved her. Stupidly, yes, I was in love with Max Winter, in the way only young women fall in love, swiftly, uncritically, mind, heart, and body in complete and total collusion.

The sudden realization that I had no one to say goodbye to, and that everything I owned could fit inside one shabby bag, was what finally brought me to my knees. I started to cry, a silent, mucusy cry, my breath coming at shuddering intervals. I cried for what was and what would never be now. I cried for my short, pathetic past and my uncertain future. She would laugh at me, wouldn't she, Rebekah? *You idiot*, she'd say. *What were you thinking, that you'd get away with this? That a love like this was possible for someone like you? Run along*, she'd say. *Work hard and earn your own way. Then find a nice boy and let this go. Max isn't for you.* My sobbing nearly drowned out the honking of the taxi.

I wiped my face with my sleeve and stomped past the roommates, now frozen in mock fear of me, slapping open the screen door so fast I nearly took it off its hinges. But there was no taxi waiting for me. It was Max Winter, stepping out of his dark sedan, feet bare, hair wet, wearing a thick blue bathrobe, remnants of shaving cream dotting his cheek and chin.

"Max!" I wanted to run into his arms but I was afraid I would never leave them.

"What's going on? A maid told me you came by. I only just got your text. I was in the shower."

"I was trying to— Max, I have to go. I'm leaving for St. Barts. Right now."

Just then the taxi pulled up behind him. Max looked at my bag and the taxi. "Why?"

"Laureen's transferring me. She wants me to run the charters there."

"Today? Right *now*?"

"Right now. I came to say goodbye. And to thank you. I have to take this job or I—or I won't *have* a job."

He drove his fingers through his wet hair, his eyes darting from the taxi to me, back to the taxi. "I mean, do you *want* to go to St. Barts?"

"Of course I don't. Not yet anyway. I won't know a soul. I have no idea what the job entails. But it isn't exactly an employment hotbed here and there is the matter of the money I owe Laureen."

"You actually don't . . . owe her anything." He winced. "Wait there. Don't move."

"What are you talking about?"

He walked over to the taxi and ducked to speak to the driver. The car backed up and drove off.

"Max, what are you doing?"

He took a deep breath. "I emailed Laureen yesterday and offered to pay your father's debts."

"You what?"

"It bothered me that she was hanging it over your head. It's criminally unfair, if not plain criminal. So I told her you'd done an exceptional job this month and asked her to put whatever amount you owed on my bill. I was going to tell you tonight, as a surprise. But now I realize I should have asked you first. I'm afraid I might have instigated this . . . this ridiculous transfer. I can't tell you how sorry—"

"What did she say?"

"She said you wouldn't want that."

"And she's right!" I threw down my bag, covered my face with my hands, and turned away from him to hide the new influx of tears. So this is why Laureen raced back.

My mortification was complete. I turned to face him, my voice pitched high. "How was I to pay *you* back for what I owe *her*?"

"It's not like that. I expect nothing from—"

"I never asked you for anything. I don't want anything from you."

"That's why I did it."

We stood there looking at each other. My chest painfully constricted. Was this what a heart attack felt like?

"Tell me something," he said. "Where would you rather go? St. Barts or Long Island?"

"Stop."

"It's a serious question."

"I can't go to Long Island with you, Max. To do what? To live where?"

"To live at Asherley with me. With us."

With one step he closed the space between us, glanced around, and awkwardly bent down on one knee on the hot gravel road, the sun directly above us. I told myself that what was about to happen wasn't real, that I was imagining this, that he was stooping to pick something up off the ground.

"This isn't how I planned to do it. I had hoped to be better dressed at least. But if this is the way it has to be . . ."

"Max, you're being ridiculous," I said, a smile fighting to break out across my sodden face. "You don't have to do this—"

"Your hand, please. I can't put a ring on it right this instant. But hear me out."

I gave him the hand that wasn't covering my mouth in astonishment. He cleared his throat and continued.

"You have made me a happy man these past few weeks. I wake up every morning in this phony paradise, away from friends and family, where I come to conduct the dullest, most heartless part of my business, cheered only by the fact that by nightfall I will get to see you. So I see no reason why we should not continue to be together. And I know we haven't known each other very long. I know I'm not an easy person to love. I have a . . . complicated life, and a complicated daughter who will probably make this a little harder for you before it gets easier. But you see, fortunately, or unfortunately, depending on your reply, I am falling in love with you. And I am the type that's intent on finishing what I start. So will you do me the honor of marrying me?"

When he bent his head to kiss my hand, I gently pulled it loose before he made contact. Even in my most ludicrous fantasies, when I imagined us carrying on beyond this past month, it never involved this, a proposal, marriage, relocation, or my living, of all places, at Asherley. Even in my dreams, even as I tried to imagine myself trailing my fingers along the boxwood at the bottom of the sloping lawn, or attending glittery political functions in the great hall, or making my way down to breakfast, one hand on the carved balustrade, the other crunching sleep out of my eyes, I could not get any closer to the estate than the iron gates.

"Oh, Max. I'm so . . . Please stand up. It can't be comfortable down there."

Stiffly he rose, brushing gravel off his now pocked knee. "Seems I have misconstrued things. I was of the mind that you might have felt the same about me."

"Oh, I do. I do. I am . . . falling in love with you, too. I think. No. I am. So you must know what this means to me. It's so kind. But you can't marry *me*. I don't belong at a place like Asherley. This is the biggest house I've ever lived in," I said, my thumb indicating the rundown townhouse behind me. "You need someone with more experience, with—I don't know—glamour. I'm mangling this. Can't we just continue like we've been doing, maybe talking on the phone now and again? Perhaps you can make a trip to St. Barts sometime soon to see me."

He had a wan smile on his face. "Yes," he said, "except for the simple fact that I want you in my life now. Don't you think I know best who belongs at Asherley, who belongs in my life, in Dani's life? I promise you if you're miserable, I'll bring you right back here, no worse for the wear."

"What about Dani? She might want to weigh in on this."

"Oh, she has. I've already told her all about you. I even sent a picture."

"And . . . ?"

"Naturally she will need some time to get to know you, to love you like I know she will. She's headstrong. But she's not in charge. And believe me, bringing you home with a ring and a promise will accelerate the bonding. She needs to know you're not just some temporary girlfriend. So I will ask the question one more time. Do you want to go to St. Barts right now, or do you want to come home to Asherley with me?"

What could I say? My epic self-sufficiency, my resistance to anyone's generosity melted away. His words had also planted a small, noxious seed of pride in me. *You're not some temporary girlfriend; he wants you to be his fiancée, his wife. He was once married to Rebekah Winter. Now he chooses you.*

"I want to go to Asherley," I said, "with you."

He grabbed me and kissed me, then lifted me around in a circle. I threw my bag into the backseat of his car and we sped off. I insisted he drop me at the end of the pier so I could tell Laureen.

"You don't want me to come with you?"

"No. I can do this alone. I'll meet you at the bungalow," I said, before kissing him.

I walked slowly to the end of the pier, savoring the smells of lunch and the sound of seagulls circling overhead looking for sandwich crusts or potato chip crumbs scattered about the dock. I thought of how I wouldn't have to clean any of these boats anymore, or hose off those paddleboards or lug that rental canoe back into storage.

When I entered the office, Laureen looked up from the desk. "Oh good Lord."

"Laureen, I came to tell you something. It turns out I can't go to St. Barts," I said. "Max Winter and I have . . . well, we just got engaged."

She fell back into the office chair and closed her eyes. "I worried something like this would happen."

"There's nothing to worry about. We fell in love, and I'm going to America with him in a few days."

She gave me a look, one eyebrow up, mouth set in a weary, crooked line. I wanted to believe she was jealous. Here she was, a woman who had worked all her life to build her wealth, and I was lazily marrying into it. Yet I got the sense from her expression, the softness around the eyes, that in fact she pitied me. Fine, I could live with that, because the man I loved was waiting for me in his bungalow. After this, I'd never, ever have to see her or set foot in this nasty little hovel again.

"I know you don't believe me right now, kiddo, but I was actually trying to save you from this very fate."

"Stop calling me kiddo. And I don't need to be saved. I'm a twenty-six-year-old *woman* engaged to be married to a man I love. And I'm sorry if my leaving makes your life harder."

She sighed, looking me up and down. "Actually, it's your life that just took a more difficult turn. If you seriously think working for me is harder than marrying a man like Max Winter, and living in a big, old drafty mansion, and trying to raise a nightmare kid like Dani Winter, you're kidding yourself. I've taken you for a lot of things, some I was right about, some wrong. But I never took you for stupid. And what happens after he gets sick of you? Or the kid chews you up and spits you out? Then what? What's your life going to look like then?" Her voice lowered. "Tell me, has he made you sign anything?"

I bristled at the baseness of her question. "No, he hasn't. But I'd sign anything. I don't want any of his mon—"

"Sign absolutely nothing until you get a lawyer. You want some goddamn guarantees that he'll leave you a little better off than he found you."

"I'm sure I'll be all right."

"Ha! Men. They kill me. They'll do absolutely anything not to be alone in the world with their sad little memories. So weak."

I was finished listening. I turned to leave.

"After it all goes to hell, and it will," she said, "don't come crawling back here. I'll be over in 'I told you so' land, making my own money, earning my own keep."

I slammed the door behind me.

★

We relocated to a suite at the Ritz and spent the next several days in a rush of errands. Max had a few more meetings. I needed to get my paperwork together, close a bank account, say goodbye to a few people. It was difficult to find appropriate winter clothes in George Town, never mind a diamond ring both small enough for my liking and serious enough for Max's.

"It's the first place Dani will look," he said, dismissing anything below two carats. "And I want her to know we mean business."

Still, we both had to laugh when I slid the simple solitaire onto a finger left scarred and calloused by ropes, its nail bed permanently damaged by an errant anchor.

"I feel like a grave robber," I said, watching it glint in the sun against its ruddy background.

The next day, I was strapping myself in for my first-ever jet ride. I'd island-hopped on small props from the private strip but had never before been on a plane that sat more than twelve people, including the pilot. I looked around at the murmuring crowd settling in. There was no denying it now. I was leaving the Caymans to live in America. I was going to be Max Winter's wife.

Before takeoff, while Max got up to fetch more blankets, his phone, tossed on the seat next to mine, pinged a text that flashed across the home screen. *If you bring ur fucking fling home daddy ill kill myself.* When Max returned with his bounty I feigned a sudden fixation with something on the wing, my face scarlet with upset.

"I cleaned them out," he said as he tucked one of the blankets around my bare ankles. Out of the corner of my eye, I watched him pick up his phone and read the text, his

65

reaction that of a man checking a weather app. He dropped the phone in the pocket of the seat in front of him, took my hand, kissed it, then settled back into his seat and closed his eyes. If true, that she would rather die than have me come live at Asherley, then Max, who knew her better than me, looked perfectly content to call her bluff. If her own father didn't take her threats seriously, then why on earth should I?

EIGHT

To go from constant heat to my first cold winter, from calm blue vistas to a jagged gray skyline, was a jarring experience that created some holes in this part of my story, which I blame on a small memory bank, granted to someone who was never meant to go through this much change. I don't remember, for instance, exactly how many days we spent in New York City. Was it three or five? Or if Max had his car brought to him or if he'd left one parked at the airport. I do remember we drove ourselves to the hotel, the traffic moving like a slow funeral procession, the better to take in the impressive buildings, some familiar to me from movies yet as alien as anything I'd ever encountered. Did we run into that brash financier Max went to college with at that fancy restaurant with the pale pink ceiling or while in line at the Broadway show? I do remember the wife, thin and flinty, looking me up and down, no doubt comparing me to Rebekah, wondering how I did it, how did someone like me manage to land Max Winter. She was in a fur, the original animal unrecognizable from the way the coat was dyed and shaped. I was wearing my first real winter coat, a heavy camel wool one with a snug belt that cost as much as a used car. She told me she'd love to come out and see us after we settled, and Max answered for me, saying that would be nice, and that we'd be in touch, muttering "never" after they were finally out of earshot.

I loved navigating the crowds, those perpetual parades, and how Manhattan felt bigger than the Caymans even though it's much smaller, the same way furnished rooms feel bigger than empty ones. But the idea that I was on a small island whose surrounding water might go unseen for days, weeks, or years was oddly disorienting. I had to remind myself that an ocean is right there, that its currents were made up of the same water I once swam in, just blacker and colder.

The morning we packed for Long Island, Max could tell I was nervous. Though he'd been intent on spoiling me in the city, I had only bought a few basics: a couple of pairs of jeans, some sweaters and sweatpants, a pair of boots, and other necessities, enough to fill my new suitcase. I wanted to avoid arriving at Asherley accompanied by a caravan of things.

"The only people who will be greeting us work for me. I pay them to like you, so what does it matter?"

He was kidding, but my need to make a good impression, to be liked by others, to satisfy their expectations, was as old as I was, instilled in me by people similarly afflicted. When your livelihood depends on the benevolence of tourists, it becomes a hard trait to shake.

These were my thoughts as we crossed the Queensboro Bridge that cold day, putting the protective canyons of Manhattan behind us. I had loved our time in New York. Far from feeling cowed by the noise and size, I had begun to feel nestled—carried, even. There was always something to look at, something new to do or eat, and there was freedom in the anonymity the crowds provided. You didn't have to drag around your history. You could go a long time, I bet, without running into anyone you knew. That seemed like a gift to me. So as sad as I was to leave, I was buoyed by Max's promise that I could take a car into the city as often as I liked, once I grew accustomed to driving on the other side of the road.

Asherley. I was almost as nervous to meet the house as I was to meet Dani. It had begun to occupy a mythical place in my mind so it was hard to believe I would actually see it, walk around inside it, and live in it. I still couldn't picture myself getting past the gate—its walls and paintings, its furniture and carpets remained indistinct, blurring in my peripheral vision.

When we left at one o'clock, the sky was dun colored, only mildly forbidding. By the time we reached the outer boroughs, the dusting of flakes had turned to flurries. The clouds ahead were low and dark; we were driving into bad weather, not away from it. Max veered south to take the parkway.

"Might take a bit longer, but there'll be less traffic," he explained.

I nodded, grateful for any delay, hoping by the time we got there my nerves would be calmer, my fears dampened. I wanted to feel excited to begin our lives together. Instead I experienced a vague unspooling, as though I'd tied a string to something in the city to help me find my way back, but the farther out we drove, Max pointing out Islip, Patchogue, Shirley, East Quogue, the more untethered I felt. Max seemed confident, happy to be going home, but I could sense the icy road just beneath the veneer of snow and the effort the tires were making to grab and hold the curves.

We drove for hours. Eventually the parkway joined together to form a narrower road, with trucks rushing past us, slapping dirty snow at our car in the tailwinds. I kept anticipating the exits, *this is the turnoff, no this must be it,* but Max drove on and on, oblivious to my mounting anxiety. I made small talk

69

about a white blocky gas station with a hand-painted mural that reminded me of home, Max squeezing my hand then quickly returning it to the wheel. By Southampton, a chill set in, one that went down to the bone. I pulled my coat tighter under my chin.

"Want the heat up?"

"No, I'm fine. Thank you, Max."

The road narrowed yet again as we cut up from East Hampton, four lanes becoming two, both completely engulfed in snow. He navigated by following the tire grooves made by a car a distance ahead, its red taillights fading and brightening depending on our speed. Old trees weighted with snow offered us some respite from the blizzard, but they also took away the day's remaining light. It was only four o'clock but it was already dark.

We finally broke out of the forested part of the drive and came upon an open road that seemed to come to a dead end at the beach. There, instead of stopping, Max sped up. We were heading straight into the water.

"Max! Stop!" I screamed, bracing for impact.

"Whoa! It's okay!" Max said, guiding my torso back against the seat as the car made a sudden transition from bumpy to smooth, the road becoming the causeway that connected Long Island to Winter's Island. My hand remained over my heart.

"Did you think I was going to drive us into the bay?"

"No . . . I couldn't see the road."

Beyond the windshield, water churned and splashed angrily against the stone shoulders of the raised road. Max glanced over at me, mindful now of my nerves. He slowed as we exited the causeway and pulled up to a set of iron gates, easily ten feet high, with thick pickets spiked at the top, *Asherley* forged in an ornate cutout. Thinner pickets of descending size extended fifty feet to the left and right of the gates, blending into the black trees. The fence didn't circumnavigate the island, Max told me. White-tailed deer lived there, and beavers and swans, but the gate kept cars from making easy passage to the house, unless you walked, braving the rocky shores before traversing the forest and its thick undergrowth. Max hit a button under his seat and the gates swung open, shoving great wings of snow out of their way.

"Looks like Gus got the plow out in time," Max said as he inched the car along another densely forested mile before Asherley. Now there was little to see out the window, just the dark shadows of tree trunks lining our narrow path. There were no streetlights, no porch lights flickering through the trees, indicating life nearby should our car skid off the road. I'd been prepared for Asherley to be secluded, but the near blackness made it feel even more remote. My fears took on a different flavor now, more primal. I thought of Rebekah careening around the narrow bends and I understood how dangerous this drive would be at high speeds, and how a fire could flatten several acres before anyone spotted the smoke. If something happened out here, who would know?

At a final bend, Max made a hard right and we abruptly left the forest and drove into a smattering of fat snowflakes the trees had been shielding us from. Before us lay acres of rolling expanse, which, reflected off the dusk sky, painted the snow a pale indigo. In the distance I spotted Asherley, its massive silhouette pocked with a dozen blazing windows. This must have been the vantage point from which Max took the picture he had shown me on the boat so many weeks ago, the day he took one of me. It occurred to me then that he hadn't taken another one, not even in New York.

"Home," Max said.

We inched into the long oval drive, and I sunk a little as the entirety of Asherley emerged, its windows glowing orange with lights or fires, giving the house the appearance of a ghostly barge closing in on us.

Because the snow and glass were the same milky-blue color, the greenhouse, at first, was camouflaged. Now here it was, too, looking as though a strange starship had crashed neatly into the side of the stone porch. This isn't a place where a person lives, I thought; here you reign. And in that moment, wearing wool socks, jeans, and a comfy flannel shirt, I couldn't have felt less regal. Max shut off the car and my ears pounded with my own heartbeat. When I saw celebrities in the Caymans I was always struck by how plain and diminutive many were without the accoutrements of fame. This was the opposite sensation.

"Ready?"

I nodded and swallowed, my eyes trailing up the side of the highest turret, where a low light glowed from within. Out of the front door a man came running towards us, using a coat as a shield against the snow blowing off the eaves.

"Ah, Elias!" Max exclaimed. "My left- and right-hand man."

Elias came around to open my door. We yelled our introductions over the weather.

"Take her," said Max. "I'll put the car away."

I ducked under Elias's temporary tarp and we scrambled up the porch steps together, through the double doors, twice as high as me, and into a wall of warm air laced with the velvety smell of roses wafting from a massive bouquet of red ones on a table near the staircase. There Elias introduced me to a young man named Gus who had thick eyebrows and was wearing a heavy coat. When I stuck out my hand, he ignored it in lieu of a brisk nod before running out the door to help Max.

"I hope I didn't frighten him," I said.

"He's shy at first, but he's a good guy," Elias said, taking my coat and disappearing into the anteroom off the foyer.

From my earlier Internet searches, I knew an unsettling number of details that made Asherley so extraordinary, like the fact that the marble floor my boots were dripping onto had been sliced out of a quarry in the Hudson Valley, and Rebekah had them refurbished by an expert who used only diamond grit pads from Italy. I also knew that the rounded, hand-carved walls of the anteroom hid two tall cabinets that had been shipped from Brussels, one housing coats and boots and the other rifles and guns, some antique, some modern. I also recognized the stained-glass crescent window above the entry door, depicting a pack of dogs leaping after a dove that once hung in a sixteenth-century monastery. I thought knowing these facts from my snooping might tamp down my sense of fraudulence, but I was wrong. I stood stunned by a grandeur not truly captured in pictures.

Elias came bounding back into the foyer. "When Max told me about your engagement I was quite surprised. And, of course, thrilled."

"Me, too," I said, rubbing my hands together. I wasn't cold. I just didn't know where to put them. "What do I do with my boots?"

"Just leave them on that mat. Katya will take care of them."

Elias was younger than I'd expected, with warm eyes and a lilting accent that made you lean closer for the words. Later

I would learn that Max had met him in Buenos Aires twenty years prior, when he and Rebekah went to buy a horse. Elias had done the books for the breeders. The two men hit it off, and Max hired him away. With each passing year, more and more of Max's investments and legal affairs fell under his command. And now he was Max's chief of staff, often traveling with him to Albany, when not at the constituency office in East Hampton.

Max burst through the front door, with Gus behind him burdened with our bags, and at the same time a large, stern-looking woman of about sixty came in from a hallway wiping her hands on a tea towel. Her hair was pulled taut off her face with a headband, and the rest hung gray and limp around her ample shoulders.

"Katya!" Max hugged her like he was her long-lost son and introduced her to me as the CEO of Asherley, whose office was the kitchen. "It's Sunday. You're not supposed to be here."

"I heard the news," she said, shrugging in my direction. "I wanted to make a roast." She added that dinner wouldn't be ready for another hour or so, but that she'd prepared something to tide us over in our rooms.

"Wonderful. Thank you," Max said, and turned to me. "Go upstairs and warm up, my dear. I have to talk to Eli for a few minutes. Katya, mind showing her where?"

Max kissed my temple and launched me into her wake. I followed her up the wide staircase, keeping my stocking feet on the thick runner, pulling my sleeves down over my hands. The house was warm but I was cold for some reason, or maybe just hungry. A tall mullioned window split the stairs left and right at a landing. The walls were flanked by paintings on either side, Max's ancestors, all men, all white and old.

74

"You must be tired," Katya said, her climbing becoming effortful.

"A little. But I'm happy to be here."

"How was the drive?"

"A bit frightening, to be honest. Lots of snow."

I almost told her I'd never seen snow before New York, but I wasn't sure whether it would endear me to her or alarm her.

"Where's Dani?" she asked.

"Still in Paris. She gets here in a couple days, I hear. I'm looking forward to meeting her."

Katya stopped on the stairs, her eyes wide. "You haven't met each other yet?"

"No. She's been in Paris this whole time and we've been in the Caymans. I thought you knew that."

Her face seemed to soften, as though she was offering a preemptive dose of pity. "My, my."

We reached the landing and I reflexively continued towards the stairs to the third floor.

"Your rooms are on this floor," Katya said over her shoulder. She was already crossing the second-floor gallery. "The third floor is Dani's domain."

I pivoted and quickly followed. We passed a long oval table, shaped like a surfboard, a slash of dramatic white veining through its black marble surface. Centered on it was another massive spray of dark red roses, their heads as big as fists. The wainscoting gleamed in contrast to the matte red walls above it, which were festooned with still more paintings, this time landscapes, seascapes, horses, and dogs. A few women.

"The roses are beautiful."

"Standing order from our florist," Katya said. "We used to grow them here, but Mr. Winter closed up the greenhouse when Mrs. Winter died." She spoke breezily, as though relaying this information to a gaggle of bored tourists. "Dani still likes having them around."

Of course she does, I thought. There will be all sorts of these not-so-subtle reminders of Rebekah. Some will be incidental to the home, which was, after all, Rebekah's life's work. And some, like this, Dani will insist upon maintaining. I had to brace myself. Soon these reminders will become background scenery and I'll begin to make my own mark. It will take time. That's all.

At the end of the gallery Katya pressed open the high double doors, releasing a gust of warmer air. The only light in the room came from a roaring fireplace, whose mouth was as tall as me. The flames' shadows danced across the enormous bed, its posts like telephone poles topped with burgundy velvet draping. These were definitely Max's rooms. I could smell him in here.

Katya pointed through an archway to another dimly lit room beyond. "I've set out some finger food and there's wine, too, in the sitting room. The dressing rooms are through there and then the bathroom's just beyond that. Gus already dropped off your bag."

"Thank you so much."

She faced me squarely, her features softer since our initial introduction. "If you don't need anything else I should get back to the kitchen and finish dinner. Give me an hour. I do hope you'll be comfortable," she said, "during your stay."

"Thank you. I'm sure I'll be fine."

After she left, I butted up against her last few words. This will all take time.

I looked around. Despite the enormous fireplace and the high ceilings, the rooms felt cozy, private. I sat on the bed to test the mattress before padding over the plush throw rugs that covered a herringbone-patterned floor, oak, well worn. In the sitting area two high-back chairs faced yet another, smaller, fire. Between the chairs was an oval table with a tray of various cheeses, fruit, and crackers. I plunked a black grape into my mouth—it turned out to be an olive—and continued through the second archway. I could see marble walls, a riot of black and white stripes, behind a glass divider—the same marble as was on the tabletop in the second-floor gallery. This was the bath area, which had modern details, sleek copper faucets, and plush white towels. To my right was a long corridor flanked by two walls of wooden doors, and my suitcase atop a center island waiting for me to empty it.

Katya's words continued to vex me. To her I was a temporary guest enjoying a stay. She thought I was too young, too unformed, too meek to make this work. Was she in the kitchen right now whispering to someone, *What is Max Winter doing with* her? Not Elias. He didn't seem the gossipy type. Maybe her audience was that young man, Gus. Yes, he'd given me an odd look, hadn't he? Or she's got the ear of some kitchen assistant, brought in especially to help prepare the roast. *Imagine everything you own fitting into one little suitcase! I hear she was practically homeless. Lost her job, was going to get kicked out of her rooming house. Max rescued her from certain penury. We'll see how long this lasts. He'll get bored of her soon. I mean, what does she bring to the table? Not even good looks. I can't believe he would pick someone like her. After Rebekah? And what will Dani make of her? Ha! Can't wait to see that. He must be depressed. I'm telling you, she didn't even say two words to me the whole time.*

I shook my head against the noise. They don't know me. They don't know what we're like alone. They don't see how easily I make Max laugh. They don't feel the air between us sweeten when we're together, even in silence, *especially* in silence. We know so little about what truly bonds a couple together. We only see the handholding or hear the bickering and form our opinions from those loaded interactions. But we don't know. Max and I, we fit together in every conceivable way. Didn't we? They'll soon see how our temperaments are perfectly calibrated. Where he is decisive and sometimes bombastic, I am willing to calmly weigh options. He's set in his ways, and I have few "ways" that are permanent, which is normal for someone his age and mine. Not to say I wasn't my own person. I knew my limits and abilities. And of course there was the sex we were having, which surprised even me with its intensity.

When Max quietly entered the bedroom he found me standing in front of the fire, my palms open to the flames. He smiled. I smiled back. The thought came to me that the last woman he might have made love to in this room was Rebekah. Did he tiptoe towards her like this, a finger over his lips? When he wordlessly removed my clothes and gently lifted me off the floor and carried me over to the bed, I wondered whether he had done this to her, thrown her backwards onto the comforter, her arms flung out like a cross. As his mouth slowly made its way from my ear to a nipple then down to my stomach, I thought, he did this to her, too, right here and not so long ago. Far from ruining my mood, these thoughts made me fiercer, clutch the blanket and a fist of his hair a little harder. I would never admit this, to him or anyone else, though. This was my secret, something that was just between her and me.

NINE

I woke from our accidental nap exhausted and breathless, as though I'd slept beneath a heavy boulder perched upon my chest. The fire was at a flicker. Max slept soundly next to me. I had no idea how long we had napped or what time it was. Looking out the window didn't help; it was already dark when we arrived. I stretched, careful not to wake Max, and pulled on my clothes. I made the bold decision to make my way down to the kitchen alone, I was that famished.

In the gallery, the now dimmed sconces lent long shadows to the roses, their great heads lowing as I passed. My plan was to follow the sounds, since I had no idea how to get to the kitchen. But no sound came from downstairs. Instead I heard someone upstairs, on the third floor, talking. It was a lost stranger's instinct to follow a voice, to try to find someone to lead me to where I wanted to go. But as I climbed the stairs to get closer, the voice suddenly became indistinct, like a low murmur that seemed to echo oddly.

At the landing I listened again. I felt something tickle my ankle and looked down. A large cream-colored Persian blinked up at me, its pupils dilated black and shiny. When I bent to pet it, it scurried past me, slinking through a door left ajar, its matted tail puffed out on high alert.

The third-floor gallery was smaller than the second. Though its walls were painted the same deep red, it had an entirely different feel, perhaps due to the dimmer light that curved off the vaulted ceiling. But it was more than that. The room was an homage, created for one person, Rebekah Winter. Instead of paintings, the walls were lined with dozens and dozens of framed photos of her, some small, some big, but each and every one was of Rebekah, smiling and not smiling, close up or far away, posing in front of something beautiful or old, in sunglasses or hats or both. Sometimes she was driving a car or riding a horse. There were several, too, of Rebekah and Dani, their bond evident. There were so many photos, craning my neck and turning to take them all in made me dizzy, a little sick. Everywhere I looked I saw long blond hair caught in the wind, too-white teeth and laughing mouths, perfect pale skin and flashing blue eyes. Rebekah looked nearly the same age in every photo, despite the passing of the years. Dani's changes from infancy to what would have been just a couple of years ago told a different story, one of a child gradually turning into her mother, her hair becoming blonder and longer, until their tresses were identical in color, length, and style. At one end of the gallery was a picture of all three of them on the porch, Max's arm around each of them. He looked so young, happy, and relaxed that it only highlighted the toll life had taken on him since Rebekah had died. At the end of this gauntlet of female perfection was another vase of black-red roses, which lent the entire gallery the feeling of a private memorial service.

The voice broke my spell. I was certain now that it was coming from the door the cat had disappeared behind. I pushed it open past a crack. I could smell cigarette smoke coming from the top of the spiral stairs winding inside the turret. There was another door at the top and it was open, too, a white light coming from inside. Careful to keep to the runner, I climbed the stairs, stopping to listen every few steps. There it was again, a woman's voice, muffled and low. Perhaps it was Katya taking a break. I stepped on a tread that creaked so loudly it brought me to a halt. I held my breath and listened. The murmuring stopped. I heard footsteps. As they neared the door, I froze with that childlike belief that stillness could make a person invisible. The door opened and there stood a tall female figure holding a burning cigarette, the other hand shielding her eyes to peer down into the blackness where I stood, pressed against the wall, trying to be small. The brightness of the room behind her shone through her flimsy nightgown, darkening her small nipples and blacking out her face. I was squinting up at the haloed form of Rebekah herself.

"Who are *you*?" she asked, finally.

My hand went to my mouth to stifle a scream.

All I could think to do was run down the stairs and out the door. My elbow caught the corner of a small silver-framed picture, one of a dozen crowding a narrow sideboard, and it fell forward with a tense smack. I stopped to right it and I saw that its glass was cracked like a spider's web, Rebekah's smile turned to a sneer. I made the split-second decision to hide the picture in the sideboard's top drawer and keep running. By the time I slowed my approach to our bedroom and slipped in next to Max, I felt boneless with terror, my heart pounding so loud I thought it might wake him.

Soon, the humiliation of my retreat caught up to me, as did the realization that that hadn't been Rebekah who hovered over me at the top of the turret but Dani. That was not a ghost I saw, but Dani back from Paris early. Oh good lord. Why did I do that? Why did I panic and run away? How could my mind have mistaken Dani for a dead woman? Why didn't I just say, *Oh, I'm so sorry, I thought you were Katya. You must be Dani. We weren't expecting you until Wednesday.* I'd extend my hand and introduce myself, like a normal person would. And later, when we told the story to Max, we'd laugh about the scare we gave each other. Instead she was probably up there right now hissing into her phone about what an idiot her father's fiancée was.

I felt Max stir. I shut my eyes, unable to face my shame just yet. This time he was the one who left quietly in order not to rouse me. I remained in bed for a little while longer, trying to muster the courage to face them. Finally, hunger propelled me down the stairs, following the sound of Dani's animated voice interspersed with Max's laugh, loud and booming, the likes of which I had never heard from him before. I crossed the foyer and made my way towards a high archway where the checkerboard floor led to an airy kitchen. There they were, leaning into each other in profile, Max delighted, transfixed by her, while Katya stood over the counter slicing the roast. I felt like an anxious jump roper waiting for the appropriate time to skip into the action.

". . . and then I call Auntie Louisa right before takeoff, when I'm already on the plane," Dani was telling a bemused Max. She was now wearing yoga pants and a snug T-shirt, still braless, her long blond hair hanging in wet strands down to the middle of her back.

"You shouldn't take off on people like that, Dani. It's becoming a bad habit."

"I know, but it's so fun."

Max finally noticed me.

"There she is!" he exclaimed, opening his arm wide to beckon me over. "I'd like you to meet my lovely daughter, Dani."

"Sorry to interrupt your story," I said, heading to the safety of Max's side. I extended my hand. "It is so nice to finally meet you."

"Nice to see you again," she said.

As Max had predicted, she glanced down at my ring.

"Cute."

"You two have already met?" Max asked.

A look passed between Dani and Katya.

"Yeah, uh . . . she poked her head into Mum's room while I was talking to Claire."

"What were you doing up there?" Dani rolled her eyes, and Max looked at me. "And what were *you* doing up there?"

"I got up to use the bathroom," I explained. "And then I heard someone . . . I thought it was you, Katya. I certainly didn't mean to scare you, Dani."

"You're the one who was scared. Daddy, you should have seen her face. It was like she saw a ghost! Who did you *think* I was?"

Max gave me a reassuring squeeze. "I bet you scared each other." He pulled out a stool next to him. "You got here just in time for some roast beef sandwiches, and I hope you like it cold. Seems we slept too long for a hot meal."

"This roast is a piece of art," Katya muttered over her shoulder. "I'm not reheating it and letting it dry out."

Dani grabbed a slice of rare beef from the platter in front of her, bit off a chunk, and threw the rest back down.

"Katya, I missed you so much," she whined, licking her fingers. Then she got up, wrapped her arms around Katya from behind, and closed her eyes. Katya ignored Dani, keeping her movements purposeful, going from the counter to the island, scooping potato salad into a bowl and depositing buns and condiments before us, all the while wearing a teenage girl like a cape.

"Honey, let the poor woman do her job," Max said. "This one ran away from her aunt in Paris and flew back early, by herself, scaring Louisa half to death."

Dani kept it up, clutching Katya, whimpering, "I'll die if you leave me, Katya. You're the only one here who loves me."

Perhaps this is typical of the age, I thought. Isn't this what makes teenagers so impossible, this careening from babyish to sullen to mature and back again? I did not have the luxury of behaving this way, but there were young people at the club, attention seekers, Laureen said, who got that way because we stopped spanking kids.

"I think Dani came home early because she was anxious to get back to Asherley. And to meet you," Max said, moving a piece of my hair behind my ear.

"Yeah, that's not why."

Max began to assemble a sandwich for me. "You take mustard, right?"

"I'm happy to make it myself, Max," I said, gently prying the bun from his hand, but he resisted, intent on serving me.

Dani let go of Katya and hopped back on her stool. "You can make *me* a sandwich, Daddy."

"I am serving our guest."

I decided women over a certain age could be divided into two camps: those who called their father Daddy well into adulthood and those who stopped in childhood, if they ever used the word at all. I was firmly of the latter camp.

My own father would have taken it as a diminutive and an indication of stunted growth on my part, for which he'd have felt personally responsible. But Max hadn't flinched at the word. In fact, after making me a sandwich, he made her one, too, using bread instead of a bun, removing the crusts, of course.

"And how long is our *guest* staying?" Dani asked, tilting her head at me, brows up in mock interest.

"She's here for good. That's the plan," he said, winking at me.

I was mindful of concealing my ravenousness, taking small, careful bites while listening to Dani chatter on about Paris and Auntie Louisa's husband, Jonah, who was only able to come over for a couple of weeks, during which time they bickered every day over the stupidest stuff, and how she made friends with a famous singer's daughter who lived in the flat upstairs by herself *at fourteen, can you believe it?* She became her second best friend behind Claire. And even though this girl's father was *super* rich, he was *super* cheap, and how Dani had to pay for everything so she'd be needing a top-up, as she put it, to which Max said he'd talk to Elias. She continued to ignore me as she spoke.

Without the filters and makeup in her photos, she looked younger than fifteen. Her cheeks were flatter too, her eyes a little closer together. She was what you'd call a commonly pretty teenage girl who, like most of them with a phone, simply knew her best angles. It never left her side, that phone. The whole time she spoke her eyes traveled automatically from Max's face down to where she kept it beside her place mat, and she would absently pick it up to check a text or a post, sometimes mid-sentence.

"We went to the Pompidou," she said, cueing up a photo and showing Max. I could see it was a painting of a woman with a stern face, wearing a red-checked dress, smoking alone in a café. "The Otto Dix," she said. "Mum's favorite."

Max looked closely at the photo, then snatched the phone out of her hand. "Was your new Parisian friend always on her phone, too?" he asked, playfully holding it out of her reach.

"She was way worse," Dani said, swatting at her phone before he handed it back to her. While checking it again, she asked me what I was on, "Like, social media wise."

"Me? Oh, nothing. I only just got a smartphone." In New York, Max had made that a priority, and I didn't fight him on it.

"Not even Facebook? That's weird. How do you keep in touch with your friends?"

I didn't want to admit to her my friendless state and said lamely, "I give them my phone number. You can have it, too, if you want." I immediately regretted the offer.

"Pass."

Max rescued the moment by suggesting that Katya call it a night, telling her that he'd clean up, that it was getting late. "In fact, stay in a guest room. I don't want you driving tonight."

Katya insisted the snow had stopped falling and by now Gus had plowed the causeway all the way to the mainland.

"With my insomnia I need to sleep in my own bed, Mr. Winter."

"Fine, I'll walk you out. Make sure your car's not buried under."

Katya took off her apron and kissed the side of Dani's head, said, "Welcome back, dear," mumbled a good night to me, and followed Max out.

The two of us just sat there for a few painful seconds. I scrambled for something, anything, to talk about, landing on the lamest of subjects.

"Was it snowing in Paris, too?"

"No."

"Isn't it the middle of the night for you now? You must be tired."

"I'm not," she said, swinging her feet off her stool. "In fact, if I was in Paris right now, I'd probably just be getting home. Auntie Louisa says Americans live on banker's hours. *Que pouvez-vous faire? Les habitudes provinciales.*" She put an elbow on the island and rested her chin on her fist, looking at me conspiratorially. "So, like, *you* totally lucked out, didn't you? Snagging yourself a rich older boyfriend?"

I had expected people to have these thoughts, but I hadn't counted on how unsettling they'd sound coming out of a fifteen-year-old's mouth.

"If you mean am I grateful that I met your father, then yes, I guess you could say I lucked out."

"Also, just because you're here doesn't mean you have the run of the place. The third floor is mine. And the turret's hers, both off-limits to you."

The question must have shown on my face.

"Yes, that was my mother's bedroom you barged into. I don't want you going up there."

"I'm sorry, I didn't know—"

"How old are you, anyway?"

I told her, knowing Max had already mentioned it.

"And you two have known each other, like, a whole *month*?" She stretched the word into nearly two syllables.

"It's been a bit of whirlwind." I glanced at the door. Max had only been gone a minute but the time crawled by.

"And you guys are gonna get married and have kids?"

"I think—I mean, we haven't really talked about—"

"So then you've worked out all the details of the prenup and you know exactly how much money he's worth and everything."

At this point she wasn't even trying to hide her disdain. I steadied myself by hooking my thumbs under the edge of the marble. Were the island not as heavy as a car, I might have had the ability to upend it with the force of my indignity.

"Dani, I know this is all very sudden. And I know it's going to take some time to get used to. *I'm* going to need time, too. But I don't feel very comfortable talking about these things with you."

Her eyes flashed. "Oh my God. There *is* no prenup. He's *such* an idiot. I mean, I know what you're getting out of all this, but I gotta say, I do not see what my father gets—"

"Dani, not another word, please." Max had entered the room, his shoulders powdered with snow.

"Daddy, I'm trying to get to know her. Isn't that what you wanted me to do?"

"This isn't how you get to know someone, my love. This is how you alienate them."

"I'm sorry, but this is just not what I expected you to bring home."

This, like a bored child who had unwrapped a gift and tossed it aside, deeming it unworthy.

"Whatever it is *you* expected, Dani, she is my fiancée and the rest is none of your business."

"I think it *is* my business. Mum hasn't even been dead for two years—"

"Dani, I'm telling you—"

"Max, it's okay. Dani's just asking me questions. I understand that." I slid off the stool. "I'm going to go upstairs now and leave you two to catch up. Good night, Dani. I'll see you in the morning."

"Yay, can't wait," she drawled, her chin on her fist.

Max shot me a stricken look as I passed.

"Also?" Dani said.

I turned to face her.

"Next time you break something at Asherley, don't hide it. We have the money to fix things."

Mute with shame, I avoided Max's eyes and left the kitchen.

A half hour passed before Max came back to the bedroom. By then I'd stopped crying, though a certain hopelessness had crept in. He peeled off his clothes and collapsed beside me like a doctor who'd just performed complicated surgery.

"I'm sorry about that," he whispered, pulling me back into the wall of his body and nuzzling my hair. "She's going to feel a little usurped."

"That's okay. I understand."

"Give it some time."

"I will."

"She just has to get used to you."

"I know," I said. "Maybe when she goes back to school and we establish a day-to-day rhythm, things will get easier."

He laughed. "Dani hasn't gone to a proper school since Rebekah died. I can't seem to make her go back."

I turned to face him, both of us now propped up on an elbow. "Is that legal? Don't you *have* to go to school at her age?"

"She has a tutor who comes three days a week. She does other requirements online. That Paris trip was supposed to involve a compressed French-language course she skipped last year, but Louisa said she barely attended. She's no dummy, but ever since her mother died, she's become very defiant. And more of a homebody."

He lazily coiled a finger around one of my stray curls. He looked so tired all of a sudden. "I'm sorry she made you cry," he said. Was my face puffy? Were my eyes still red? "I should have given you more warning, but I was worried you'd reject me if I told you you'd be living with me *and* an unruly, spoiled teenage brat. I'm a terrible father, I know."

"No, I think she's still grieving, and you bringing me home must be very unsettling for her. I'll try my best to . . . I don't know . . . do anything to make it easier on her."

"You're a good person. I love you for that."

He kissed me.

I looked around. "Whose room was this before?"

"This room? Why?"

"Dani called the turret her mother's room. Was that also your bedroom up there? With Rebekah?"

"Yes. I moved down here after she died. This was a spare room but I prefer it. The turret was always too bright for me."

"So is that Dani's room now?"

"No. Her bedroom's on the third floor, but she does spend a lot of time up in the turret. I've begged her not to, begged her to go through Rebekah's stuff, give some of it to charity.

91

But she freaks out if anyone goes up there, as you've discovered. Incidentally, what did you break?"

I squeezed my eyes shut against that memory. "A picture of Rebekah. I'm so sorry. I shouldn't have hidden it. I should have said something."

"I told her to take all the photos down before she went to Paris."

"Well, they're still up. They're everywhere. On the walls, on the tables. Dozens of them."

Max fell back onto his pillow and closed his eyes, exhaling deeply. "Fuck."

I fell back, too, and for a while we both lay blinking into the velvety darkness of the cold bedroom, before Max got up to stir the fire.

TEN

Max was up early the next day and I shadowed him, using him as a shield for my reentry into life at Asherley. If he sensed this was what I was doing, he was sympathetic enough to say nothing. When we reached the top of the stairs, I could hear a different woman's voice, coming from the foyer downstairs, not Dani's or Katya's.

"Max, are you up?" she yelled.

"Ah, Louisa," Max said to me. "I promise you this will be less painful."

Max's sister was older than him but looked younger than I had expected. Next to her was a man who stood at least a head shorter, with white hair and a matching moustache. Louisa's eyes shone bright when she spotted me. Here might be a friend, I thought, taking in her wide-open face. As soon as we reached the bottom of the stairs she pulled me into an athletic embrace that was over by the time I had a chance to raise my arms to return it.

"It is *so* nice to finally meet you. I'm Louisa, Max's older, bitchy sister," she said, still clutching my shoulders to take in my face and hair, and repeating my name until she got the pronunciation right. "And this is my first husband, Jonah."

"She's been saying that for twenty-six years. Someone should break it to her that I'm as good as it gets." Jonah hugged me, too, adding, "You're a slip of a thing. It's a wonder you don't float away in a storm."

Louisa hooked her arm in Max's and then mine and we drifted into the dining room, following the smell of coffee.

"Max, I've had it," she said. "That kid thinks she can just bolt from people to cross the Atlantic or wander around New York all by herself like a stray cat. You have to have a talk with her or I can't take her places anymore. I'm old. I get nervous."

"When she gets kidnapped, don't pay the ransom," Jonah offered. "That'll teach her. In fact, I know a guy who can arrange a lesson."

The dining room table was the size of a small pool, and on the sideboard a breakfast buffet, not unlike the ones at the club, awaited us. I was drawn to the window, needing a glimpse of Asherley's grounds in the daytime to orient myself. I still felt stuck in that vague in-between place. I wasn't in the Caymans anymore, but I was not fully here yet either.

A snow-covered lawn sloped down to a stand of spindly black trees. Beyond that was Gardiners Bay, a greener, angrier version of the ocean I grew up looking at. Gray clouds hung low at the horizon. As I stepped closer to the window I spotted an icy spire poking above the treetops. Its incongruity gave me a little jump.

Louisa joined me at the window. "I have always hated that god-awful thing. Rebekah was the only one who understood the greenhouse. I still think it's a stain on the whole aesthetic."

"It is riveting, though."

"So are mushroom clouds. And I don't want to see one of those on my lawn, either."

94

Over breakfast, I could feel my shoulders start to drop as a part of myself I'd stifled around Dani began to surface—a confidence, I guess, at least in showing my affection for Max. I let my hand graze his forearm now and again. I laughed a little too loud at his and Louisa's stories about growing up on the island. The conversation between Louisa and me was easy, chatty, and light. She asked all the usual questions a sister might ask of her brother's new love: where was I born, who were my parents, what was my schooling, the broader strokes of my life that eventually led to meeting Max and ending up here, ensconced on Long Island and betrothed in a little more than a month. Every new detail I offered seemed to delight rather than disgust Louisa.

Dani, thankfully, slept through breakfast, as was, apparently, her habit. And if Katya was the one responsible for cooking the delicious spread—bacon, scrambled eggs, a quiche—we didn't see her. The only person who made an appearance was a rather sullen Gus, who came in from time to time to take away the dirty plates and cups or bring in a freshly filled coffee carafe.

"I thought he just worked in the barn," Louisa whispered.

"Katya doesn't think he has enough to do in the winter," Max replied with a shrug. "And he'll have less to do once the rest of the horses go."

Louisa said how sad she was that most of the horses had been sold, the final two retiring to a stable in Montauk soon. Max reminded her that they were Rebekah's passion, one that Dani didn't share.

"She's got to find something to do, something to care about," Louisa said.

"She likes playing with makeup and clothes," Max said, sneering a little. "And her phone, of course."

"Like every single fifteen-year-old girl on the planet," Louisa said. Max seemed on the cusp of a testy rebuttal, until a look passed between them.

"Yes, that's true. She is still a teenager, still quite young," he said, fussing with his fork. "But I do expect a little bit more from her. She's got privileges when it comes to her education. I want her to take advantage of them."

Louisa abruptly stood and asked me if I wanted to take a tour around the property with her. I looked at Max. This was something he'd said he wanted to do today.

"Go. Jonah and I have some business to catch up on," he said. "Louisa's just as qualified as I am to be your guide."

We bundled up and headed out back through the breeze-way off the kitchen. When we passed the door that led to the greenhouse, I couldn't help but try the handle. It was locked, so I peered through the dirty glass. Everything inside looked slightly ransacked, as if it'd been abandoned in a hurry. Tipped-over chairs, rows of misaligned tables covered with dried bags of dirt and stacks of green plastic starter pots scattered throughout. Along the highest wall were the remnants of dead rosebushes, now whacked back to stumps.

"Rebekah had two green thumbs. Do you garden at all?" She caught herself before I could answer. "What am I saying? You were born on a boat, for God's sake! You must sail then."

"A little. I mostly operated fishing boats. Small yachts and such. Will the greenhouse stay shut up like this?"

"I don't know. I hope not. It's an astounding feat of archi-tecture, I'll give it that. And you don't rip something like this down just because you're sad. But Max seems intent to lock it up and leave it to rot. Do you want me to talk to him?"

"That's all right," I said. "I'm sure he has his reasons."

Or reason.

The air had a snap to it, the new snow quite deep in spots. Louisa had a natural athleticism, her legs all sinew and muscle in the manner of women who grew up on acreages, surrounded by horses and water. She was nearly twice my age, yet keeping up with her left me feeling breathless and ungainly in my new boots.

"You know, when Max called and told me he'd met some-one special, I didn't think he was ready. But that's often when it happens, isn't it? When you least expect it, there is love."

"I'm still stunned. I really never thought that something like this would happen to someone like me." I wanted to add that I still didn't believe it was happening, that a little over a month ago I was dropping fish carcasses off Rum Point Beach and cutting my own hair. But to say this out loud would be to conjure my recent past, which I worried would resurface and cancel out all this good fortune.

"What do you mean, someone like me?" she asked with a laugh. "You're perfectly primed for this sort of thing. You're young, open-hearted. And lovely to look at."

"Ha. Thank you. *Lovely* is a nice word for not exactly the bombshell people expect Max to be with. Especially after Rebekah," I said. "I think I've already disappointed Dani. She's used to having a glamorous mother."

"Has she been that bad?"

"I wouldn't describe it like that. She's just— I'd find it dif-ficult to be welcoming, too, if I were her."

"You can't let Dani interfere with what you have with Max. She'll come around eventually. She's got a lot of good qualities, you know. She's gutsy, vivacious, has a big appetite for life. I've always said she's fascinating and frustrating by equal measure. Besides, bombshells are overrated. *I* can see what Max sees in you. I know my brother. He brought you home for a reason."

She sounded sincere, which made me blush. I quickly changed the subject.

"Does Dani do that often, run away like she did from Paris?"

"Well, technically she's not running away. She's usually running back to Asherley. She's flagged cabs in Manhattan and convinced them to drive her out here, and she has the number of every water taxi company up and down the Eastern Seaboard. She's quite handy with a boat, too. Maybe that's an interest you two can cultivate. She's a hell of a sailor. Just like Rebekah. Proves talent isn't always genetic. Interesting how that works. I once knew of a child who, despite also being adopted, had the identical gait of—" Louisa stopped and placed a hand on my forearm. "Are you all right?"

"I—I didn't know. Did you say Dani was adopted?"

"Yes. Max didn't tell you?"

"But . . . the resemblance between her and Rebekah."

"An illusion. Pull back the hair and there is no resemblance. She dyes and cuts it to look just like Rebekah. Has since she was eleven. Far too young to start but Rebekah never said no to her. None of us has, sadly. But anyway, Max has never thought of her as less than his own flesh and blood. That's probably why he hadn't mentioned it. From the day they brought her home, I don't think I knew a more wanted thing in my life than that baby . . ."

It didn't matter. Of course it didn't matter. But why hadn't Max told me? I didn't have a chance to ask Louisa more questions, because we'd reached the barn, where, centered on the lintel, there was an ornate *R*.

Inside, we stomped the snow from our boots and I was hit with the smell of animals and damp hay, a nauseating sweet fecundity that reminded me of both life and death. Around a corner scurried the pale fluffy cat I had seen in the house the night before. The way its flesh swung beneath it indicated to me that it might be a she and that she might even be pregnant. Gus soon followed, rubbing an eye.

"Sorry to bother you, Gus," Louisa said. "It's always tricky to know when to come by when one lives where one works."

He barely looked at me, offering another shy nod while wiping his hands on his jeans.

"Where are you keeping Isabel these days?" She turned to me. "Such a gentle thing. I wish Dani would take up riding her again. When's she moving, Gus?"

"April, I think. Her and Dorian go once the snow melts."

We followed him down the long hallway past the horse heads bobbing in the dim light and stopped in front of the last stall. There, Louisa introduced me to Isabel, a penny-colored mare with a crooked white diamond between her eyes. When I nervously attempted to touch it, she flinched with a whinny, returning her nose to Louisa's hand.

"Don't take it personally," Louisa said, caressing Isabel's neck with assertive strokes. "She's like that with everyone. She was Rebekah's favorite. You can't be nervous with these animals. If they sense any weakness they won't trust you to handle them."

While Gus cleaned the stall and Louisa cooed loving words into Isabel's ear, I wandered into the tack room next door. I let my hand caress several worn saddles astride a rough-hewn rack and thought about why the news of Dani's adoption unsettled me. Of course it made no conceivable difference to my feelings for Max, but it might have prompted an important conversation between two people poised to spend their lives together, who might perhaps have children. I would have asked, for instance, if Max and Rebekah had adopted because of medical reasons or simply because they wanted to. And what if Dani's problems stemmed from mental illness? Surely information about her birth parents might help with a diagnosis and my ability to parent her. I was entitled to know these things.

Louisa joined me in the tack room, guessing at what preoccupied me.

"Look, I don't know how Max would forget something like this," she said. "It's not some deep, dark family secret."

"I'm sure you're right," I said. "It's just a reminder, I guess, that we haven't really known each other very long."

We left the barn without saying goodbye to Gus and headed to the boathouse, built with the same gray stones and brown fish-scale siding as Asherley. A large balcony cantilevered over the bay, below which were two slips poking out from under heavy doors, like a cat stretching its front legs into the water.

I was surprised to find that the air was colder inside than out, our breath escaping in small, white bursts. Louisa flicked a switch and turned on the ground lights that lit the room's perimeter, giving the cavernous A-frame the feel of an abandoned lodge. There was a small, well-equipped gym behind a glass wall on a riser, along with a pool table and a well-worn leather sectional facing a walk-in fireplace big enough to heat the entire space. We were eye level to what looked like a fifty-foot sea carcass, wrapped in a tarp and suspended above the larger slip.

"What sort of boat is this?" I asked, tracing my hand along its covered hull with more confidence than I'd handled the horse.

"To me it's just 'big.'"

By its shape, I thought it could be a Dufour or perhaps an Odyssey. I loosened the tarp where it puckered at the transom to reveal the name: *Winter's Girl*.

"I believe this was the last thing Rebekah gave to Max before she died," Louisa said.

"Great name for a boat," I said, feeling tired suddenly.

"Yes, Rebekah was the cleverest thing."

Suspended a few feet above the other bay was a smaller antique speedboat, sleek and wood-hulled, with what looked to be a newer motor. I recognized the model from its low-slung aft, like an empty hot tub, padded in robin's-egg-blue vinyl.

"Is this an Aquarama?" I asked, grasping its Bakelite wheel, thick and cold and pleasing to the touch.

"Good eye. Yes, one of the smaller models. My grandfather bought it new but never named it. I had always hoped Dani would claim it."

"It's beautiful," I said, caressing the aged, puckered varnish.

"Yes," she said, "yet another thing at Asherley that could use a little TLC. You got here just in time."

Louisa suggested we make our way back to the house, leaving the rest of the beach for a less blustery day. The air felt tinged with an unease I could not name. I reminded myself, again, that Max and I had only known each other for just over a month. Gaps in information were to be expected. Dani's adoption would have eventually come out in conversation. It's not like I'd had a list of questions for Max, ticking them off one by one until I was satisfied enough to make this leap. That's the thrill of whirlwind romances: not knowing exactly where you'll land once the storm subsides.

ELEVEN

It was almost lunch by the time we returned to the house. Louisa led me through a wing I hadn't toured yet, knowing we'd find Max and Jonah, and now Elias, holed up in the study. It was a man's room, designed by a man, no doubt, and for men. The brown paneling extended across the ceiling, and the walls were embedded with hundreds of books, leather-bound, their titles etched in gold. We entered quietly, so as not to interrupt Elias, who was talking about Max's reelection campaign the coming fall. Max had mentioned to me the possibility of another run, but little about what that entailed. Louisa took the armchair next to Jonah, while Max extended his arm, beckoning me over to the couch where he held court. Walking across the oceanic rug to take my spot next to him, I was filled with a self-conscious pride that was both female and unfamiliar.

"Do I have realistic competition?" Max asked Elias.

"Yes, but this time you have a machine behind you. And your numbers are good. Plus, now that you don't have to win a primary, campaigning should be cheaper, but we'll still have to cash in some bonds, unless you get over your aversion to fundraising."

Max gave me a squeeze. "Who are the Dems putting forward, do we know yet?"

"Guy named Tom Armstrong," Jonah said. "Sells trucks out on the bypass. County executive in the nineties. Man of the people, blah, blah, blah." Jonah looked at me now. "Bet you didn't bargain on hitting the hustings when you left paradise."

"We haven't really talked about it," I answered, glancing sideways at Max. "We haven't talked about a lot of things."

Louisa pointed to her watch. "Husband, let us be off."

"You're not staying for lunch?" I asked, conscious of sounding needy. I had hoped Louisa would be around when Dani finally came downstairs so I could take notes on how she handled her.

"Two meals in a row will put Max and me over our limit," she said. "We love each other, but we don't really like each other that much."

"Elias?" I asked.

"No. I'm only dragging work here because you kept Max away for so long. But I swear, from now on, work talk only at the office."

Before they left, Louisa promised to take me around East Hampton, to shop for a few more things and introduce me to some of their friends. "We can surprise those two at the constituency office. See if they're really working," she said. She lowered her voice. "And don't let that little brat steamroll over you. You're the grown-up, she's the kid. Remember that."

Max and I stood shivering at the front door, waving away both cars. When we turned around, there stood Dani, bare-foot, wearing shorts, her belly exposed in the winter. She was chomping on a celery stick. I jumped.

"Whoa, take a Xannie," she said.

"Good morn— I mean afternoon," Max said.

"Auntie Louisa pissed at me?"

"Well, she said she doesn't want to take you to Paris anymore."

She shrugged. "Oh well. Paris is boring anyway."

"Will you deign to join us at lunch?"

I regarded her anew, my eyes drawn to her hair, the thin line of dark roots growing in, the faded pencil reimaging her brows. She seemed to be wearing yesterday's makeup.

"I already ate. Gus is going to drive me over to Claire's."

"To do what?"

"I don't know. Go tobogganing?"

"That sounds like fun," I said.

She gave me a tight smile. "Yeah. And after that we're going to set our hair in rollers and then make crank calls to boys." She headed back up the stairs.

"Dani," Max called after her, watching her take the steps in twos. "Come here, please!"

She kept on climbing.

"I have to nip this in the bud," he said, about to follow her.

I grabbed his arm. "Leave her, Max," I said, with confidence I attributed to Louisa's parting advice.

"All she's done is snark around you."

"It's day two. Let her take her space."

"I also want to talk to her about Rebekah's photos. She can put them in an album or something, but they have to go in storage."

"They don't bother me. It's her mother. She probably misses her even more now that I'm here."

He placed his hands on both of my cheeks and held my face, tilting my head slightly this way and that, examining my eyes, my angles. "Who are you, oh little wise one, and what have you done with that innocent young woman I met under the sun last month?"

105

"I do want to talk to you about something."

"Uh-oh. What did I do—except ruin your entire life by bringing you here?"

I grabbed his hand and led him back to the study, quietly shutting the door behind us.

"What is on that mind of yours?"

I inhaled deeply. "Max, why didn't you tell me Dani was adopted?"

"What are you talking about?" he asked. "I'm sure I mentioned it."

"I'd remember that."

He put his head down as though looking for something on the floor. Then he looked up. "Is this bothering you?"

"No. I always assumed, with time, we'd fill in certain details about each other's lives. But this feels like a big omission."

"You think I deliberately failed to mention my daughter was adopted? For what purpose would I hide this information from you?"

"I don't know."

"I thought I'd mentioned it. If I haven't, maybe it's because it rarely crosses my mind. I think of her as my own, so much so I sometimes forget she was once someone else's."

"That's what Louisa said."

"Well, she's right. This isn't a *secret*. I don't know why I didn't tell you. You can find it on Google if you search far back enough. But why is this troubling you? Is it a problem?"

"My God, no," I said, and sank into an armchair. I landed on what I always say when I feel more embarrassed than indignant. "I'm sorry, Max."

"There's nothing to apologize for," he said. He stepped over to one of the French windows as a vehicle pulled up in the drive. We watched Dani hop into a small truck, and the wheels crunched snow as they took off.

"She treats Gus like her personal chauffeur. I don't like it," Max mumbled. He turned to face me. "I'm sorry. I'm sure there is a lot of stuff I've failed to mention."

He came over to where I was sitting and placed his hands on either arm of the chair. "What other questions do you have? I'd be happy to answer them."

"Max, if I offended you, I didn't mean to," I said, shrinking into the seat.

He launched himself off the chair and stood upright, shoving his hands in his pockets. "You want to know why we adopted, I suppose." He didn't wait for me to reply. "We couldn't get pregnant. We tried for years. Went through all the tests you go through, Rebekah more devastated than I when the answer remained elusive. A definitive *it's your fault, no, it's her fault* would have been better than the awful mystery of it all. Then, around the time the doctors threw up their hands, a baby became available through a private service. I needed some convincing, but once we held her, we never looked back."

Emboldened by his honesty I asked him what he knew about her birth parents, or at least her birth mother.

"Enough to know that she was far better off with us," he said.

I realized my legs were shaking. I touched my face. It was clammy and hot.

"Are you okay? What is it?"

"I just feel terrible about all this," I said, waving my hand vaguely.

"About being here?"

"No! No, I feel like I just smacked into a hornet's nest. Max, are we having a fight?"

He laughed loudly. "Believe me, you'll know when we're fighting. This is just us still getting to know each other. And in that vein I suppose we should talk about the conversation you and Louisa walked in on."

He told me he'd been ambivalent about reelection but now was leaning towards another run. He quite liked the work, more than he thought he would. It gave him purpose. Dani, too. She liked to be involved.

"But it's a big disruption, a campaign," he said.

"Do you want to do it?"

"Yes."

"Why?"

He looked at me thoughtfully. "I guess I should say it's because I've been blessed with so much, I feel the need to serve. That's not untrue. But it's got more to do with self-interest, I'm afraid. Asherley, the land around it, makes me a major stakeholder in Suffolk County. I want to do what I can to protect it."

"Is Asherley under threat?"

He smiled. "Depends on your definition of threat. For instance, that causeway? It means we might technically no longer live on an island, which might affect how we're taxed. To me, that's a threat. And I'm in a position to do something about it."

A small knock on the door interrupted us. It was Katya.

"Sorry to bother you, Mr. Winter. Who's staying for lunch?"

"It's just going to be us, Katya. And I think we'll take it upstairs, if you don't mind."

"I'll take it up now, then," she said, and ducked out.

"After a big fight like that, I like to make up," he said.

My eyes lingered on the door. It felt strange for things to be reversed so suddenly, for me to live someplace where others worked for me, came and went in hushed rooms, brought me food, washed my delicates, changed my sheets. I didn't want to become imperious, accustomed to a widening gap between me and the people who worked here. I might be marrying a wealthy man, insulated from the messier bits of life, but that's not who I was raised to be. I needed to participate in my own care, our care. I would talk to Katya later, find a way to help that wouldn't impinge on her duties and income. That's how I would grow more comfortable here, earning a little of what was being given to me so freely.

We ate our lunch on the four-poster bed—whole garlicky leaves of romaine lettuce, fried sardines, chunks of buttered sourdough—until I was full, and then napped again at dusk. When I woke, Max was gone from the room, though he'd left a fire going. I grabbed my phone off the nightstand to check the time, embarrassed by my indolence. Soon it would be supper and what had I accomplished that day? Walk, eat, make love, and nap. Off to a purposeful start. No wonder Dani wanted nothing to do with me. I could imagine what she was telling her friend Claire. *She's lazy, plain, such a mouse. I have no idea what my father sees in her. She just follows him around hiding behind him like an idiot. When she's not eating, she's sleeping, when she's not sleeping, she's running around after him. God, it's so embarrassing.*

I had resisted checking Dani's Instagram account since we'd arrived at Asherley. But lying there, I was overcome with

109

the impulse, if only to confirm my paranoia that she'd made some mention of me.

I was not wrong. There were three new posts. One was from yesterday, a looped slice of video, presumably taken in the back of the cab from the airport. It was a grainy close-up of her face quickly morphing from serene beauty to cross-eyed goof, over and over, the caption reading, "On my way to meet my future stepmonster." The comments were mostly chiding: "Man, she's gonna *love* you! Hahahaha," and several cartoon faces exhibiting mania and disgust and some thumbs-down signs as well. Her last two posts, both from a few hours ago, featured her and a much prettier dark-haired girl, presumably Claire. The picture was treated with filters that removed imperfections, brightened eyes, and gave their already smooth skin a doll-like sheen. In both shots they were squeezed into the frame, their breasts pressed together. In one, they had cartoon dog ears and noses. In the second, both wore tight tank tops, while Dani, side-eyeing the camera provocatively, licked the side of her friend's face. The caption read, "Yum. Missed my Claire Bear."

Though the pictures unnerved me, this could well be perfectly normal behavior for fifteen-year-old girls. There must be a way to ask if Max monitored her social media accounts without admitting to my own prying. I didn't want to be a stepmonster, an interloper nosing around in places I didn't belong. What would Rebekah have done? Would she have set limits, threatened to take away Dani's phone, or would she have complimented her, celebrated her bold displays of unabashed intimacy? Maybe she'd join her in the frame sometimes.

I tossed my phone aside and stared into the waning embers, pulling my sweater tighter around me.

TWELVE

I did one thing well during those early weeks at Asherley: I stayed away from Dani as much as possible. She had her own routine. Monday, Tuesday, and Thursday a sweet-faced tutor named Adele, not much older than me, would arrive promptly at eight-thirty, Dani meeting her sometime after nine, her hair drying down her back. They would work in the study, freshly abandoned by Max, who by then would have left for his constituency office in East Hampton, when he wasn't away for two or three days in Albany. At first I assumed I'd go with him on those trips, but spouses didn't do that, he said, and besides, I'd be at loose ends wandering the streets of another unfamiliar city all day, entirely bored at night. He worked through dinner, he said, sometimes with other colleagues who also liked to maximize their time in the legislature so they could be with their families more often. So far, there hadn't been any events worth bringing me to, he said, opting to invite only Dani to a small zoning meeting at the library one night, because it was "her thing" and she knew how to live-stream it on his social media feed. He said I'd be uninterested, that it was nothing special, and that I'd be on his arm during the big events in the summer. But the truth was, Dani didn't want me there. Of course I said it was no big deal, that he definitely should take Dani, because it afforded them much-needed time together, and that it was, after all, her thing, not mine.

He kissed me and said, "Thank God you don't care about these things. I know Dani will come around soon. How did I ever get so lucky?"

Of course I felt lucky, too, my alternative life playing out in my mind whenever I'd stare out over the black bay. While I missed the sun, and the color blue, I did not miss Laureen, or my shabby room, or anything to do with the charters. I did not miss leaving work smelling like fish and arriving there smelling like cigarette smoke. When I did think of the Caymans, it was not so much with longing but with regret that I hadn't appreciated the heat until I came to a place where I was almost always cold. I meant to ask Max if we'd go back there next winter, when he usually set aside time to spend at the club. I wondered if Dani and I would be friends by then, and how Laureen would greet me, and why I cared.

Still, when Max was away it felt imperative he not know how lonely I felt. So I feigned stoicism, waving him out the door with a brave smile. Then I'd turn to face the empty house, moving like a listless pinball from room to room, regarding this painting, moving that vase, opening this drawer, closing that curtain, eventually ending up in the dark pocket of our bedroom at the end of the day, either waiting for Max to join me or to call me or neither, often unsure which to expect.

One morning, I went to say goodbye to him in the foyer, this time for two nights, and he told me Louisa had booked us a table for lunch that day.

"You mean you've asked her to babysit me while you're away."

"I asked her to take advantage of my absence in order to spend more time with my lovely fiancée, which she is thrilled to do anyway. You shouldn't find it hard to believe that she likes you."

"Well, it's good to know I'm not universally loathed here."

He pulled me into an embrace. "Your suggestion to give Dani space was a good one. She's eating dinner with us now. That's a good sign."

True. After sulking in her room for a week or so, she was technically taking meals with us when Max was home. But Max's inquiries about her day were often met with single-syllable words and sounds.

How was Adele today?

Good.

What are you reading right now for English Lit?

Books.

How's Claire?

Fine.

Delicious chicken, isn't it? (I'd usually comment on the food.)

Shrug (indecipherable).

Care to enlighten us with anything else going on in your life?

Nope.

After eating a runway model's portion, she'd excuse herself and go upstairs for the rest of the evening, where she enjoyed her own TV and laptop. What did she need with the rest of Asherley? What did she need of me?

With Max gone it meant another few days alone with Dani in the house. Before Katya arrived, I made myself an egg sandwich and a thermos of coffee. Since the horses frightened me almost as much as Gus did, I gravitated to the boathouse, the quietest place on the property and where I felt most myself. The door was locked, so I ate my breakfast on the woodpile, in full view of the house, taking in the smell of musk rising from the bog as it thawed. Swamp maple saplings poked at me, one lodging a sticky bud in my hair that coated my fingers in sap when I pinched it out. I oriented myself by noting Shelter Island on my left, Gardiners Island on the right, and Plum Island straight ahead. On a rare clear day, you could see all three islands from a second-floor window, probably farther still from the turret, but I hadn't been up there since that first night, when I mistook Dani for Rebekah.

Cawing ospreys circled overhead, smelling my sandwich. I tossed some of the crusts into the switchgrass, even though I knew they'd be too cautious to land. I could see their fat nests pocking the still-barren parts of forest. There'd be eggs soon. When the birds were strong enough to leave the nests they'd make their way back down to the Caribbean for the winter. But not me. I live here now, I thought, finishing my sandwich. This is my home and this is the land I'd come to know, and these are the birds I'd recognize and the trees I'd learn to identify.

Gus, up early, too, spotted me from the barn. I waved only to be polite, something he interpreted as a summons. As he walked towards me, I felt dread. What would I talk to him about? I hopped off the woodpile to greet him. He glanced nervously over at Asherley. I followed his gaze to the top of the turret, where a shade dropped like an eyelid shutting. I wondered if she'd been sleeping in Rebekah's room regularly, against Max's wishes. I turned back to Gus, determined not to let her ruin my day.

"I didn't mean to interrupt you," I said. "I was only waving good morning."

"I thought maybe you wanted to get into the boathouse. I have the key."

"Oh yes, I do, as a matter of fact," I said, eager to get out from beneath Dani's spying eyes.

I followed him inside and he felt along the wall for the light switch. I wandered over to the boats, and it occurred to me what I could do to occupy my time.

I pointed to the Aquarama. "Can that boat be propped up?"

"The slip has a cover. I can just lower it down onto some blocks. But that's an antique. It was Mr. Winter's father's."

"Yes, and the hull hasn't been refinished since the middle of the century. Can there be heat in here, too?"

"Mrs. Winter just used the fireplace if it was chilly. She didn't come down here much in the winter."

"I see," I said, bristling. He must have sensed I'd never started a proper fire before, because he promptly disappeared upstairs and returned carrying an electric heater.

"Perfect. Thank you," I said. "Also, do you know if Max—if Mr. Winter—has any reefing tools?"

Gus disappeared again, this time through a door behind the bar, and bumped around in a storage area. I removed my ring and placed it on a shelf beside the boat, the one with no name. My father once told me it was bad luck for a boat to remain nameless. A boat, like a person, needed a name, he said, or else it was cursed to drift forever.

Gus returned carrying a dusty briefcase, lifting its lid as if he were a game-show model, showing off an array of shipwright tools that would look, to someone unschooled in basic boat refurbishment, like a finicky set of weapons. I picked up the reefing hook, used to pull old caulking out from between planks. Its C-blade was still sharp, its handle worn and burnished. There were elegant bits and smaller blades, too, that, because they'd been stored properly, glinted in the light.

"They're very well taken care of," I said.

"These were Mr. Winter's grandfather's tools," he said, with a note of pride.

"Well, I think it's time they were used again. Thank you, Gus. You've been very helpful," I said, giving him a prompt to go back to what he was doing. But he hovered still.

"Do you want me to start today?"

"No! No. *I'm* going to do it. *I* will refinish the boat. I just need to go into town for some supplies."

He looked perplexed.

"I know how to strip a boat. It used to be part of my job." I asked if there was a vehicle I could take into town. He pulled keys from his pocket, describing the truck I had seen him use to take Dani to Claire's. He offered to take me, but I was desperate to do something purposeful, even if it was just to drive twenty minutes to the hardware store in East Hampton.

I left him to the task of grounding the boat and made my way directly to the garage. As I passed by the side of the house, Asherley maintained its gravitational pull on my body, the turret like a heavy eye that followed me as I walked. I succeeded in not looking up, exhaling when I entered the garage and was again out of view of Dani and the house. Strange that I didn't feel as menaced inside the house as I did when I was outside looking at it, walking around it, regarding it. Perhaps it was the gray sky against the gray stones and the dirty glass of the greenhouse, but the nip in the air sent a chill to my marrow. Things would be different in the full flush of spring, I told myself, when it got warmer and greener. It's hard to feel lonely or frightened in the summer, when I would get back out on the water, and in my element. I was determined that by then Dani and I would have become better friends. We could take the big sailboat out. I could be her crew. She would show me her favorite nooks along the banks. We'd putter up secret inlets, looking for robins' nests and beaver dams. She'd tell me stories about Rebekah that I'd welcome without feeling threatened or jealous. Eventually they'd be replaced with our own stories, the things we did together as a family. If Max and I had children, Dani would take them under her wing, snapping pictures of them sleeping or running, teaching them how to sail, too, and posting pictures to show her friends what a perfect big sister she was. I had to believe these things were possible. I had to be able to envision this kind of future for us.

I backed out of the garage carefully, thrilling to the feeling of independence that driving anything always gave me. It was the first time in weeks that ease crept into my body. I was embarking on an errand alone to fetch supplies to start a project of my choosing. I didn't need to go to an event at the library to feel purposeful. I could find my own projects. This drive was an opportunity to reorient myself, to get a feel for driving on the right side of the road, and to remind myself there were things I could do here to fit in beyond loving Max Winter.

I took the winding road through the forest slowly, tires scraping the mounds of dirty snow piled along the side. Soon it would be spring, then the second summer since Rebekah's car accident. Max once pointed out to me the tree she'd hit, now cut down to a black tabletop of a stump, nestled in skeletal ivy.

"There," he said. "That's where the fire started. See all the way to the edge of those trees over there? All burnt."

We paused that day, the car idling. I watched his profile, somberly handsome in the twilight. I realized that every time he left Asherley and every time he arrived home he must think of her. Every time he drove through this part of the island he must remember that horrible night. How the fire trucks roused him. How he must have smelled the smoke before he saw it. He probably knew she was dead before he was told they'd found her remains, the shell of her car. For him and Dani this was living history, this part of the forest. This patch would always be scorched to them no matter how big and green these new trees grew. Of course I understood that. How could anyone not understand that?

I had begun to relax when the causeway came upon me, the sea churning on either side. This was the first time I had driven over the narrow passage myself, and Max was right, it was disorienting if you looked left or right. The trick to avoid vertigo, he told me, was to stare straight ahead and drive.

After I bumped off the causeway and back onto the mainland, other houses began to poke through the forest, one or two pretenders to Asherley, stone mansions newly built, plus a few simple saltboxes here and there. These were ostensibly our neighbors, and I wondered if I'd ever know them. If my vehicle broke down and I banged on their doors in distress, would they believe me that I lived at Asherley? Would they say, *But you're not Mrs. Winter, Rebekah died years ago*, before slamming the door in my face?

East Hampton came upon me quickly, its pretty neatness reminding me, in parts, of seaside George Town but with bigger vehicles and wider roads. The town really only consisted of two main shopping strips, so the hardware store wasn't difficult to find, nor was parking. Walking into the store, as always, my father was there in the smell, a combination of plastic packaging, leather, and cleaning supplies. I took my time down the narrow, cluttered aisles, savoring the flood of nostalgia, remembering what my father had said about certain brands of epoxy and what clamps worked best, which varnish to use on mahogany. Waiting in the cashier's line, I was proud of my selections, rehearsing in my head how I'd explain the process to Max, imagining him puffing up at my knowledge and self-sufficiency, and the care I would take in refurbishing the boat. I also realized I'd forgotten sandpaper. When I turned around to fetch some I bumped directly into a small woman wearing a long fur coat and large sunglasses.

"You forgot something," she said, and shoved a wallet at me. It took me a second to realize it was *my* wallet, and that it was Dani standing there.

"Thank you. I— What are you doing here?" I was more alarmed than surprised, uncertain whether this was a generous or menacing act on her part.

"Gus was driving me into the city."

I wanted to explain myself, to say that I had always charged things to Laureen's accounts when I shopped for her, and I never seemed to need a wallet or purse when I was with Max, who swatted away all attempts I made to pay for anything. I wanted to tell her I wasn't a complete idiot for forgetting this at home, inside my own purse, which was probably hanging off the back of a chair in the kitchen.

"You are a lifesaver. Thank you so much."

"Sure," she said, turning away.

"I'll see you at dinner."

"Probably not," she replied over her shoulder.

The door banged shut behind her. The line had inched up, leaving a large gap between the checkout counter and me. Perhaps it was common here, that fur-clad teenagers suddenly appear, hand you money, then disappear, because no one around me seemed disturbed. It was as though some strange comet had streaked through the hardware store and I was its only witness.

THIRTEEN

The morning of Max's second day away, I went to the barn to find more tarp and walked in on Gus about to decapitate a small animal with a shovel.

"Stop!" I yelled. "What are you doing?"

He pulled back the shovel and rested his arm on the handle, exhaling loudly. "It's almost dead anyway."

I knelt down to examine its tiny body, its silent mouth reaching for food. It was a kitten, maybe three weeks old. Gus told me the barn cat had given birth deep inside a gable. When he spotted the cat around the property recently, avoiding the barn completely, he assumed she'd abandoned them. Sure enough, when he dug into the crevice between roof beams, he discovered only one of six had survived.

"So she *was* pregnant." I don't know what possessed me to intervene; I didn't believe it was cruel to kill suffering animals. When a mother cat abandons her kittens, it's usually for a good reason. But the kitten, though hungry and filthy, seemed otherwise hearty, intact, with the same long hair as its mother. I scooped it up and headed straight to the kitchen, where I found Katya stuffing a chicken with lemons.

"What is that?"

"A kitten," I said. "What can we give it?"

"I don't want it in my kitchen."

I ignored her and wrapped the squirming kitten in a tea towel to contain it, then perched it in a bowl next to me.

I pulled the kitchen laptop towards me. "What do month-old kittens eat?" I said out loud as I typed the sentence into the search bar.

Katya, pulled into the drama, silently read the elaborate kitten care instructions over my shoulder, which included round-the-clock feedings for at least another week, sterilizing equipment, and helping them with everything from temperature regulation to going to the bathroom.

"Wow. More work than a baby," I said.

"Well, you wanted more to do around here."

I looked up the closest pet store, which stocked kitten milk powder and other supplies, then called down to Gus, for the first time sending him on an important errand.

"It'll be dead by the time I get back," he said.

"Let's take that chance."

I hung up and washed my hands. Then I dug out a glass turkey baster and warmed up some watery milk for the kitten to drink.

"Where are you going to keep it?" Katya asked, her voice stern. I looked around the kitchen. "Nope. Not here. I am not going to have a dirty animal in my spotless kitchen. And no, you cannot bathe it in this sink."

I didn't want to leave it in the barn. The chemicals I'd be using in the boathouse were noxious, they'd irritate her, maybe even poison something this small. No, it needed to stay warm, and near enough so that I could hear it, to keep up with its feedings. Even for a week. I glanced down the hall that led to the back door. With its warmth and proximity, the greenhouse would be a perfect place to incubate a kitten until it was healthy enough to be spayed or neutered, along with its mother.

I asked for the key.

"I don't know where it is," Katya said. "And even if I did, Mr. Winter forbids anyone going in there. Ever."

"I'm sure he'd rather I keep it there than in our bedroom," I said, holding out my hand for the key. "I promise, if anyone gets in trouble, it's going to be me."

Keeping her eyes on me, she reached her hand into the sugar bowl above the sink. She placed the key on the counter next to the damp tea towels. "I did not give this to you. You just found it."

I scooped up the kitten from the bowl. The corridor that led to the door was dark. I lived here and yet I had a sense that I was trespassing on Rebekah's prime territory.

I slid the key into the sticky lock, fussing with it a bit until it gave in my hand. I was shaking. I eased open the door. Inside the air was heavy and close. I inhaled deeply as the kitten stirred. Nothing grew here and yet it smelled sweet and loamy with possibility, the oddly angled glass generating a naturally intense heat. I held out my free hand as I walked down the middle of the star, shadows competing with the sun to caress my skin. From the outside, I had agreed with Louisa's assessment, that the greenhouse was interesting but ultimately a cold, jagged intrusion on a classic aesthetic. But inside it was warm and light-filled, magic from every angle. Even the gnarly rose stumps looked like they could be revived with just a little water and attention. I could smell and feel the life that had once been in here. From beneath a table I pulled a wooden crate that housed green pots of dead seedlings and carried it over to the sink by the door. I placed the bowl with the now sleeping kitten in the sink. Using a piece of dusty canvas, I created a makeshift cubby in the crate for it to sleep in. All

I needed was a blanket, and the conditions for it to thrive in this place would be perfect. I turned on the tap and let the brown water run until it was clear. When I placed the kitten in the warm water, it turned out not to be gray at all but the same beautiful cream color as its mother, with darker orange stripes. Its eyes, cleared of gunk, were a bright mossy green.

"So you *are* pretty," I said, dipping her in the water and shaking the dirt loose. Afterwards, I wrapped her—for it was indeed a female—back up in the tea towel and carried her to a sunny spot to dry. "And you're going to get me in a lot of trouble."

I could see why Rebekah had loved it in here. It had none of the draftiness of Asherley and, even barren, a warmth that reminded me of home. This place could be beautiful again, too, I thought. Why build this lovely, useful structure if it only thrived while Rebekah was alive?

I kissed the kitten and placed her on an empty sod bag, away from the bare earth so she didn't get dirty again.

I would talk to Max about this place.

Dani stayed away the rest of the time Max was gone, and I was happy for the break, as was her tutor, it seemed. I missed Max, spoke to or texted him a couple of times a day, glad to hear Dani had told him she'd gone to Louisa's New York pied-à-terre so that I didn't have to. Max was unfazed; she did it often, he said, promising she took homework with her. Fine. If this wasn't a problem for Max, I wouldn't make it a problem either. That would be my new philosophy. Follow his lead.

With her away, I thought I'd find myself bounding down the stairs in the morning, skipping through the dim corridors, exalting in the freedom of feeling neither watched nor ignored. But in a strange way, Dani's absence exacerbated Rebekah's presence. Wandering in and out of all the rooms, holding the kitten, familiarizing myself with each one's purpose and view, I saw Rebekah's hand everywhere. In the parlor, I ran my fingers along the French wallpaper looking for the seams, remembering where she had stood in those first photographs I pored over. In the third-floor gallery, the kitten buried in my neck, I lingered over each photo, noticing that the glass in the picture I'd broken had already been replaced. It looked to be an older photo, black-and-white, taken somewhere in Europe. Rebekah stood on a bridge, a line of blurry ancient buildings behind her. She was wearing a light-colored trench, her fists deep in her pockets, smiling impatiently at whoever took the picture, likely Max. I imagined her demurring at first, saying, *Enough with the camera, Max, let's just go to dinner*, and Max saying, *No, one more, the light here is perfect. Fine*, she'd say, *take it quickly. I'm getting hungry*. This photo was the product of a loving eye, *his* loving eye. I thought again back to the awkward moment Max snapped my picture on the boat. Why had he not taken more photos of me like he did her? Now, looking at my reflection in the photo's glass, holding a mangy little animal, my hair matted from being stuffed under a hat, my face dirty from working on the boat, I knew the answer.

I turned away from the photos and made my way to what I assumed was Dani's actual bedroom, where she slept when she wasn't up in the turret. Surprisingly, the door wasn't locked. Inside was a teenager's dream room, though three times as big and quite at odds with the rest of Asherley. Instead of stodgy antiques and quiet rugs, there was a large denim-covered sectional facing a flat-screen TV as big as a small theater's. On the glass kidney-shaped coffee table, a tangled game console shared space with a clean crystal ashtray and spent sticks of incense. She had her own microwave perched on a small robin's-egg-blue fridge. Band posters were interspersed with nice art and some African-type masks. Kilim rugs were scattered across the floors, artfully overlapping each other. Her four-poster bedframe had the same ornate quality as ours, though hers was painted white, the drapery pale pink, the comforter and pillows a riot of pinks and reds, the patterns expertly mismatched in a way I attributed to Rebekah's eye. The dressing table was covered in dozens of tubes of lipstick and compacts of blush and eye shadow. There were also several more framed pictures of Rebekah, some with Dani as a baby, and more recent ones of her looking adoringly at Dani, a mother in love. I hadn't seen these ones before, not in the gallery nor online. These were intimate, candid, imperfect. Something of real love was captured in the frames. They made me feel indescribably sad.

Without touching anything, I quietly left the bedroom. Now to the door at the end of the gallery. I knew it led to the turret, to Rebekah's room, which I had only glimpsed behind Dani that first night. I wouldn't stay long. I'd just look out those same windows from which Dani always seemed to be watching me, monitoring my movements around the grounds. I closed my hand around the glass knob. It turned easily, but the deadbolt kept me out.

During those nights and days Max was away, I was finally busy, so busy I barely slept or showered. Between refurbishing the Aquarama and feeding the kitten every few hours, I was charged with a humming sense of purpose. For the first time since I'd arrived at Asherley, I began to feel useful, especially when I fed the kitten her bottle. I had named her Maggie, after Miss Marguerite, one of Max's ancestors in the paintings whose shock of white hair reminded me of her.

I was determined to learn more about the family I was marrying into, not to feel like I belonged at Asherley—I would never feel that—but at least to show Max I cared about its history. Katya pulled down some books about the people in the portraits, flipping to the most important ancestors. She generously spent an afternoon in the kitchen pointing out key facts, only losing her patience once or twice, complaining she had a lot to do, you know, and this was cutting into her precious work time.

"No, no, *that's* Lady Carolina," she said, correcting me, pointing out the difference between two paintings of a blond woman in the same blue dress. She explained that Lady Carolina, the mother, was a favorite of President Rutherford Hayes while he was a bachelor, before she married Max's great-great-grandfather. Marguerite Winter Duplessix, their daughter, was courted by a Union general, someone famous she couldn't remember, before she turned him down and married a local French farmer.

"Apparently she was an excellent letter writer, threw great parties, and was no lady. Rebekah loved her, ate up any information about Miss Marguerite. She found a large bolt of that blue satin perfectly preserved in the attic and had it made into that little skirt around her makeup table."

She said it as though I'd been up there and was familiar with Rebekah's bedroom.

"You mean in the turret?"

"Yes."

"I'd love to take a look at it," I said breezily, hoping Katya would slip me another secret key. She ignored the prompt while tracing a pencil down a long to-do list that included a weekly flower order.

"Katya, do you think we can order something other than those roses? Wouldn't it be nice to get lilies or daisies, something fresh for spring?"

"It's not spring yet," she muttered. Then, as if to make up for her brusqueness, she asked about the kitten.

"She's sleeping. I emptied the litter."

"He won't like it, you know."

"The kitten?"

"You being in the greenhouse."

At that moment I received a text from Max. *Can't wait to see you tonight. Getting in late. Wait up. xo*

"I'll talk to him," I said, pocketing my phone. "Another few weeks and I can get her spayed. After that she can run free on the island and we can lock it up again."

Truthfully, I had no plans to lock up the greenhouse again. While crouched on the floor, Maggie heartily latching on to her kitten bottle, I had begun to fall in love with the place and imagined cleaning the windows and planting rows and rows of vegetables on the tables, green beans, tomatoes, cat grass in pots, maybe some yellow marigolds, and taking great sheers to Rebekah's red-black roses. Those hours in the greenhouse had revived my spirits. I had no intention of cutting off my supply of warmth and light.

I helped Katya clean up after lunch, then gave Maggie another quick bottle and headed down to strip another layer of varnish off the Aquarama before Max got home.

When I opened the door I was surprised to find Gus inside, holding his phone in front of the boat and talking out loud to someone on the screen. It was Dani. He spun around wearing the face of a man caught in the act of doing something that was, on the surface, quite benign, yet both of us knew it wasn't.

"Sorry," he said to me. He turned away and spoke into his phone. "I have to go."

I stepped towards the boat. My eyes possessively scanned the hull, the tools, his phone.

"She was just curious about what you were doing in here. So I thought I'd show her."

"She's more than welcome to come down here and see for herself," I said. I didn't like his expression, the way he had looked at me with pity almost. "When is she coming home?"

"I'm just heading out to get her. Unless you need something."

"No, thanks."

He left without another word. I looked around the boathouse and shuddered at the thought that Dani didn't even need to be on the property to spy on me.

FOURTEEN

When I heard the sound of wheels on gravel, I didn't even pause to wash my hands. I dropped my brush and bolted from the boathouse and up the path. Max was home, later than he said he'd be, but he was home! There was so much to tell him about the boat and the kitten, so much to hear about his days and nights in Albany. I breathlessly rounded the corner of the garage and jumped into his arms, heedless of how dirty I was or how laden his arms were with bags.

"I should leave more often," he said, laughing, as I kissed him all over his face.

"Never, never, never leave again," I said.

He dug his nose into my mess of curls. "Am I smelling . . . what is that? Formaldehyde? Have you been embalming the dead again?" He looked at my hands, my nails stained by my efforts. "Where's your ring?"

"In the boathouse. Come. I have a surprise for you."

"Great. I *think*. Listen, I also want to talk to you about something." I pushed his bag off his shoulder and tugged him by the sleeve over the side lawn.

"Me first."

I planned to thrill him with the boat first, then tell him about our new furry tenant convalescing in the greenhouse. I opened the boathouse door with a flourish and we were both freshly hit with the smell of varnish, which had begun to turn

131

the boat back to a gleaming liver color. Only two or three more coats to go.

Max, his mouth half-open, took a few steps closer to the boat, one hand floating towards it, careful not to disturb the finish.

"This was my father's boat. He never let me touch it. I'm . . . speechless."

I couldn't place his tone, whether he was grateful or angry. "I wanted to surprise you. Please say you don't mind."

He turned away from the boat and came towards me, his face slowly relaxing into a beatific expression. Was he tearing up? He swept me into his arms. I wrapped my legs around him, and as he walked, he murmured into my ear.

"What did I ever do to deserve you?"

"So you don't mind?"

He shook his head, placing me down on the leather couch and unbuttoning my plaid work shirt, then my jeans. For all of this ardor and my eager compliance, his expression was not triumphant. He seemed, for lack of a better word, mournful, as though preemptively sorry for what he was about to do. When I held his face in my hands, he avoided my eyes.

"Hey. What is going on in that head?"

"That I want to get you naked right now."

"I can see that," I said, helping him with my jeans. They bunched at an ankle and he angrily worked off a running shoe to free them. Stopping for a moment, he looked at me again with that same sad expression.

"You didn't want such a big life, did you? You might have been content on that little island tinkering away on a boat like this."

I leaned forward and kissed him. "Not without you."

It was still bewildering how well he knew how to please me, without my ever having to explain my body's intricacies to him. He simply knew where to touch me and with what part of his body, using the right level of fervency. Knees bent, body slack, I lay there while he pleased me again, my fingers spidering through the hair on the back of his head. Moans filling my ears, ones that were loud enough to drown out the sound of approaching footsteps. When I saw Dani in the doorway I snapped my knees shut on Max's ears.

"Wow," she said, laughing. "This boathouse has seen a *lot* of action lately."

Then she slammed the door shut, sending up angry dust motes in her wake.

Max sat upright, keeping his eyes shut tight as though with enough concentration he could turn back time. After what seemed an eternity, he muttered, "I'll talk to her about this."

I dressed, enraged. "About what? About knocking? About privacy? About . . . sex? Oh my God, I'm going to throw up."

"Look, it was bound to happen. These things *happen*. We live with a nosy teenager."

He bent to retrieve my shoe, waiting a beat. "What did she mean about the boathouse seeing action?"

I looked at him squarely and snatched my shoe from him. "Gus helped me ground the boat before she went to New York," I said, my voice flat. "She's been spying on me. I'm guessing she would like you to think that I am fucking him."

Max collapsed against the wall and let out a dark laugh. "I see," he said, shaking his head.

I wanted to tell him Dani was more than just a nosy teenager: she watched me from the turret, went through my purse for my wallet, followed me into town, had Gus chronicle my activities. I wanted to say I'd been at Asherley for more than a month and things were not thawing. They were becoming worse. She was getting chillier and meaner and odder. She wasn't following me around because she was nosy. She was trying to menace me, threaten me, to make me afraid of her, so afraid that I would leave. That's what she wanted. She wanted me gone. And barring that, she wanted to wreck what I had with Max. And I wanted to tell him that if she kept it up, she might succeed.

Max unpacked and made some calls and I took a long bath to soak the varnish off my hands and the smell out of my hair and skin. Halfway through dinner, Dani joined us. I could barely look at her.

We ate quickly, silently, Max telling us about Albany and how the big issue is zoning for condos since more young people want to live in Suffolk County but can't afford a mansion. He knew older residents would resist. Dani said they'll change their mind when they can't sell their big, fat homes and that letting young people get into the housing market more affordably would only help them build a future here. Of course I was impressed with her acuity, only fifteen and holding court on local issues while all I could do was nod and listen, the gulf between them and me wider and deeper. They carried on, the two of them, as though there had been no mortification in the boathouse. Dani, in fact, was chattier than usual. So I was surprised that she folded me into the conversation towards the end

134

of dinner with a compliment on the job I had done on the boat.

"Now I didn't get a *great* look at it, but I could tell the boat looked very shiny and new," she said. "Was it hard to strip off all those layers?"

"Not if you're using the proper chemicals," I said, noting the time. The kitten needed a feeding soon.

"So you just rub a chemical on the wood in little circles and it eats it out while you just lay back and wait?"

"Yes, sort of."

"Maybe you could show me how sometime," she said. "You seem to really enjoy it."

"Yes, I'd love to," I said, only then picking up on her innuendos. I threw my napkin onto the table.

"Dani," Max said, a hint of a warning in his voice. "I would like to talk to you about something important, if you don't mind." He shot me a look, one that said, *Go. I've got this*.

Dani collapsed back into her chair with a huff.

I snatched up empty plates and found Katya in the kitchen putting on her coat. She usually left right after serving dinner on nights I insisted on doing cleanup.

"I just fed Maggie," she whispered, hoisting her purse onto a shoulder. "She should be okay for a few hours. But she's a restless little thing. Running all over in there. Three days and she's got her strength back."

"Thank you, Katya, so much." I dropped the plates onto the island and turned on the water full strength to rinse the dishes. She gave me a look. "I'm *going* to tell him. Things are a little tense right now." I motioned to the dining room.

"Okay. Well, good luck," she said.

I finished filling the dishwasher and soaking the pans. While their muffled conversation in the dining room continued, I reached into the sugar bowl for the greenhouse key and tiptoed down the hall for a quick visit. It was dark inside and silent, but the air was sweet and warm. Her water dish was full, the litter clean. I felt inside the back of the crate. No Maggie. I spotted the shadow of her tail draped over the side of the shelf above. She must have climbed the bags of dirt. Restless, indeed. And spry. She was feeling better.

As I headed back to the kitchen to wait out the storm, she leapt. Hard to believe such a tiny thing could instigate such a commotion, but by the time I turned around again, the shelves were raining down after her, their weight collapsing the table, sending stacks of clay pots and bags of dry dirt smashing on the floor and a terrified Maggie scampering into her crate. Then it was over except for the dust.

Max and Dani came running down the hall, their confused voices in unison: *What is going on? What are you doing in here? What is that* thing *that just ran under the table?* The calamity lasted only three seconds, but it felt like an hour.

"What the *fuck*?" Max's eyes darted around the greenhouse. Dani seemed to be in a daze.

"I can smell her," she whispered, closing her eyes and tilting her head back to breathe deeply.

I knelt down and pulled the kitten out from the back of the crate. I thought she was purring, but her tiny heart was beating so fast she was vibrating with terror.

"Everybody, meet Maggie. Maggie, meet everybody," I said with a nervous laugh. Still on my knees, I held the kitten tight, to protect her and myself from their reaction. "Gus found her in the barn almost dead. I've been feeding her for a couple of days."

Max glared at me, his hands opening and closing. Dani fell to her knees next to me, reaching for the kitten. Reluctantly, I poured the scared thing into her arms.

"She's about a month old," I said to Dani. "I've been giving her kitten formula. She can start on watery wet food next week. In another month or so I can get her spayed. Then we can find a home for her."

"Who let you in here?" Max asked, in a voice I barely recognized.

"I couldn't keep her in the boathouse while I was using chemicals. And I didn't want her in the barn. It's too far for feedings," I said, leaving out the fact that I found Gus creepy. "I didn't know where else I could keep her. She requires constant care right now."

"Who gave you the key?"

"I found it."

Dani was lost to us, having formed her own language with the kitten, girly coos and high-pitched sounds.

"Katya knows better than to let anyone in here."

"Can I take care of her, too?" Dani asked. "Please, please, please?"

We were side by side on our knees, the closest we'd ever been.

"Yes! Of course you can. If your father says so."

"I'm not asking him. I'm asking you." She nuzzled Maggie's neck, her eyes pleading. If I had known a kitten could create this détente, I would have arrived from the Caymans with a crate of them.

Max, ignoring this miracle happening between us, walked over to the pile of debris and poked his foot at the broken clay pots and the spilled dirt on the ground.

"I'll clean all this up in the morning," I said. "I promise."

He turned to face me, his expression still livid. "Dani, take it out of here. Now."

"Her name is *Maggie*, Dad," she said, remaining next to me on the floor.

"I said take it and go."

Dani looked at me for direction.

"It's okay, Dani," I said, trying to stay cheerful. "After I talk to your father I'll bring you her things and some formula if you want to feed her tonight."

Dani nodded. I helped her to her feet. When she and the kitten were well down the corridor, I turned to face Max, clearing my throat.

"Max, please let me explain. I would have brought her down to the boathouse sooner but—"

"You've been busy this week." He sounded calm. "I'm gone three days and you take it upon yourself to fix a boat that wasn't broken, and then you bring a sick animal into the only place on the property I don't want people to enter. As you can see," he said, his arm sweeping the room, his voice pitching louder, "this place is *unsafe*. The glass, it needs to be reset. Those frames, they're all rusting out. In fact, that fan, *that fan* weighs at least fifty pounds. It could fall out of the roof at any time and onto someone's head and you've been running around in here chasing a kitten? I don't *want* anyone in here. Not you, not my daughter, not Katya, and certainly not that fucking animal!"

There was nothing about Max that I recognized in that moment, not his face, nor his tone of voice. Backlit by the moon and looming over me, he was a mere outline of the man I thought I knew. I froze, speechless. Sensing my fear, Max shook his head as though to break a spell.

"Oh God, I'm sorry," he said. "The way I spoke to you just now. It's . . . I haven't been in here in a long time. Forgive me. Please."

"It's all right," I said.

"Now give me the key."

I passed it to him.

"Please. Leave me alone for a minute."

I picked up the kitten's things, her crate, her litter box. Before I left, I stole a glimpse of him through the dirty glass door. I'll never forget how lost he looked, arms slack at his sides, eyes closed, head bowed slightly. Walking through the kitchen with tears running down my cheeks, I was torn between anger at the way he had spoken to me and sadness for a man I'd left alone in his dead wife's most treasured spot, a place she created and loved. Smell is a talented time machine. I saw how Dani instantly remembered Rebekah. He's also inhaling her memory, thinking back on a time when he might find her in there, wearing a straw hat, perhaps, white-blond tendrils falling around her shoulders. I saw them now, dappled by the sun, him sneaking up behind her, wrapping his arms around her. Unlike me, she'd be wearing gloves to protect her perfect white hands, and a dress, probably, something feminine and flattering, cinched at the waist. He's kissing her neck and she's smiling as she cuts a dozen roses for the table, blades glinting in the sun.

For every step forward I made at Asherley, I suffered several back. While the kitten had seemed to bring me closer to Dani, she had caused a rift between Max and me. Outside Dani's bedroom, I heard cooing and giggling. I put down Maggie's crate and took a moment to wipe the tears off my face. Then I knocked, listening as Dani skipped across the bedroom floor. When she opened it, I went to step inside, but she pushed me back with her body.

"Careful! I don't want to let Maggie out," she said, now through the crack in the door.

"Oh. But I brought you her stuff. Let me just—"

"I got her bottles and formula from the fridge. Just leave that outside the door. My friend Claire's here and she knows how to take care of kittens."

Over Dani's shoulder, I saw her friend lying on her side on Dani's bed, one arm aloft holding a string to taunt Maggie.

"Nice to meet you," Claire called out, without lifting her head.

Dani gave me a bright, wide smile. "Okay, so, night-night," she said, before shutting the door in my face. The silence was broken seconds later by the sound of teenage girls laughing.

I stood there in the gallery surrounded by a hundred triumphant Rebekahs.

Perhaps Maggie had done something cute to elicit those giggles. Perhaps they weren't making fun of me at my most vulnerable. But Dani was cruel, and it was clear now that her happiness was achievable only in direct proportion to my sadness. Even if I were to look upon that moment between us in the greenhouse as an appeasement, it was only temporary, the price, this time, a kitten. When she grew bored of Maggie, then what would I need to throw at her to keep her at bay?

As for Max, I still loved him, felt it acutely that night in the empty spot in our bed. But when he had asked to be alone in the greenhouse, he was asking to be alone with her, and it was the only thing in the world I could truly give him.

FIFTEEN

Once I had made up my mind to leave, a calm came over me. The fight was over. In fact, it felt less like leaving than like Asherley itself was pushing me out, rejecting me like a body rejecting an unfamiliar organ. The memory of Rebekah was stronger than any future I might have here. Dani was certainly content to live off it, and last night I had got the sense, finally, that Max might be, too.

The sun was barely up by the time I had packed my small suitcase and checked flights. I wanted to avoid a scene. I left behind the few winter belongings I'd acquired since I'd been at Asherley, taking only what I'd need for the Caymans in early March. I had enough money in my own account to get me to the airport, purchase a one-way ticket, and stay at the hostel until I found work. My plan was first to prostrate myself at Laureen's swollen ankles and beg for my job back, or any job, really. I would tell her she'd been right, not just about Max but about me, and my stupidity, the arrogance of thinking I was special enough to turn a fling into a marriage. If I couldn't appeal to her sympathies, then I'd walk up and down Seven Mile Beach knocking on every office door of every hotel and restaurant. It was high season. Surely someone needed extra waitstaff or cleaning help.

I wrote Max a letter and left it on his dressing table. It was short. I said I loved him very much but I couldn't stay where

I wasn't wanted. I thanked him profusely for these past few months; they had been the best of my life. Something like that. I wish I'd kept it. I think back often on that morning when I called the cab, whispering that I'd meet the driver down at the gate in an hour since I did not know how to open it from the house. I crept across the second-floor gallery to the top of the stairs. There I listened for sounds. Everyone was asleep. Katya hadn't arrived. Would she have stopped me from escaping? Probably not. She had the same middle-aged pragmatism as Laureen, which I had come to admire and hoped one day to emulate. Imagine not caring what people think. Imagine having the courage to talk back to people you don't like, who don't like you, or better yet, not reacting at all, simply shrugging it off and moving on with your day. I wanted to be more like that. I would let this experience toughen me up. I would recover and be better for it. And yet none of these thoughts, however true (or not), stanched the flow of my tears. This was a big love. I would grieve its loss for a long time.

I carefully placed my bag on the tile floor of the foyer. When I crept into the anteroom, I glanced at the gun cabinet next to the one that housed my fleece. I recognized the handguns, the same kind we kept on the boats in case a shark or a large stingray threatened a client, or, though I never told Laureen, a client threatened me. I considered a few more months here, with the tension ratcheted up even higher. I could never hurt Dani, but she could hurt me, or herself.

If you bring ur fucking fling home daddy ill kill myself.

That these scenarios even crossed my mind meant it was time to go.

143

As I shut the cabinet door, I heard footsteps. I closed my eyes and prayed. I wasn't religious, but I asked a power from above, any power at all, to give me the strength to keep walking out that door. I left the anteroom clutching my fleece to my heart, knowing Max was prepared for a different kind of battle, which I knew already I would lose by the way he said my name in a low, hollowed-out voice, my letter wafting from his hand to the floor.

"Don't go."

"Max, I'm sorry. But I have to." I picked up my bag.

He grabbed the handle, gave it a gentle tug, and placed the bag on the floor behind him. "No. This is not what I want to happen. You can't leave." He looked more exhausted than I did, ashen-faced, unshaven, his eyes bloodshot. "Stay. I love you."

"I can't. This has become too hard. For everyone."

"I'll make it easier."

"You can't."

"Yes. Yes, I can."

"I don't belong here, Max. You know that."

"You do. I thought you were happy here."

"I thought so, too, until last night, when I realized I'll never be enough. Especially not for Dani."

"Nonsense. Last night should never have happened."

"I know. I shouldn't have opened the greenhouse."

"You did nothing wrong. *I* should never have spoken to you like that. I behaved like a monster. I can't tell you how ashamed I am of myself. I didn't come upstairs last night because I couldn't face you. And now you're— I don't want to lose you. Stay. I need you. *We* need you. More than you know."

When the heart rules the body, it will always betray even the soundest, wisest corners of your mind. It's hard to believe now how easily I could be persuaded by sentiment, how the feeling of being needed could murder all my resolve. It's part of being young, I suppose, that malleability, the best and worst part, but there I was, crying "Oh, Max" and flinging myself into his arms, smelling that musty smell of a long, sad night on him.

He held me tight for a while, murmuring that he had wanted to come up to our bed a thousand times, to put his arms around me, to comfort me, but he thought I wanted to be alone with my kitten, and that a night apart for him to contemplate what he'd done and how he might make it up to me might fix some of what he had broken.

"I should have come to you. I should have begged your forgiveness right away. Dani, too."

"Max, she's never going to come around."

"That's not true. I saw something last night. A glimmer. Something softened in her. You saw it, too. With the kitten."

Before I could tell him how quickly she had hardened, he reached into his front pocket and held up my engagement ring, given to me after a different taxi had once nearly separated us.

"Remember when you met me by the car yesterday, before you took me down to see the boat? I told you I had something I wanted to talk to you about. This isn't how I planned it, but here it goes. I can't bear to be away from you. Put this back on, because what I'm trying to say is we should get married. As soon as possible. Why wait?"

There were many good answers to that question, chief among them being the way he had looked in the greenhouse,

145

haunted and aggrieved, confirming we'd be wise to put more time between Rebekah's death and the start of our marriage. But there was such naked need in his eyes. I was flattered to be wanted this much, to know that Max Winter was desperate to marry *me*.

So instead of no, I said, "I don't know why we're waiting, Max. Yes. Let's do it. Let's get married right away."

The first person Max suggested I call was Louisa. Perhaps he felt I needed to be buoyed a little before we broke it to Dani. When Louisa squealed with delight at the news, I could have cried.

"Have you told Dani yet?"

"Not yet."

She offered to come over right away to help with the planning. "I'll make it so all you have to do is show up," she said.

I thanked her and told her that wouldn't be necessary. We wanted it to be very small, and I had plenty of time to tackle most of what needed to be done. "But I would love your advice, Louisa."

"Well, here's some: Don't worry about what Dani says or does. Just plow ahead. She'll catch up. She always does."

Finally Max texted Dani to come down and join us in the den. I still hadn't told him she had absconded with my kitten. When she made her entrance holding Maggie, my heart hurt all over again. She was trailed by Claire, an arresting beauty whose height and bearing made her seem closer to my age than Dani's. Though Claire was dark where Dani was blond, her eyes icy blue where Dani's were brown, they dressed alike, both wearing pastel cotton shorts that they likely slept in, and both were braless, the points of their nipples tenting their loose white T-shirts.

I spoke first. "You must be Claire. We sort of met last night."

"Yeah. I was a little distracted. She's just so cute," Claire said, giving the kitten a scratch behind her ear, then drawling, "Hi, Mr. Winter."

"Claire. Dani, we have something we want to tell you. Claire, would you mind waiting for us in the kitchen?"

Claire went to leave.

"Stay," Dani commanded. "Anything you tell me I'm going to tell her anyway."

Max looked at me for permission. I shrugged. Now was the time to cultivate some of that grown-woman insouciance. Whatever Dani's reaction, I would weather it, as Louisa suggested. As for Claire, I was glad for her to stay, if only to witness the fact that good things can happen to not so beautiful women, too.

"First of all," Max began, "I want to apologize for how angry I got last night in the greenhouse. I had no right to yell like that. It was wrong. *I* was wrong."

"It's okay, Daddy," Dani said. "*I* know no one is supposed to go in there."

"Yes, well, with everything that's happened . . . it's just made me realize how short life is, and how lucky I am to have you both in my life."

Dani began to pet Maggie more aggressively, perhaps less to soothe the kitten than herself.

"You know I love you very much." He looked at me. "I love you both. And I know we got engaged pretty quickly. Well . . . we've decided to push up the wedding. We haven't really talked about the details yet, but it will be here, and soon, and though we'd love your blessing—"

"You're going to do it anyway," she said with a shrug.

"Yes, Dani, we are."

"So why do you want my blessing?" She looked at me and then at her father, back and forth, trying to knit us together in some logical way in her mind, her chin quivering. I almost felt sorry for her, standing there barefoot, holding a squirming kitten.

"Well, may I be the first to say congratulations, to both of you," Claire said, smiling and nudging Dani.

"Yes. Congratulations," Dani said, her voice flat, her eyes dead. She handed the kitten to Claire, took a breath, and walked over to me, opening her thin arms wide.

"Oh, well, thank you," I said, and entered her awkward embrace.

Then she walked over to Max and searched his face before giving him another stiff hug.

"I hope you'll both be very happy," she said, returning to stand next to her friend. "Can we go now?"

"Of course," Max said, unable to hide how pleased he seemed by her rough attempt at sweetness. "Thank you so much, Dani."

"Sure, Daddy. Let me know if I can help you in any way."

When the door shut behind them, Max and I looked at each other with astonishment, mouthing *Oh my God!* Then we threw up our arms in silent victory.

I was reeling. In twenty-four hours we'd gone from the disastrous boathouse interruption to the greenhouse confrontation to my near abandonment, to a quickie wedding.

Dani had not flung herself onto the carpet in paroxysms. She had not lit herself on fire.

We both collapsed onto the couch.

"Maybe she didn't want to make a scene in front of Claire," I whispered.

"I don't care why. Let's just be grateful."

He took my hand and kissed it, closing his eyes. Perhaps Max was willing to see any progress through rosy lenses, but nothing in me trusted her yet. Arm's length was as close as I wanted Dani Winter to get to me or my wedding plans.

SIXTEEN

I suppose it shouldn't have been surprising that wedding planning came easily to me. I had always been organized and frugal, but I became uncharacteristically decisive by employing one simple rule: anything that Rebekah had done for her wedding, I would not. Louisa became my best resource, because there were, to my disappointment, no pictures of Max and Rebekah's wedding to reference. Louisa told me Rebekah hadn't allowed cameras that day. She had thoroughly documented their courtship (and subsequent honeymoon in Venice), but had wanted her wedding to pay homage to Asherley's bygone era. She even asked guests to drop their phones in a basket when they entered the house. I envied that directive, privacy being my natural inclination. Louisa told me when Rebekah had caught Jonah furtively monitoring the score of a baseball game on Max's laptop in the den, she poured her drink on the keyboard.

"They didn't speak for weeks, which killed him. He was in love with Rebekah, though to this day he'll never admit it," Louisa said, rolling her eyes.

As for the menu, Louisa told me they had only served food sourced on or around the island: venison and pheasant stuffed with ramps, wild garlic, and mushrooms, and strawberries and cream for dessert. No wedding cake. Rebekah found cake gauche.

What would we serve? For such a small affair, and it being informal, I decided we'd have a catered barbecue: corn on the cob, potato salad, a roasted pig, lobster rolls, cake, and ice cream.

Max gave me his guest list over breakfast one day, family, friends, neighbors, and a few close political associates from Albany, fewer than forty people in all. I insisted we invite Katya—I didn't want her to work—but Max drew the line at Gus. He was strictly an employee.

"Besides," he said, "I think Dani's got a little crush on him, and I don't like it."

This took me aback. She certainly ordered him around and gave him odd directives, like keeping an eye on me. But if anything, he often seemed reluctant to be around her. When she crossed the lawn to visit Isabel, he'd often leave the barn. Same if I found him in the kitchen eating something. The minute Dani came in, especially if she was in pajamas, he'd bolt.

When I didn't reply, Max asked outright. "You've never noticed any flirtation between them?"

"No. Never. Not on his part anyway," I said, remembering the trouble Laureen told me she'd once gotten up to in the Caymans.

"Anyway, she needs more friends her age," he said, and looked down at the list. "Is there anyone you'd like to invite?"

This was a gentle question, a necessary one, too, though Max already seemed to know the answer.

"I don't think so," I said, trying to keep the sadness from leaching into my voice.

He took my hand and kissed it, then pressed it to his heart. "You are very much loved here. You know that, right?"

I nodded.

The most significant person in my life, other than Max, had been Laureen, and I couldn't imagine her wide, sunburned face among the intimate crowd. Still, after he left for work, I wrote her an email, to let her know that a wedding was in the offing, counting on her prediction that there was still time for my affair with Max to blow up in my face.

Her reply was terse.

Honestly, I didn't think I'd hear from you again. But you've always been a surprising person. Am just back from St. Barts. Found someone to run the marina, and two new captains for the smaller boats I'm still running from there. Sadly, I have to ground the Singularis until the lawsuit is settled. Sucks because she was my big moneymaker. God I hate the British more than the Americans if you can believe it. Well, congratulations then. I'm glad it wasn't a total disaster and I do hope you'll be happy in America. John-John will soon retire due to his heart. My health is mostly good.

I could hear her Australian twang in those blunt sentences and see her stomping through the streets of Gustavia trying to rustle up marina help, decent boat captains, and fishing guides. That would have been one of my jobs, had I gotten on the plane that day. My alternative life haunted me sometimes. I saw myself jotting down the day's tasks while sitting on the balcony of my small company condo, the outside painted lemon yellow probably, the inside decorated with a tacky shell motif. I'd check the time, then race to the airport, waiting in the overly air-conditioned arrivals lounge for the next clients to deplane. But that was not my life. Instead, after a breakfast that someone else prepared for me, and seeing my fiancé off to work, I entered

Asherley's formal dining room to plan my wedding, parting the heavy damask curtains so the sun could hit my shoulders. If Laureen could see me holding court at the end of this polished table, so shiny the whites of my eyes reflected on its surface, what would she say? Would she note how comfortable I looked, surrounded by clippings from bridal magazines, a cup of coffee cooling on a place mat? Or would she say I looked like a fraudulent wannabe, a sorry substitute for the stylish Rebekah? *She's nothing but a scrubby beach urchin*, she'd say. *Not one person of her own to invite to her wedding. That says something about a person, doesn't it? That she has nobody but Max. When a woman only has a man to count on, she's taken a very wrong turn in her life.*

When Max called just then to tell me a reporter from *The New York Times* wanted to cover our little ceremony in the Hamptons, I remembered that Laureen often picked up the Sunday *Times* at the airport.

"It'd be for the Vows column," he explained. "I'd normally scoff at this sort of thing except Elias thinks we could plug the election. And a lot of people out here read that silly column, apparently."

"If you don't mind, then I don't," I said.

Then came another surprise. Dani began to make regular appearances in the dining room. At first she'd wander around bored, dropping the increasingly chubby Maggie on the floor while she poked through the magazines piling up on the table. I'd play with Maggie, answer any questions Dani had, then she'd scoop up the kitten and be off.

A few days later, she stood behind me to look at an assortment of dresses cued up on the laptop, evening gowns mostly. I still felt intimidated by the idea of a flouncy white wedding dress, kept trying to find one in which I could picture myself. We said nothing to each other at first, our demeanor like a couple of doctors silently contemplating a medical slide.

Finally Dani pointed to the most prominent dress on my screen, a shimmery velvet tube dress, in pale coral, with a boat neck and dolman sleeves. "You're thinking *that*?"

"I don't know. I mean, it's your dad's second wedding."

"Yeah, but it's *your* first. This shit's for the mother of the bride."

In the reflection on the screen, she tilted her head thoughtfully. "And velvet will age you."

I wanted to say I wouldn't really mind looking older, but she was already out the door, Maggie trailing behind her.

The next day, after Adele drove off, Dani swanned back into the dining room, making her slow promenade around the table while the kitten chased a feathered string she held in her hand. I'd begun to look forward to seeing her, if only to note what she wore that day or what she did with her hair. That day's outfit was black yoga pants and a white poplin shirt. She had on pink lip gloss, her hair piled in a bun. The dark roots on the back of her head grew in a little faster than the front, or maybe she just touched up the front more often, but she was due for a hair appointment. She collapsed in a chair opposite me, picked up a magazine, and began flipping through the pages.

"Where were you planning to shop for your dress?"

"I'm sure I can find something nice at a department store. Barneys or someplace like that."

She was silent.

"I mean," I went on, "the wedding's in a month. Buying a dress at a high-end bridal shop would take too long."

"I know a place that can do quick turnarounds if you're off-the-rack," she said. "And I think you are. I mean, you don't have any boobs. Claire's mother got her wedding dress there a few years ago. Only took three weeks. She bought a sample."

"I don't want to spend a fortune."

"Like you have a budget."

Maggie climbed up her yoga pants and nestled under her chin. She was doing a good job of taking care of the kitten but not of socializing her. She played too aggressively, climbed curtains, and scratched couches. I decided not to make a fuss about it, grateful she at least kept the name.

She gathered up Maggie and stood. "I'll make an appointment. If you want. Unless you just want to go alone, or with Aunt Louisa, which is totally fine, I really don't care."

Was she serious? I worried that if I showed too much eagerness, she'd take it back. She'd say she was just kidding.

Still I replied, a little too brightly, "That would be great, Dani. Thank you!"

"Cool. I'm heading to Claire's. Tell Dad I won't be home for dinner."

"You can leave Maggie here if you want. I'll cat sit."

She hesitated, eyeing me for a second. "Fine, but don't get too attached. She knows *I'm* her real mother."

Ten steps forward, five back.

She handed over the kitten. I looked down at sweet, dumb Maggie squirming in my lap. Her teeth were all in now. And though she couldn't quite break my skin with her tiny fangs, she started swatting angrily at my fingers and pulling them towards her mouth, testing, as kittens do, how hard she'd have to bite before she drew blood.

★

That night, in our bedroom, while I smoothed moisturizer on my elbows, I told Max about Dani's offer to go dress shopping with me.

"Dani? You mean Dani Winter?"

I shrugged, pretending it was no big deal.

He came up behind me at the dressing table, kissed the top of my head, and regarded me in the mirror. "I'm going to call you the stepdaughter whisperer. How did I get so fucking lucky?"

The way he looked at me just then—marveled at me, really—sent a rush of pride through my body.

"Incidentally, where do you want to go for the honeymoon?" he asked. "April anywhere in Europe is ideal. Fewer grubby tourists."

"Won't we be grubby tourists?"

"Speak for yourself."

"I don't know. I sort of hoped we could bring Dani. If she wants to come with us. You were just in the Caymans, after all. I feel like we'd be abandoning her again. I thought we could make it a family trip."

He tensed up. "That's a nice idea. But she's got school until June. That's part of our homeschooling agreement."

"Then we'll wait," I said. "It'll give me time to think of a great place. We don't have to rush off, do we?"

"We don't, no," he said, removing his cuff links and placing them in a dish in front of me. "But campaigning begins in the summer."

"Right. Of course."

He looked at me with concern. "Look, I love how much of an effort you're making with her. I do. But I wonder if you should ease up a bit."

"Well, I *am* going to give her a wedding gift."

He weighed his next words carefully.

"Listen to me. Dani can be very hot and cold. I just don't want to see you get disappointed if she suddenly pulls away. You're going shopping with her. That's great. Taking her on a honeymoon—maybe. But it's *your* wedding day. *You're* the bride. *You're* the one who receives gifts. Not Dani. She is quite literally a girl who has everything."

"I just want everyone to be as happy as me," I said. "Especially Dani."

He sighed and put his arms around me, kissed my neck. When I reached up to caress his thick hair, he took my hand to examine it.

"You keep taking off your ring. Do you hate it that much?"

"Oh no, I love it. But I'm still working on the boat," I said, getting a good look at my fingers. My nails were a wreck. The wrinkles in my knuckles were stained brown from the varnish. I pried my hand away. "I have one more coat to go."

Far from being deterred by his warning, I was excited about my gift to Dani. I planned to name the Aquarama *Dani's Luck*, a play on Daneluk, her ancestral name. I had already ordered the stencil online; it would take me two days to paint on the letters. Then I'd drape the boat until the big day. If we were closer by then, I would unveil it after the ceremony. I'd ask Max to bring her down to the boathouse, where I'd be waiting. He'd cover her eyes with his hands. Dani would be impatient, as always. "For God's sake, what is going on?" Then they would come in and he'd remove his hands. Dani would slowly take in the gleaming boat that I'd sweated over, varnished, and now named after her. Her eyes would go from me to the boat

157

and back again. "For *me*?" she'd say, smiling, while Max's eyes brimmed with tears. *How did I get so fucking lucky?*

"Where did you go just now?"

I shook off the daydream.

"Do we have enough?" he asked.

I looked at him dumbly. I had missed the first part of the question.

"Enough tables and chairs. Or should we rent more?"

"I'm sorry, Max. For the reception. Yes, rent, definitely."

He still looked concerned. "All right, then. I'll get Gus to call around. Forty people. Maybe eight round tables. Some for food, the cake."

"That's a lot."

"Rebekah fit twenty tables in the great hall for our wedding with room to spare."

Of course she did. The room probably magically expanded to accommodate her needs—straight out of a Disney movie. The coffee poured itself. Plates floated so guests wouldn't have to carry them *and* a drink.

I knew it was stupid of me to ask, but I did it anyway. "Max, I have an interesting idea for our reception."

He closed his eyes and threw his head back. He already knew what I was going to ask.

"Before you say no, I want you to think about it." Like a trial lawyer, I had prepped responses to his arguments. "You said yourself that the great hall might be too big for such a small event."

"Well, then, the dining room."

"There's no access to outdoors for smokers, and the powder rooms are too far."

"Why not a tent?"

"It'll still be early spring. The weather will be unpredict-able. What if it's a chilly, rainy day?"

"What about the barn? The horses are moving soon."

"It smells. Plus there's only one bathroom and it's too far. The guests will have to walk over muck if it rains."

"The boathouse, then." He moved over to the bed, opened a book and pretended to read, indicating the discussion was over.

"The boathouse is too small, Max. And it'll take weeks to air out the varnish."

He slapped the book shut. "The greenhouse is not safe."

"We have time to do repairs. Gus can help."

"It's filthy."

"I know how to wash windows."

"Look. I love you. I want to give you everything you want, so I hate saying no to you. But that's my final answer. The greenhouse is closed and it's staying that way."

SEVENTEEN

Louisa was on her second martini when I told her about Dani's offer to come dress shopping with me. We were sealing the last of the invitations while enjoying an early dinner in town.

"Told you she's full of surprises," she said. That's when I realized, with some disappointment, that she'd put Dani up to it.

"How much did you pay her?" I asked.

She smiled, patting my hand. "Look, all that matters is Dani's going with you. It'll be a great opportunity to get to know each other. To finally bond."

"I was hoping you'd come, too. You have such good taste."

And you can protect me from her, in case she plans something nefarious.

"So does Dani. No, this will be good, just the two of you. Seven . . . eight . . . ," she said, counting the small pile of gold envelopes.

"If you have any dress ideas or suggestions, feel free to pass them on." I had stopped asking for details about Rebekah's wedding after Louisa told me, jokingly, that I seemed more fixated on Max's first wedding than my own.

" . . . Thirteen . . . fourteen . . . Surprise us, dear. I'm sure you'll look terrific in anything you put on as long as it's not too fancy. You'd get swallowed up in a ball gown. Just wear something that looks like *you*. A month is enough notice for invitations, don't you think? It's not high season or anything. And we are holding it on a Friday."

That had been Louisa's suggestion, so as not to compete with better-prepared couples that had long since booked their caterers and florists.

I shrugged. "If people can't make it, they can't make it."

"Darling, *everyone* will make it. They'll be very curious to see who the hell Max Winter's marrying."

After Rebekah, I wanted to add, imagining guests stifling giggles as I made my way alone down the aisle of that cavernous room, holding a clutch of wilted wildflowers in my hand.

"Oh and of course, Elias," Louisa said, finding his name on the list, "and his husband, I can't remember his name. Polo player, handsomer than Elias, if that's possible. Max said you're having the ceremony in the great hall." She scrunched up her nose. "It might be too late to rent a tent."

"I had a much better location in mind, but Max shot it down."

"Oh?"

"The greenhouse."

Her eyes flashed wide open. "Oh my God, yes!"

"Max said absolutely not."

I didn't mean to re-litigate the issue, nor inspire Louisa to action. But she was adamant.

"Don't worry. You shall have your greenhouse reception. Just let me deal with Max." Her eyes drifted to my hair. "Now what did you do to your lovely curls?"

I touched it, embarrassed. I forgot that I'd parted it to the side and straightened it, the result, admittedly, of looking at too many photos of Rebekah, who often wore her hair this way.

"Well, *I* like your hair just as it is. I'm sure Max does, too."

"He's never really commented on my hair," I said, uncertain if that was a good or bad thing. "Anyway, I was just experimenting for the wedding."

On the way to our cars we passed a clothing store with headless mannequins in the window, dressed in every conceivable style of white linen shirt, their balletic feet pinioned to the floor. Louisa pulled me inside. A brief stop turned into an hour-long spree, pushing back the poor saleswoman's closing time. At one point, Louisa took over for her, tossing item after item over the top of my dressing stall, commanding me to step out so she could see, vetoing some of the things I liked and insisting on some of the things I didn't. It was fun, in a way, to be regarded so intently by someone who was so decisive, who held maternal sway over me. She scanned each outfit, a finger to her mouth, adding a scarf, a sweater, a belt to a dress. When it came time to choose what to buy, she laughed out loud. She meant for me to have *all* of what passed her muster, an obscene pile she scooped up like a human backhoe and deposited on the counter.

"I can't possibly go home with all this, this . . . *stuff*. It's ridiculous. I don't need all these clothes. Where would I wear them?"

"Dani tells me you *do* need new clothes," she said, "and that you've been wandering Asherley for weeks in the same four things. We can't have that. If you're going to be a Winter, you have to start dressing like one," she said, with a joking flare.

"I have clothes," I mumbled. In truth I had only two pairs of jeans, but quite a number of tops and T-shirts that I hoped had camouflaged that scarcity. It didn't bother me that Dani noticed what I wore, but it stung that it distressed her enough to tell Louisa.

When I placed Max's credit card down on the counter, Louisa flicked it away.

"Consider this your trousseau—a wedding gift from Jonah and me," she said, and gave instructions for the packages to be delivered to Asherley the next morning. There was no arguing with her. What could I say except thank you? Before we parted ways, my phone rang. It was the bridal shop. Dani must have given them my number. They had a cancellation the next afternoon. I took it.

"Perfect," Louisa said. "While you're in the city, I'll talk to Max about the greenhouse."

I texted Dani to tell her I took the cancellation, but she didn't reply. I pulled up to Asherley and checked my phone again. Still no reply. The lights in the turret were on, which meant she was still up. I put on my nightshirt and washed my face. I thought of texting her again. It was a big house; that wouldn't be weird. *Hey, still haven't heard back if you want to come dress shopping tomorrow. The appointment is in the afternoon. We should leave here by noon.*

No. I had to go to her. The more I shrunk from her, the more she sensed my fear and attacked. What was the big deal? She arranged the call. She had offered to come. I was merely knocking on the door to confirm our departure time.

As I approached the third-floor landing, something was off. I thought perhaps I'd gone up the wrong way, that I'd stumbled upon a previously unseen level of Asherley, because though the gallery felt familiar, it was empty, cavernous, the walls scattered with dark red squares. Every

163

single picture of Rebekah had been removed, every glamour shot, every sweetly posed close-up, every picture of her embracing Dani, their hair twining together, each was gone, leaving behind a shadow where the sun hadn't hit the walls for years.

My stomach turned. Had Dani finally obeyed Max's request, one he'd made even before I arrived at Asherley? Why this change and why now? Did this bode well for us or not? I could hear music coming from behind the door that led to the turret, a sort of tinny synth with a bass like a heartbeat, not loud, just insistent, like a faraway nightclub. I placed my hand on the knob and turned it, giving the door a little shove. It opened easily. Now the music got louder, bouncing off the walls of the spiral staircase. I was also hit with the smell of pot, my memory flashing to my roommates' parties, when I'd walk in to a wall of smoke after my shifts. I didn't know what to expect with a stoned Dani; she was bad enough sober.

My voice cracked when I called her name once, twice. I couldn't quite muster the nerve to project my voice over the music, afraid of her still. I gently stomped my feet as I went up the first few steps, hoping this would announce my arrival.

It worked. She poked her head out the door at the top, then flung it open, not remotely concerned that she held in her hand a lit joint.

"Hey, you! Wait, wait." She aimed the remote in her other hand over her shoulder to turn down the music. She was wearing the same flimsy nightie she'd had on the first time she confronted me at the top of the stairs.

"Come up."

My feet were frozen on the steps.

"I don't want to bother you, Dani. But I texted you to tell you tomorrow—"

"Come *on*, seriously," she said, beckoning me with an arm. I took a tentative step up. "You know you want to."

She was definitely stoned. I took a deep breath. I'd make it brief, then leave. As much as she was right about my curiosity, this wasn't the time to take a tour.

To cover up my nervousness, I spoke as I marched up the rest of the stairs with as much confidence as I could rally. "I just wanted to tell you the bridal shop called and there was a cancellation so I have an appointment tomorrow afternoon if you still want . . . to . . . come . . ."

The room rendered me momentarily speechless, its majesty closing in around my shoulders. It was white and round, with curved, crisscrossed beams up above, as if we were suspended in a giant birdcage. The bed in the middle of the room was covered in clouds of white pillows, with a lamb's-wool throw tossed across it, punctuated by a circle of peach fuzz curled in the center: Maggie sleeping. The bed was perched on a platform, as though just sleeping in here was an event. Around us were a dozen windows, each black with night, adding to the sense of disorientation, of not knowing which way was the sea, which the forest.

"It's . . . stunning."

It was, to be sure, the most beautiful room in the house. But why wouldn't it be? Rebekah had designed it for herself, and of course for Max. Dani watched me as I walked over to the bed, my fingers moving slowly across the thick wool throw. *Max once slept here. With her. They made love on this bed. She got ready at that dressing table with the blue satin skirt. He adjusted his ties behind her in that mirror.*

My handed drifted to Maggie.

"Ack. Don't wake the baby," Dani said. Her face was garishly made up, her eyes weighed down by fake eyelashes. She took a final hit, struggling to focus.

"I only came to tell you about the appointment," I said.

"Come on. You've wanted to come up here since you got to Asherley. You even tried the door a few times." Her tone was confusing, both seductive and accusatory. She gave me a self-congratulatory shrug. "I baby-powdered the knob."

This proved I wasn't paranoid. She was not only watching me, she was setting traps.

"Yes, well, I was probably looking for you," I stammered.

"Sure. I get it. I understand a lot about a lot of things, you know."

She sauntered over to the dressing table and stabbed out what was left of her joint into an open jar of face cream, then gulped back what was in the coffee mug—wine, likely, from the fermented smell in the air. The dressing table was covered in makeup, the tops missing from lipsticks, broken clamshell compacts strewn about, potion bottles of varying heights and purposes like a tiny crowded cemetery. This was old makeup, dusty, probably Rebekah's, some of the colors nearly used up. Her hand hovered over a clutch of lip colors, their tips glistening. She plucked a red shade from the crowd.

"Dior named this one after my mother. It's called Rebekah's Red," she said, dramatically rolling her r's.

She pressed it to her lips, smearing it over a pinker color, then handed it to me. "Go ahead. I want to see what it looks like on you."

"I don't think so."

"Pleeease. I'm just trying to get to know you. We're just hanging out. Like girlfriends." She took my hand and placed the lipstick firmly in my palm and lifted the stick to my lips. "Go on."

I was sickened by her strange prompt, but I gave my lips a few weak dabs with the flattened tip so as not to set her off.

"Oh my God, like this!" she said, losing patience. She grabbed the lipstick and clutched my chin in the claw of her hand, gathered my lips in a loose pucker, her mouth so close I could smell the wine on her breath. She was fifteen, I kept telling myself. This is a fifteen-year-old girl. Fifteen-year-olds shouldn't be smoking pot and drinking alone in their dead mother's bedroom. As she drew on my lips with a color I knew would be lurid, I thought frantically what I could say to stop this game. She let go of my face.

"Wow, yeah," she said, squinting at her own work. "That is really *not* your shade."

She turned my face to the mirror. My mouth was clownishly stained and her grip had left my cheeks dotted white. She picked out a different color.

"Don't bother, Dani, you won't find a flattering shade. I don't normally wear lipstick."

I couldn't go back to our room with my mouth like this. Max might be home by now. There was a door ajar. The bathroom. I crossed to it, continuing to talk to her as though nothing about this episode was abnormal, as though she wasn't a wasted teenager putting her dead mother's lipstick on her future stepmother's mouth.

"So, as I was saying, we'd have to leave here by noon, but I totally understand if you're busy . . ." I felt inside the room for the switch and flicked on the light.

167

It wasn't the bathroom. This was what I could only describe as a sunken oasis, not a closet so much as an exclusive boutique, with an island in the middle that was larger than the Aquarama. On the island were the pictures of Rebekah that had disappeared from the gallery, most of them now freed from their frames and spread out in seemingly organized piles, as though Dani were in the middle of an elaborate art project. The backgrounds of some of the larger headshots had been cut away and layered over one another, dozens of Rebekah faces in various emotional states. I felt my knees wobble and I turned to leave, but Dani, now close behind me, gave me a slight shove inside.

"I know, right?" she said with glee. "Isn't it sick? Check this out."

She hit another switch, and a set of large doors slid sideways into their wall pockets, exposing a collection of gowns, organized by color, from white sequins on the left all the way to black satin on the right, with every conceivable shade in between. Dani began to flick through the dresses methodically, conducting a sartorial show-and-tell, like a bored instructor.

"Met Ball, Tonys, second Bush inauguration, first Obama." She paused, catching her breath. "Dior runway, Met Ball, Oscar de la Renta sample, Emmys, her last Met Ball. Oh my God, my *fave*." She pulled out a strapless white poufy cocktail dress embroidered at the hem and waist with black flowers. "Givenchy. Vintage Audrey Hepburn . . ." She intently scanned the remainder of the dresses at the darker end of the scale. "I'm going to try . . . *this* one on, and *you* . . ."

I took a few steps back. So many dresses, so many occasions for them to appear together as a couple, and Max had

168

yet to take me anywhere fancier than a French bistro in Southampton.

"I'm not in the mood to try on clothes, Dani. It's very late—"

"*I* know! This!" She yanked out something black and long, thrust it towards me. "This'll fit. It's stretchy," she said. Her smile was wide, genuine. "Please?"

The second I took the velvet thing from her hands, Dani stripped, tossing her nightie in the corner. I averted my eyes from her nakedness, but not before noticing she already waxed off most of whatever pubic hair she might have at her age. Everything felt wrong about this.

"I should go. We can talk at breakfast."

"Come *on*. We never do *anything* together. Just this one time?" She wriggled the Givenchy over her hips, turned around, and lifted her hair. "Zipper, please and thank you."

I placed the velvet dress on the island and did up the zipper, the bodice swallowing up her spine. She turned to face me, dropping her hair back around her shoulders.

"Now you." She reached for the hem of my nightshirt and lifted it over my head with such force it caught on my nose.

"Dani!"

I covered my breasts, the dire facts of the moment closing in on me. I was now naked in front of a teenage girl.

She snorted. "Of course you wear granny panties," she said, bending to form a funnel with the black dress, lowering it in front of my legs. "Step in, step in! Use my shoulder," she commanded.

If only to cover my body, I stepped into the dress. Dani shimmied it over my hips. I gathered the rest of it over my breasts, quickly surmising that it was strapless. She spun me around and zipped the back. Then she took one look at me and bent over laughing. The bodice, once filled with Rebekah's ample breasts, now wilted hollowly over mine.

"Oh my God, you're so *shy*," she teased, pinching the breast pockets, accidentally clamping one of my nipples. "Have you and my dad even had sex yet? Or are you *waiting for your wedding night*? Oh wait—I know the answer to that!"

"Dani, stop. I feel ridiculous."

"I know what this needs!"

She yanked open the top drawer of the island and pulled out two fleshy disks. When I reached around back to unzip myself out of the dress, she shoved the disks down the front, roughly handling my breasts until they were perfectly in place.

"*So* much better." She spun me around to face the mirror, and placed her chin on my shoulder as though she was regarding her best work yet. "Gorge, right?"

I could barely meet my own eyes in the mirror.

"Don't you love it? Here, put these on, too." She wrapped a string of pearls around my neck, gathered up my hair in her fist.

I flung the necklace away from me. "No, Dani. I don't love it. I really have to go to bed now." I ripped the disks out and threw them to the ground. I could hardly believe I had let her game go this far.

"Just one more thing, pleasepleasep*lease*. Hold this." She slapped a stick in my hand. I looked down. It seemed to be attached to a stop sign. It happened fast. She raised the hand holding the sign until it covered my face and she snapped a picture. I flipped the sign around, bracing myself to read something rude. But on the front was a neatly trimmed picture of Rebekah's face, life-size.

"Isn't it hilarious?"

"No, Dani," I said quietly. "This is not hilarious. I find this all very frightening."

I reached behind me, gripped the tiny zipper clasp and pulled hard, not caring if I ripped the dress right off of me. It slid down my body and I stomped out of it, then scrambled to put my nightshirt back on.

"Good night, Dani. I imagine you won't be up to a long trip into the city tomorrow. I think it might be best if you just rested."

She looked at me and blinked hard a couple of times.

"Oh shit. I'm so sorry. I was only trying to have some fun with you. I didn't mean to scare you." Her voice was like a child's. She put her fingers to her cheeks. "Are you going to tell Daddy I'm doing bad things up here? Oh, please don't tell him."

"I won't. But maybe you should talk to your father. I'm worried about you."

She dropped her pleading expression, her lips now curling into a sneer. "Aww. She *cares*. Oh, that's so *nice*. I don't give a shit if you tell my dad because he doesn't give a shit about me, or if I do bad things, as long as I don't do them anywhere else but at Asherley."

"Dani, that's not true. If he knew you were up here smoking pot and drinking alone and messing around with your mother's things, he'd be very worried."

"He told you that?"

"He doesn't have to. Come on, Dani. He loves you very much."

"You *know* that? How do you know that?"

"Now you're being ridiculous." I wanted to scream, *Don't you remember? It was your mother who was hard on you, not your father!*

Dani shut her eyes for a second in contemplation. When she opened them, her demeanor was calm, her voice steady. "I know you think he loves me, because that's what he wants you to believe. I mean, what father doesn't love his own daughter? But you know and I know that I'm not his real daughter."

We stood facing each other. She looked calm, sober, her expression resigned, as though she'd long ago come to terms with this terrible fact and had learned to live with it.

"Good night, Dani. You're wrong about your father. He loves you very much." I wiped the lipstick off my mouth with the back of my quivering hand and left the room, shutting the door behind me.

EIGHTEEN

I didn't debate about whether to tell Max the next morning. I couldn't keep this secret. I'd tell him as soon as possible, not only what she was doing up there but what she had said to me about him. All teenagers feel unloved and unseen by their parents at some point, I knew that. But of course he loved her, and he'd take it upon himself to demonstrate to Dani just how much, in ways that would be indisputable. At first, she'd be mad at me for breaking my promise. But soon she'd see it as the result of my growing affection for her.

I threw on sweats and splashed cold water on my face, then peered at my mouth in the bathroom mirror. My lips were still stained with Rebekah's Red. I gave my mouth a final scrub with a hot cloth. Then I took a nailbrush to my stained fingers until they were pink. I pulled at the skin on my cheeks, noting my pores, the dusting of freckles. Should I start wearing makeup? My eyebrows did need plucking. Had they always been so unruly? All these years, while other girls and women were cultivating their vanity, my gaze had been elsewhere, on other people, on a horizon line, or on the dashboard of whatever boat I was piloting, not on my face and its flaws. Now suddenly they were all I could see. Even our rooms, once my cozy, dark oasis, now felt stuffy compared with Rebekah's, my one closet a sad home for the few things I owned before yesterday's spree. They were delivering the new clothes today. Maybe once

I started wearing nicer outfits, Max would want to invite me to events.

From the top of the stairs, I was surprised to hear Dani, already up and laughing in the kitchen. How she was not incapacitated by a hangover was a testament to her youth—or the quality of the wine and pot.

When I entered the kitchen the two of them were positioned exactly as they had been my first night at Asherley, knees together, heads bowed towards each other, this time a kitten on Dani's lap. When she saw me, her whole face lit up. Even Maggie came to attention, her ears perched high on her head.

"Good morning," Dani said in a cheery voice. "I was just telling Daddy about our night."

My gut sunk. "Oh?"

"Sounds like you guys had fun," Max said, a hint of hope in his voice. I took a seat beside Dani and leaned over to scratch Maggie's head. She'd gone from being a dirty little creampuff to a sleek, muscular kitten, with a gleaming, well-cared-for coat.

"What time did you get in?" I asked Max, entering the conversation cautiously.

"After two, I think," he said. "I slept in the den so I wouldn't wake you. I made scrambled eggs. I'll heat some up for you."

"No, they're fine like this," I said, spooning some onto a plate. "What else did you tell your dad?"

Dani shrugged. "That we hung out. Did each other's makeup. Just girl stuff." Then she lowered her voice and cupped a hand at her mouth. "I might have been a little stoned, Daddy."

Savvy move. *I'll tell my father before you do.*

Max exhaled, less angry than exasperated. "Dani, I told you, no smoking pot. Where did you get it? Claire?"

"She was also drinking," I blurted out.

"Is that true?"

"I might have had a little sip of something."

"Do I have to change the lock on the wine cellar again?"

"No, Daddy. I won't do it again."

Dani shot me a look, not a vicious one, more like the way you'd silently congratulate your poker partner on a clever move. "I didn't peg you for a tattletale," she said. "I know *I'm* no snitch."

"I'm not tattling, Dani. Last night I told you I was worried about you. And I am." Then I pulled out my trump card. "And while I'm not your mother, I don't think even *she* would have been very pleased with your behavior."

She closed her eyes and tilted her head back. When she opened them to reply, her response came out like a pent-up roar.

"What the *fuck* do you know about what my mother would or wouldn't have *liked*? You don't know a fucking thing about her. Or me. Or my *father*, for that matter—"

"Dani, Dani," Max said quietly.

"Who do you think you *are*?" she continued, pointing a finger at me. "Coming here and thinking you can move in and—"

"Dani, I mean it."

"—just insert yourself into my life, into *our* lives, telling me how to live *my* life—"

"I'm not trying to do anything—"

"What have you even *done* with your life? I'm amazed you lasted this long, to be honest."

175

"Jesus Christ, Dani! Would you just shut the fuck up!"

We both fell silent. I had never seen Max so red or heard him yell so loud. Judging from the way Dani's anger instantly dissolved into anguish, neither had she.

"Daddy," she said, her chin trembling, her voice small. She lowered her head into her chest and began to cry.

Max put his arms around her, murmuring, over and over, "I'm so sorry, sweetie."

She leaned her head into his chest, arms flaccid around Maggie. Between sobs she said, "I was just . . . trying . . . to be . . . nice to her."

Now I was the one rolling my eyes.

"I know, honey," Max said, and mouthed "I'm sorry" at me over her shoulder. "But you know I hate it when you use drugs. You're too young. It's worrisome. To both of us. That's all she was saying."

Dani pulled away from him. "I don't need *her* to worry about me, Daddy. I need *you* to." Clutching Maggie tightly, she stepped off the stool and wiped her face with the back of a hand. "Just *you*."

As she passed by me, she shot me a small triumphant smile, one that announced the end of an excellent performance. The door swung behind her.

Max exhaled. "I'm sorry about that. And I'm sorry I yelled like that."

"You don't need to apologize to me. I wonder if you don't yell often enough," I said, in a way that surprised me with its bite.

"I know. I let her get away with a lot." He buried his face in his hands and gave it a hard rub. "Argh! This isn't getting any easier for you, is it?"

I shook my head. That was the simple truth. It was getting harder.

"What can I do to help?" he asked.

"I don't know. More rules? More boundaries? I mean, she's doing drugs. She's drinking alone, at fifteen. She says you don't love her. That doesn't bode well for her, or for us."

"I know. I know. Her problems aren't new to this house. I really thought the worst of it was over. Lately, though—" He stopped. Was he going to suggest this new round of bad behavior coincided with my arrival? "Maybe she needs to go back to rehab."

"Rehab? When did she go to rehab?"

"Last year. She wasn't eating enough, she was partying a lot. I was worried she was heading for a breakdown. I even tried to take control of her money so she couldn't buy anything I didn't know about, drugs in particular. But she rallied. Pushed back. Went to a therapist in town for a while, then stopped going around the time she stopped going to school. Since then I haven't had much luck making her do anything she doesn't want to do."

"Well, tell her it's back to therapy. I don't know. You only have a few more years with her, and then she's on her own."

"We. *We* only have a few more years with her," he said. He reached for my hand. "We are a team. And with any luck, we'll have our own spoiled brats to tame soon enough."

I smiled. We had only discussed the matter of children once, casually, over our last dinner at that fish shack. "Well, our brats won't be spoiled," I said, "if I have anything to do with it."

"Another very good reason to marry you."

"Maybe we should postpone the wedding. It's not like we booked a hall."

"No. No more waiting. Pick out your dress, and let's get on with it." He paused for a moment. "Dani's not going with you to the city. She's grounded until the wedding. And I'm going to lock up our liquor."

"I have a feeling she never really wanted to go," I said, quite honestly relieved. Perhaps last night was her way of sabotaging plans, even subconsciously.

"Why don't you see if Louisa will go?"

"No," I said, so quickly I had to backpedal slightly. "I mean, it's really not a big deal, Max, picking out a dress. It'll clear my head to have some solitude."

Mostly, I didn't want Louisa to know about this rift. She'd interfere, and I wanted to repair things on my own. Besides, she'd said she was going to talk to Max about the greenhouse. I didn't want to be with her when she initiated the conversation, in case Max thought I'd put her up to it.

"I don't like the idea of you driving to New York alone."

I gave him a look. "I've piloted some very big boats for very big clients in very bad weather. I can certainly get a car to a large city with a GPS."

He laughed and wrapped his arms around me. "I remember that wildly independent girl. Do you have a dress in mind?"

"Something really fancy," I said. "With a big tiara, and a huge train. How would you like to see me in that?"

"For all I care you can marry me in a garbage bag."

I kissed him for that.

Max gathered his wallet and keys. "Don't wait on dinner," he said. "I'll be late again. A meeting with the county executives."

"Max, wait."

He looked at me. "What is it?"

Ask, ask, ask.

"Why do you never bring me to events?"

His shoulders dropped, as did the corners of his mouth. "Oh no. Oh, my dear. I just assumed you didn't want to go to those things. Plus, I wanted to give you some time to settle in, take this on bit by bit. Why, do you *want* to come to events?"

"Maybe. Sometimes."

"Then you will. But not tonight. You'd gnaw off your arm out of boredom." He kissed my forehead. "Good luck today. And things with Dani, they'll get better. I promise."

He left me in the kitchen to pick at the cold eggs.

I showered and dressed quickly, taking a coward's early exit from Asherley to avoid Dani. As I headed to the garage, crunching purposefully across the gravel drive, there came that familiar sense that I was being watched. Tiny hairs on my neck lifted. I kept walking. I did not look up. If Dani were indeed up there peering down at me from the turret, eyes full of resentment, I would not give her the satisfaction of unnerving me further than she already had.

I sat in the car for a second to gather my thoughts, feeling sorry for her, for the way she had left the kitchen sobbing, even if it was theatrical. Doubts began to trickle in. Maybe taking her to the city was what she needed, what we both needed. More closeness, not more distance. An apology. Some forgiveness. A discussion about a fresh start. I reached for my phone. Maybe I should text her. *I know your dad said you're grounded, but if you still want to come, I'm waiting out front. Come. I'll take the blame.* Instead I scanned her Instagram, something that now came automatically to me when I wondered where her mind was or what she was doing.

There was a new post, from this morning. It was hard to make it out in the bright light of the car, but it looked to be a black-and-white candid of Rebekah. She seemed to be falling forward, laughing, hair piled on her head, wearing a dress. She had a fist under her chin, the other held up to block the person taking the picture, as though she was running a paparazzi gauntlet. The photo was artistically blown out so I couldn't decipher the background. I opened it wider with my fingers. A stray dark tendril poked out from behind Rebekah's blond hair and a doomy realization fell over me. Whatever filter Dani had added blurred out the edges of the face so that if you weren't scrutinizing the photo as closely as I was, you'd think you were looking at an old picture of Rebekah. But this wasn't Rebekah. It was a photo of her, and I was standing behind it. That was a lock of my hair, my arms. That was my ring on my hand. The caption read: "No one will ever replace you, no matter how hard they try." The likes numbered in the dozens already, with not one commenter aware of the ruse. "Beautiful mama," wrote one person, "RIP Rebekah we loved you," "Thinking of you Dani," and on and on.

My hand shook; I felt on the verge of throwing up. I went to dial Dani's number, to scream at her to pull down the post, but to confront her was to admit I was a lurker, too mortifying to contemplate. And to tell Max was to admit to worse. Even the photo, with Rebekah's laughing mask, and the position of my arms, implied antic complicity on my part. Max would be incensed. How could we recover any sense of normalcy?

I texted Dani to tell her I was heading into the city, that I assumed she didn't want to go, but to stick around later because I wanted to talk to her about last night. Even if it meant admitting I snooped, I had to tell her to delete the post, and I had to do it in person, to show her how much it upset me, and how much it would hurt Max. Pulsing ellipsis indicated her imminent reply. One minute passed, then two, before it finally disappeared. She was giving me nothing.

"Fuck you," I muttered, feeling like a fool again. I threw the car into gear and spun out of the garage and down the barren drive, leaving a cloud of gray dust in my wake.

NINETEEN

Nothing had prepared me for entering a store like this, a two-story bridal-industrial complex, filled with women shopping in pairs, mothers and daughters mostly, for whom this would be an idea of heaven. There it was again, that mother-shaped hole inside me that made itself painfully known. Of course this was a place for mothers and daughters. A mother would pluck all the right gowns from the racks and toss them over the changing room door. The daughter would try each one on. Each time the daughter stepped out, the mother's face was the first thing she'd search out, even before her own in the mirror. The mother would cluck a no to all but the one dress of which she was certain. That's what my own would have done. Or she might have made me a dress, something pretty and flattering that I'd have been proud to wear. It struck me that I didn't know, and this made me sadder than the plain fact of her absence. Time was stretching my memory of my mother so thin, I was beginning to lose even an outline of her. Tears stung my eyes, the stresses of this morning catching up to me. I dabbed them back with the tips of my fingers before giving my name at reception.

"Did you bring anyone to help you make a decision today?" the woman behind the counter asked me. "You're limited to two people."

"No. It's just me today."

She smiled tightly. "Did you bring pictures or an inspiration book?"

I was in that common nightmare, trapped in a classroom where everyone's writing a test I'm entirely unprepared for.

"No. Was I supposed to bring something?"

"No, no. It's just that usually women come here with a pretty good sense of what they're looking for. Helps your assistant pull the right dresses for you to try on."

Her eyes traveled from my hair to my shabby T-shirt to my worn jeans. I imagined her struggling to picture my transformation into a bride.

From behind came a voice. "We do have an idea of what we want. It's a casual wedding, so we thought we'd start with some tea-length gowns. Pull whatever you have in ivory."

I turned around and there was Dani, standing behind me in dark sunglasses, wearing a tan mackintosh and slouchy boyfriend jeans, clutching a metallic purse.

"Dani! How— What are you doing here?"

She shrugged. "You said you had an appointment."

"Yes, but I thought . . . your dad grounded you. How did you get here?"

She rolled her eyes. "Gus, duh. And you can't tell Daddy that either."

"Is this your guest?" the receptionist asked, sounding way too happy for me.

"Yes," Dani said, stepping past me to press against the reception desk.

"Sisters? Friends?"

"Yeah, uh, neither," she said. "I'm Dani Winter. She's marrying my father, Max Winter."

"Oh, well, congratulations!" the woman replied, in a way that made it difficult to discern whether she actually recognized Max's name or was just doing a good job of pretending.

"Did she tell you their wedding is in a month?"

"No." The receptionist touched her neck. "That changes things."

"Yes," Dani said. "It does. It means we should really only look at samples. Unless we find something we like off the rack. In that case, you should send someone in to pin. We'll take care of alterations. I have a good seamstress on Long Island."

"Of course," she replied.

"Also, can we have one of the private rooms?"

"Um. Yes."

"And some water, please. Room temperature. I'm super parched."

"Right away."

I stared at Dani in disbelief, my emotions a riotous jumble finally settling on something akin to confused gratitude. I was, for the first time since we'd met, more happy than terrified to see her, despite everything that had happened last night and this morning. And her manner, which I would have taken for rude, seemed to be interpreted by the receptionist as purposeful and direct. In fact, she seemed to happily obey this girl who rattled off designers and terminology like an old pro. Then again, she was Rebekah Winter's daughter. She probably knew the inside of every changing room up and down Fifth Avenue. Even Georgina, the elderly saleswoman assigned to us, thrilled to her every command. We were ushered upstairs and shown to our plush dressing area, where we waited for Georgina to pull the first batch.

"I apologize for last night," Dani said without quite look-ing at me. "And also for this morning. I know you were just trying to be helpful. But seriously, I'm fine. I don't know what got into me."

"Thank you, Dani, for saying that. And I'm sorry, too."

"For what?"

"For telling your father you were drunk. For mentioning your mother." I thought about bringing up the Instagram post. But things were going well. I decided to wait until later, when we were alone, in case she threw some kind of public fit.

"Anyway," she said, "I'm going to lay off the pot. It's mak-ing me lazy and fat."

"You're hardly fat."

"Well, I *am* lazy."

I left that one to simmer, marveling at the differences between our adolescences, the ones that went beyond class and money. We were quiet until Georgina returned, pulling a clothes rack that looked entirely made of meringue.

"Here we are," she sang.

In a strange way, the drama in Rebekah's closet had removed any remaining shyness about my body. After the first misfire (an off-the-shoulder mermaid thing), it became clear that a floor-length gown would indeed swallow me whole, ivory went best with my skin tone, and beading was ridiculous.

The trying on and discarding of clothes and outfits and iden-tities seemed to be an entirely female endeavor that I had only been introduced to since meeting Max. In my old life, being poor meant having few clothes. But it also meant I wasn't des-tined to constantly become different versions of myself. Yet here I was again, Cinderella discarding rags for a ball gown, a hovering stepdaughter to boot, one who was becoming less and less ugly to me by the minute. Watching the stern pride she took in touching the materials, examining the hems, the buttons, the beads, discussing these details with Georgina, warmed me. Finding something I liked became less important than finding something *she* liked on me, in the hopes that this would be what drew us closer. At one point, while she struggled to close a tiny clasp on my sash, her hair was near enough to my hand to lovingly stroke it, yet I resisted.

"This thing . . . is . . . a little *bitch*," she whispered.

Don't smother her with affection. It's like socializing a feral cat. Let her come to you.

"There!" Dani said. "What a pain in the ass. But . . . look."

I turned around, Georgina chasing my hem to tug it straight.

When it hung limply on the hanger, there had been nothing remarkable about this dress. But the way the cap sleeves cupped my shoulders, how the ivory silk bodice held my waist and the chiffon skirt brushed my ankles . . . it simply *looked* like my dress.

"Well, now," Georgina said, placing her hands on her waist.

"What do you think?" Dani asked, her poker face cracking.

"I . . . *like* it," I said, lying. I had instantly loved it, but I wanted to know what she thought before I went all in. I didn't want to have to backpedal embarrassingly if Dani turned her nose up at it.

"You can't *like* it," she scolded. "People don't *like* their wedding dresses. You have to fucking *love* it. Do you? Do you fucking love it?"

"I think so. I—"

"Because I fucking love it!"

"Then I fucking love it!" I replied, louder still, taking a little leap. I motioned towards her for a hug, but she turned to Georgina and resumed an all-business air.

"This is the one," Dani said.

"In under an hour. Impressive," Georgina said.

"It's because of Dani. I would have dithered all day."

I turned back to the mirror. Dani came behind me and gathered up my hair in a rough bun.

"Wear it like this . . ." she said, tilting her head. Our eyes met in the mirror. There was a flash of something, not love, not friendship, but maybe an alliance.

A short film replayed in my head, stopping on a frame from a few months ago. I saw myself piloting a dozen drunk men to the middle of the Caribbean to catch and kill fish they did not eat. There was another still: me in a stained golf shirt, trailing Laureen to her car as she barked instructions at me. Then I was cross-legged on a rickety twin bed eating cold noodles out of a Styrofoam cup. A party I wasn't invited to raged on in the kitchen I shared with strangers. *Look at you now. This is real life. Your* life. *You live in a mansion on an island. In a month you will marry a man you love, who loves you, too, the only obstacle to your happiness his difficult daughter, who might have just granted you a blessed reprieve.*

TWENTY

Leaving the boutique, wearing my jeans, sneakers, and T-shirt again, my hair back up in a ponytail, was to feel like Superman exiting the phone booth as Clark Kent. We walked to a restaurant Dani liked near Central Park. She kept her distance, pointing out landmarks with a perfunctory air.

The restaurant was a sea of older attractive people, men with no hair or a lot of white hair, women who'd had excellent work done on their faces and expensive haircuts; I wasn't properly dressed for this place either. We were seated immediately. As the waiter pulled out her chair, Dani's phone dinged a text. She glanced at it.

"Daddy," she said, wincing. "Making sure I'm still at home." She typed a quick reply, then put the phone away. "Again, you *can't* tell him about today. I mean it. He'll be so mad."

"I'm sure he'd be happy to know that we were able to spend a little time together. Without fighting. Especially after this morning."

Now my phone alerted me to a message, which we both knew could only be from Max. *Home after midnight. Hope today went well. Can't wait to hear about your dress. Love Mx*

"Promise," Dani pressed.

"Fine. But he won't believe I picked that dress out by myself."

"Miss Winter, how are you?" The waiter poured two glasses of water and told us the specials. It clearly pleased Dani that they knew her name, that they knew she preferred sparkling water, and that I was witnessing this. But if she thought I envied being fifteen and a regular at a fancy restaurant, she was wrong. There were other, better things she could be mastering at this age, especially with her fortune, like concerts, or posh camps, or ski trips. Not adult rituals like this. I also noted we were closing in on two entire hours together, the longest we'd spent in each other's company.

Dani confidently ordered the chicken dish, which made it easy for me to do the same.

"You know," she said once the waiter had left us alone, "I don't go up to my mother's old room that often. Not like I used to. Only when I really miss her. The closet still smells like her."

I could have cried. "I understand that," I said, stopping my hand from covering hers in comfort.

"You don't, though."

"I do. I also lost my mother when I was young. I remember rolling myself up in her comforter. It smelled like her for years."

She furrowed her brow, her mind making room for this unexpected bit of information. "I didn't know about your mom," she said. "Daddy never told me."

"There's a lot we probably don't know about each other. But you can ask me anything you want. Go ahead. We can make it like a game. We'll take turns."

"How did your mother die?"

"Breast cancer."

"How old was she?"

"Mid-thirties. That's two questions. Now I get to ask you one."

189

She ignored me. "Were you there when she died?"

"Yes. I was."

"What do you remember?"

I felt a pall come over me. To conjure these memories was always to risk tears. But Dani had never shown this much interest in me.

"Well, she had been in the hospital for a while. A couple of months. I suppose I thought she'd come home. No one told me the truth about her illness, that it wasn't something she'd recover from. One day a teacher drove me to the hospital. I knew why. I remember feeling like I never wanted the car to stop. My father was waiting for me in the emergency room area. He told me that my mother had slipped into a coma. They led me to her room. It was dim. She didn't look or sound like herself. Her cheeks were all hollowed out. She had one of those . . . death rattles. It was awful to watch, to know there wasn't going to be a goodbye. My father didn't want me to see her struggling, so a nurse took me to a room down the hall where I waited for him to come and tell me that she had died. I seem to remember waiting a long time."

As expected, there were tears in my eyes by the time I finished.

"That's sad."

"Yes. I still miss her, too. Especially today. But I was glad you were there."

"I remember the night *my* mother died, too."

My heart sped up. Max had only ever painted broad strokes about that night. I'd been reluctant to prod him for details, afraid I'd renew his grief.

"All I told the police I remembered was that it was super hot that day and Mum and I went swimming and then my

190

father came home from a fundraiser in New York. We had pizza, then I went to bed and I was asleep when she took off in her car." Dani looked around the restaurant. "But I remember a lot more."

She pressed her fingertips into the tines of her fork, taking note of my interest before continuing.

"If I tell you what I remember, do you promise not to tell anyone ever, not even my father?"

I knew that keeping a secret from Max would allow Dani to wedge something noxious into our relationship, which she could drive deeper at any time, but the need to know her story was stronger than this fear.

Without waiting for my reply, she began. "It happened during that really hot week in July, remember?"

I shook my head.

"Right. Well, anyway, it was super hot all summer, but that week broke records and our air-conditioning went out. First time ever. Some guys came to look at it, but they said they needed a part, so it would take a few days. There were phone calls, one in particular with my dad that seemed to really piss Mum off, and another one she took in the greenhouse. I heard her yelling. When she came out, she seemed strange. Nervous. She kept biting her nails. Pacing. She told Katya, Go home early, it's too hot to work. And she gave Gus the day off too. Then she said, Dani, get in the car. I thought we were going to meet Dad in the city, check into a hotel, see a show, until the heat broke. Or maybe go to Auntie Louisa's. She said no. She wanted to stay home that night. She drove fast into East Hampton. She always did. We went to the hardware store. Her phone rang while she was parking. Dad again. She told him she was buying fans because the air-conditioning broke. I could hear his voice get louder. She whispered something like, I'm telling you this ends tonight, and hung up. The guy at the store said they were sold out of fans and suggested we check Bridgehampton or Montauk, but it was getting late. We'd never make it, even with the way my mom drove. She said, We're going to have to tough it out, kiddo. It'll be like camping."

Dani took a sip of water. So did I, surprised to find wine in my mouth. I was so transfixed, my focus on Dani had sharpened to such a keen point, that the room and everyone in it had disappeared.

"Anyway. Mum drove fast back to Asherley. It was so dry out. The water in the bay was as low as I've ever seen it. She said, Let's put on our bathing suits. She made a big thing of lemonade and we went down to our beach. She didn't want to swim. She sat on the chair and kept looking at her phone while I splashed around. I said, Come in the water with me, and she said, That's okay, Dani, I like watching you. Do a somersault or something, do some tricks, so I did. And then I noticed the curtain move in the turret. I was a little scared and I said, Mum, someone's in your room. She turned around. It was Dad. He waved from the window and Mum went, Shit. He wasn't supposed to be home, I guess. She wasn't happy to see him. At all." Dani leaned in and whispered, "I think maybe my dad was cheating on her."

The word left me momentarily stunned. She could have slapped me across the face and I wouldn't have felt a thing. *How is that possible? He adored Rebekah.*

"That's what I *think*, anyway," Dani said, and sneaked a sip of my wine. "I mean, he's *never* home. You know that now more than anyone."

"Yes, but I always thought they were happy. I always thought they had a perfect marriage."

She shrugged. "Mum said people know five percent of what goes on in anyone else's marriage. I mean, he might have loved her before I came along. He even said to her once, You love Dani more than me, and she goes, Maybe I do? What's wrong with that?"

Her eyes lingered on me, as if she was testing the effects of her words. Max painted a different picture, of a mother who was hard on Dani, and a father making up for that with leniency and love.

"Married people say things they don't mean all the time, Dani."

"Maybe. But when I said Mum took that call in the greenhouse? I was listening. I heard her say, Max, you promised me that this wouldn't keep happening, that this would stop, so why is this still going on? Something like that. I mean, what was *that* about except cheating?"

Our meals arrived. Dani dug right into her chicken as though she hadn't just detonated a bomb on top of my life. I was dizzy with hunger, but when I picked up my utensils they felt heavy, the meat looked too tough, the Brussels sprouts too much like fists to cut into. The idea of putting food into my mouth revolted me.

Dani noticed my distress.

"Do you want me to stop talking about it?"

"No. Keep going," I replied too quickly. "If you want."

"Okay," she said, chewing. "So yeah, my dad, he came down to the beach acting all happy. But Mum wasn't happy to see him. She was super tense and was all, What are you doing home? You were supposed to stay in the city. And he said, I missed my beautiful girls, barely even looking at me. When he went to kiss her she squirmed. He said, It's getting dark, Dani. Get out of the water. Let's all go back up to the house. We can order in so we don't have to cook in this heat. Are you going to eat that?"

It took me a second to realize she was talking to me.

"Oh. No, I'm—"

She stabbed a Brussels sprout with her fork and transferred it to her plate. "So. I get out of the water, shower really fast because I *knew* they were gonna try to squeeze in a fight while I was upstairs. When I came back to the kitchen, they stopped talking. Mum had tears in her eyes. The pizza guy came. We barely touched our food. Between the heat and the tension, you could cut the air with a knife." She slashed her knife in front of me.

"So dinner was done. I knew Daddy was gonna bark at me to go to bed. I said it was too hot in my room, I want a fan, I won't be able to sleep. But then I thought, wait a minute, I'd know more about what's going on if I 'went to bed.'" She mimed air quotes. "So I go, Okay, fine, Daddy. I thought I was being a genius, but then they went into the greenhouse again. And that's when the fighting really took off. I couldn't hear much, just, like, muffled yelling and stuff. But while I was crouched at the top of the stairs to try to hear more, the doorbell rang. I jumped. It was past eleven, late for visitors. I got scared. I heard his steps across the foyer. He answered the door. I couldn't see who was there, but it was a woman. They spoke all hissy and low, like they were trying to keep it down because I was 'sleeping'. I heard him say, Let's go somewhere else to talk.

"Now they were all in the greenhouse and things got really quiet. The silence was worse than the yelling. It felt like they were in there forever. I leaned over the banister to see if I could hear anything at all. I couldn't. So I tiptoed down the stairs. I got as far as the door to the greenhouse. The glass was dirty, but I could see him, my dad, and there was my mother . . ."

Dani went quiet for a moment, her forehead wrinkling, as though these events were happening in real time in front of her.

"It was the last time I saw my mother. Before I could get a look at the other woman, she yelled something. My mother's name, I think. I ran back up the stairs. Behind me I heard my dad yell, Rebekah, Rebekah! Then he said, Wait, you can't leave. Don't leave. I kept running, all the way up to their room in the turret, just in time to see my mom's car take off down the drive. I figured she was mad. That she just wanted to go for a drive. She did that sometimes."

Her shoulders dropped, and she looked at her hands in her lap. "Daddy was still in the house with that woman, so I raced down to my own room and closed the door because I knew he'd check on me. I slipped under the sheets and lay very still with my eyes shut. Not tight. That would look fake. I read you have to keep your eyebrows relaxed and your mouth slightly open, so that's what I did. And I waited. And waited. And oh my God, my heart was beating so, so fast and *finally* I heard him come upstairs. He stopped outside my room. My heart was going boom, boom, boom. He slowly opened my door, crept to the side of my bed, so I fake woke up. I sorta stretched and I go—sounding all groggy—Hey, what's wrong? He said, Nothing, honey. I brought you a glass of cold water. Here, he said, sit up and drink. It'll help you cool down. He told me Mum went into town for a sec. I got

195

worried. I said, Why? He said, She remembered we had a fan at campaign headquarters and she went into town to get it for you, sweetheart, because it's so hot in here. I said, Why didn't you go? And he said, Mum needed some air. She'll be back soon. And that's the last thing I remember.

"I woke up the next morning like a pile of bricks were on my chest. I could smell burning through my window, though I didn't connect it to Mum. Daddy was already sitting next to me, sitting in the same spot, like he never left. He looked terrible. He said, Hi, honey, voice all raggedy. I have to tell you something really sad about Mum, he said. And I knew. I knew he was going to tell me she was dead. I knew it. He said, Mum had a car accident out by the causeway. There was a big fire. She died in it. There are police downstairs. They might want to talk to you about what you remember about last night, he said. But the most important thing is I loved your mother very, very much. You know that, right? I said, Yes, Dad, I know that. And you know how much she loved you. Never forget that, he said. I won't, Dad, I said. Because if the police don't know how much we all love each other, he said, they might take me away from Asherley, and from you, and you'll be all alone. We don't want that, do we? Do you understand? And I said, Yes, I understand."

This was the first time since I'd met Dani that she had showed any vulnerability; she was on the brink of real tears.

"But here's the thing. The police didn't ask me anything except for when did we eat dinner, what time I went to bed, that sort of thing. Nothing important. So I said nothing about that woman. They seemed more interested in talking to my father. Daddy whispered to one of the police,

She's only thirteen. I wasn't a little girl and they were treating me like one." She shook her head. "Anyway, I'm telling you all this because that's why my dad won't let anyone in the greenhouse. He feels guilty about what happened that night. With Mum. With that woman. I caught him a few times standing in the dark, inhaling the air. You *can* smell her in there."

She was quiet for a moment. Then she shrugged, her demeanor shifting.

"Oh. I almost forgot. You texted me this morning, said you wanted to talk to me about something?"

I had completely forgotten about this morning's events, now buried under the night Dani just recounted. "Oh, uh, yes. It was about . . . the picture you took of me last night, when I was . . . Could you please erase it from your phone? I don't want your father to ever see it." I thought I was being clever, focusing only on the photo she took, leaving out the part about her posting it, but she called my bluff.

She slapped her hand on the table. "I *knew* it! I bet Claire a hundred dollars that you lurk my Instagram. You're a fucking lurker! Ha! That's so creepy, I *love* it."

"I don't know what you're talking about."

"All *right*, Stepmommy, if you *say* so."

The waiter suddenly appeared at our table. But when I looked up to ask for the bill, I was shocked to see Gus hovering over us.

Dani leapt up. "Oh shit!"

He nodded at me, looking embarrassed.

"Hello, Gus," I said. "Actually, Dani, I thought *I* would drive you home. I'd prefer to, in fact. I feel like we have a lot more to talk about."

She ignored me. "You were going to text me when you were circling the block," she said to Gus. "Did you have to *park*?"

"I *did* text you," he hissed back, and pointed to the dark sedan at the curb out the window. "Meet me out there. I don't want to get towed."

Max was right. Something was off about their relationship, and familiar. Too familiar. They were bickering like a tense couple.

"Sorry, I gotta run," she said to me. "Can you put this on Daddy's card without him knowing I ate with you? Oh, and he can't know about Gus, or what I told you." She slung her purse across her shoulder. "Okay?"

She spun around.

"Wait. Dani."

"What?"

"Tell me what . . . what happened to that woman."

She crinkled her nose. "What woman?"

"The one who came to the house that night?"

"Oh, I don't know. I never saw her again." Then she cocked her head at me thoughtfully. "Know what? *I* think you're going to make a beautiful bride."

Then she left. I watched her hop into the front seat with Gus. While I waited for the check, I looked at her Instagram feed. The photo was gone.

"Oh thank God," I whispered, closing my eyes and placing my phone over my heart, grateful that she decided to just be mean to me, and not cruel.

TWENTY-ONE

Dani's story played over and over in my mind during the ten-block walk back to the parking garage. All the way out of the city, through the suburbs, down the middle of Long Island, over the causeway, and into the forest, I went over the scenes she'd described, how Rebekah talked on the phone, paced and bit her nails, how she drove into town like a madwoman, how she fought with Max and got angry at a woman who came to Asherley, so angry she fled in a car and died.

Of course Max would feel guilty, if indeed that woman had been his lover. But she couldn't have been. Max cheating on Rebekah was impossible to imagine. Maybe she was a lost stranger looking for directions. But I'd have to believe she got lost crossing the causeway, heading to a gated island. I thought then of the way Dani had relished my astonishment, leaned deeper into the story the more it distressed me, and a darker thought crossed my mind. Dani had made her up, had executed a deliberate misinformation campaign to mess with my affections before I married her father. To what end? Well, for starters, if I believed him capable of being unfaithful to Rebekah, what hope for fidelity did I have? He *was* away a lot, and he had plenty of opportunity. But then why would he want to marry? Why not just go on being a swinging bachelor? Max loved me, of this I was sure. One conversation with him would expose her game and dispel these doubts, even if it meant breaking my promise not to tell him Dani had ignored her curfew. I could leave out the Gus part, tell him she'd driven with me.

Passing through the iron gates and then the last stand of oaks before Asherley, I tried to remember where Rebekah's car had crashed. She must have been going fast. I couldn't find the stump, but I could make out parts of the burnt forest that had begun to blend into the old growth. Soon it would be as though the accident had never happened. The forest would forget, and maybe so would the island's inhabitants.

At the end of the long drive, a bright moon accentuated Asherley's spires and cast a pall over that incongruous greenhouse. I imagined driving through the glass at high speed, sending shards flying in a million directions, releasing all the bad memories. There was no light coming from the turret and yet, even dark, it maintained its sentinel quality.

I drove into the maw of the garage and sat for a while, weighing the cost of betraying Dani at the most fragile intersection in our relationship. We were just beginning to form some semblance of a bond, however tenuous. It was a month before the wedding. The damage would be irreparable, the repercussions, knowing Dani, arriving in unpredictable ways. Yet to *not* tell was to stew over the plausibility of Dani's claims.

I checked my phone. No new texts from Max since the one at dinner. No *Drive safe*, no *I'm thinking about you*, no *Text me when you get home*. A new feeling welled up inside of me, niggling and dark. There it was, the doubt Dani had hoped to plant in me with that story. Then and there, I vowed to rip it up by its roots before it grew into a malevolent weed.

As I reached for the door handle, I heard a small thump and saw a shadow pass across the rearview mirror. I froze, only my eyes moving. There it was again. I pivoted around in time to catch the barn cat, Maggie's mother, padding across the back of the car. I was about to exhale when I caught a glimpse of something, no, some*one*, standing alone in the dark of the garage. Adrenaline flooded my limbs. The shape moved towards my window. *Someone was in the garage with me.* I slapped at the lock, a scream escaping my throat.

"Ma'am! Ma'am, it's okay! It's only me!"

Gus crouched down at my window.

I shoved open the door. "Jesus Christ, Gus, you scared me half to death!"

"I'm sorry, ma'am."

"Don't sneak around like that!"

"I wasn't. I—I came out to see if you needed any help with bags or anything. I was going to leave, but you stayed in the car a long time. I worried maybe you were sick or something."

I sat for a moment, a hand on my sternum. It hurt to pull oxygen back into my lungs, they'd emptied so suddenly. I stepped out of the car, my legs wobbly. "I was just gathering my thoughts."

Here I was alone again with Gus. What if Max were to pull up right now and see us leaving the garage at night? Would he laugh off Dani's inference a *second* time?

He peered into the backseat. "You need help with anything?"

"No. Everything's being delivered."

"Okay, well, some packages came for you earlier. I put them in your dressing room."

"Oh good," I said. I had hoped to put Louisa's gifts away before Max came home. "Thank you."

"I really didn't mean to sneak up on you like that. When you didn't come out of the car right away . . . you sure you're okay?"

"Yes. I'm just tired. When did you two get in?"

"About a half hour ago."

He stood there expectantly, as if he wanted to tell me something else.

"Well . . . good night."

"Yes, I—"

"What is it, Gus?" I barked. I didn't like being near him. Tonight, at the restaurant, I had seen a different Gus, impatient and familiar with Dani, convincing me Max's concerns were well placed.

"Well, I just wanted to say, ma'am, that . . . I'm glad Dani has someone like you in her life now."

"That's nice to hear."

"She's not a bad kid, you know. She's just been through a lot."

"Losing a mother is hard, I know," I said. "Well, good night, then."

"Again, I'm sorry, ma'am. I really didn't mean to scare you."

"Please don't call me ma'am."

"Sorry. It's a habit from the first Mrs. Winter."

I practically sprinted across the gravel drive to close the gap between the garage and the house the way a child leaps from floor to mattress to prevent the monster under the bed from grabbing at her ankles. It wasn't Gus I feared, or even Dani. It was the way the memory of Rebekah constantly shifted and changed. The minute I pinned her down as *this* way, she became *that* way. Was she a bad mother or a good one, a devoted wife or a scorned one? I had a stubborn need to define myself in relation to her, so the more elusive Rebekah remained, the more confused I felt here.

I went straight to my room and collapsed into bed. Dark ruminations about Dani's story and the episode in the garage eventually morphed into my dream, the one that always ended with Rebekah holding me under water until I jerked awake with that feeling of dread in my chest and the sense that I had barely escaped something dire. The sun was not yet up. Max growled and sleepily pulled my back into the cave of his body. I hadn't heard him come in. I spun around to kiss him, deeply, hungrily.

"Good morning to you, too," he said. "What a nice way to be woken up."

"I missed you," I said. We kissed some more, his hand snaking up my nightshirt. "When did you get in?"

"Very late. I hope I didn't wake you."

"I was out cold, I guess."

"How did it go?"

"How did what go?"

"Did you find a dress?"

It felt like a dozen years ago, our time at the store. Had I imagined Dani's helpful presence, her support and compliments?

"As a matter of fact, I did."

"Among the many attributes about you that I love, you are also decisive."

"Well, it's not fancy, but it's very me."

"Was Dani helpful?" He cocked an eyebrow, trying to make his face seem angry, to no avail.

"You know about that? That she came to New York?"

"She texted me when you guys were driving back together. Would you have told me she went with you?"

"Max, she made me promise not to."

He collapsed back onto his pillow. "How can I lay down the law around here if you keep her secrets?"

"I'm sorry."

"She said she had fun with you, though. Did you have fun?"

She told me you were a cheater. Are you, Max? Did you cheat on Rebekah? Will you cheat on me? Maybe you're already doing it. Maybe that's why you never invite me to events, or on overnight trips to New York, because you're seeing someone, maybe that woman, the one who came to Asherley. Why don't you marry her?

He snapped his fingers in front of my face. "Where did you go just now?"

I closed my eyes and opened them again, as if to erase the evidence of my thoughts.

He lifted his head off the pillow to get a better look at me. "There was a funny look on your face, an angry one that I've never seen before. Right here," he said, pressing his finger in between my eyebrows. He scowled, imitating what he'd seen.

"I didn't look like that," I said, laughing, trying to lighten the mood.

"I'm telling you, a little drama just played itself out on your face. I saw it. What were you thinking?"

"I was thinking nothing. I was thinking how excited I am for the wedding, now that I've found a dress. And I was thinking how grateful I was that Dani was there to help me."

He looked at me, bemused. "I haven't quite figured out when you're lying to me."

"It's *true*," I said, smiling, lightly punching his arm for effect.

"Lying by omission requires talent, and you, my dear, don't have it. Lucky for you, I find your attempts at mendacity a tiny bit sexy."

"I do have a question." I could broach the subject without betraying Dani. After all, we were going to be married, and wasn't infidelity something about which you'd naturally ask your betrothed? "Did . . . Rebekah ever cheat on you?"

He frowned. "What makes you ask that?"

"I don't know. Maybe because you've been married before and I haven't."

"I don't *think* she cheated on me. Are you going to ask me if I ever cheated on her?"

I nodded.

"Is this because I've been away so much?"

I nodded again.

"I promise after November you'll be sick of me. Whether I win or lose, things will slow down. And there are a number of events in the Hamptons this summer that I'm taking you to, so many you'll be sick of that part of the job, too." He searched my face to see if his answer was satisfactory. "Look. I am many things, some shitty, some just plain venal, I know. But I'm no cheater. I never have been, I never will be. I'd divorce you before I cheated on you, and I'd only do that if you stopped loving me, which you won't, correct?"

"Correct."

He spilled over on top of me. "You do believe me, don't you?"

"I do."

And I did. I made the choice to believe him. Doing so also meant I didn't need to betray any more of Dani's secrets. If she was testing my trustworthiness, I had just laid an ace.

Max reached for his watch on the bedside table. "Let's go out for dinner tonight, just the two of us. I'm glad you're getting along better with Dani, but you were my friend first."

I kissed him and walked over to the window. Whenever I threw open the curtains, I always expected to be hit with the sun, but gray clouds menaced the horizon. Still, I felt hopeful, determined to throw myself with chilly efficiency into the remainder of my wedding plans. Dani would soon grow bored of me, the same way she would tire of Maggie when she became a moody cat with territory to conquer and sharp claws to enforce her boundaries.

After a long shower, I made my way downstairs. As I neared the kitchen, I heard Louisa's voice. Then Max uttered the word "greenhouse," and I pressed my back against the paneling by the archway, ashamed that my first instinct was to eavesdrop.

"I disagree completely, Max. I think the great hall is far too formal for a small spring barbecue."

"Did she put you up to this?"

"Actually, she told me *not* to say anything," Louisa said, thankfully. "She begged me to stay out of it. I can't understand why you're so adamantly against the idea. It's such a good one."

"For Chrissakes, what can't you understand?" Max hissed, his voice cracking. "I don't want to hold my wedding in that filthy glass cage."

"I was in there this morning. It won't take much to prep it."

"How the hell did you get in there?"

"I used to live here, remember?"

"I don't go nosing around your house when you're not around."

"You don't own half my house. Anyway, all we have to do by my estimation is tighten some panels, lay down a temporary floor, clean the glass, and air it out. The boys that did our pergola could get it done in a week."

"Why do you care so much about where I hold my wedding?"

"Because I quite like her. And I'd like her to be happy here. Because I think she's working wonders with Dani."

"Ha! *That* tide could turn pretty swiftly."

"You have so little faith in that girl."

"I know her, Louisa."

Footsteps echoed from the main staircase behind me—Dani making her way down to breakfast. Gathering myself, I walked into the kitchen at a quick clip.

"Louisa, what a nice surprise," I said, smiling widely and phonily, rushing to kiss her cheek. "Good morning, Max."

"Morning, my love. Coffee's ready. I'm making scrambled."

He was trying to conceal the dark mood their fight had put him in.

"What brings you here?" I asked Louisa while pouring my coffee. My hand was shaking.

"Oh, you know, I was in the neighborhood and all that."

Dani came in holding Maggie, wearing shorts and a pair of green wellies with long yellow laces. "Look, Mags, a kitchen party," she said, rubbing Maggie's scruff on Max's face.

207

"And *she* wasn't invited," he said.

"Don't talk like that in front of Maggie, Daddy. I don't want her to feel unwanted, too."

"She *is* unwanted. By me. I'd like her gone by the wedding."

"And to think he used to be such a nice little boy," Louisa said, turning to me. "Max told me you and Dani found a dress. I'm so pleased."

"I am, too," I said, looking over at Dani. "And I was very grateful for the help."

Dani shrugged. She was preparing Maggie's slurry, heated up as I had shown her.

"It's a cute dress," Dani said. "It's got this little sash—"

"Shh!" Louisa pointed at Max. "It's supposed to be a surprise."

Dani rolled her eyes, then placed the kitten on the floor next to the saucer. She began her little ritual of collecting components of her breakfast from all corners of the kitchen—spoon, blueberries, cereal, milk—into one *mise-en-place* on the island before assembling everything into a bowl like a mad scientist.

"By the way, Dani," Louisa said. "I sent invitations to Claire and her parents, but there's still time to add someone else."

She was eating while standing, scrolling through her phone. "I don't have any other friends." She turned to address the kitten. "Just you, Boo."

"Might help if you went to school," Max said, "or anywhere beyond Asherley, for that matter." He was buttering toast like he was angry at the bread.

No one could ignore the tension in the air.

"Well, Daddy, I *am* grounded," she replied. "And anyway, I *do* go to a lot of places. I go to Claire's. I go into town. I go to the city. I went to Paris with Auntie Louisa, didn't I? And yesterday I went to New York with *her*," she said, her thumb pointing towards me.

"Against my wishes," Max said, putting his hand on my shoulder. "And you put *her* in a tricky spot, asking her to lie to me about that."

Dani eyed me. "I didn't ask her to lie," she said. "I just asked her to omit some things. And did you?"

We locked eyes.

"I didn't say anything to your dad that you hadn't already told him, Dani."

I don't know if she believed me.

"Welp, good talk. I think I hear Adele driving up."

She took her phone and her bowl and fled the kitchen. Maggie, transfixed by her bootstrap, was left with no choice but to chase her.

When she was well down the hall, Louisa spoke up.

"Why are you being such an asshole to your daughter?"

He took his coffee over to the window and looked out towards the barn. "When we move the last horses to Montauk, I'm going to ask the stables to take Gus on full time," he said. "There won't be much around here that a landscape company can't handle. We don't need anyone living on the property anymore."

"Max, you can't fire him for driving Dani around," Louisa said. "What's the boy going to say to her? No?"

"It's more like a transfer. Besides, she's sixteen soon and she'll learn how to drive herself around."

"I actually think it might be a good idea, too," I said.

Max turned around.

"Oh? Why this change of heart?"

"I just think Dani might be relying on him too much. She needs more friends her own age."

"Yes, exactly."

Louisa abruptly changed the subject. "Have you two given any more thought to where you'll hold the reception?"

Max gave her a weary look. "Yes, Louisa, as a matter of fact, we have. And I'm sorry, but the greenhouse is off-limits."

"My dear, would you mind leaving us alone for a minute? I would like to talk to my brother."

I tried to signal her with my eyes to give up the cause. "Louisa, I'm perfectly happy to have the reception in the great hall. Really."

"I know you are," she said. Max remained by the window, waiting for part two of their battle. "But that's not what I want to talk to him about."

The undercurrents were starting to feel like riptides. I stood, hoping Max would stop me. But he said nothing.

"I'll be down at the boathouse, then."

"I'll bring you your breakfast there in a minute," he said, with a comforting wink.

I grabbed a coat on my way out the back door. To be dismissed like that was humiliating. Rebekah would have laughed and said, *Louisa, whatever you have to tell Max, I'm sure you can tell me.* My greenhouse request wasn't supposed to have unearthed Rebekah again, but it had, and now I felt like even she had chased me from the house. The horror on Max's face the night he found me in there with Maggie came back to me. By this point I wasn't even sure I wanted my reception in the greenhouse. Perhaps I only wanted to occupy a space sacred to her in order to chase out a memory that left me feeling lacking. I was discovering things about myself I didn't like, things that were entirely new, that had frightening depths. I began to imagine that Louisa had shooed me from the room to continue to assuage Max's guilt over *what happened that night.* There it was again, Dani's story reinserting itself, weaving itself into my narrative. Perhaps Louisa also knew about the other woman, knew that he felt guilty about how she'd upset Rebekah so much she drove off in a rage. Maybe she was telling him right now that he had to forgive himself, that perhaps it was Rebekah's indifference to him that left him no choice but to stray, and it wasn't his fault the other woman confronted him at his home. That's what sisters do, they defend you, they bolster you, they even lie to you if they have to.

When I opened the door to the boathouse, I was disappointed to find Gus there. He stood cranking the bigger boat down onto its slip, its tarp now removed. It was indeed an Odyssey, about thirty feet, old but in excellent shape.

"Oh, hey there," he said, turning the wheel on the pulley. "The stencil arrived for *Dani's Luck.* Thought I'd give *Winter's Girl* a tune-up. I hope you don't mind, I—"

"I do mind, Gus. I'm sorry, but I would like to work in here alone. Can you do this another time?"

I was taking it out on him, my inability to assert myself with Louisa and Max. I was becoming one of those people who boss the help around because they feel powerless in their own lives.

"Sure, ah . . . okay. I'll just . . ."

"Also, Mr. Winter doesn't know you drove Dani to New York yesterday. And I'll leave it that way for now. But you need to clear those requests with him in the future. Or perhaps me, if he's not here."

"But that's always been part of my job. It's why Rebekah hired me."

At the mention of her name I flared up again. "Well, Gus, things have changed around here!"

He was about to walk away, eyes downcast, when I heard the imperiousness, the scorn, in my voice. I was disgusted with myself.

"Wait. Gus. I'm sorry. I didn't mean to yell at you. It's just . . . it's been a very weird twenty-four hours."

"That's okay. I understand."

I felt emboldened suddenly, to prod a little, to ask questions I didn't dare ask Max or Louisa, let alone Dani.

"I get the sense you two got along well. You and Rebekah."

"I guess we did."

"She's a hard subject to bring up around here. I have so many questions about her. I've been wondering, naturally, what she was like. As a person, I mean."

He thought for a few seconds, casting about for words. "Well . . . she was great with the horses. She liked . . . nice things. She was busy all the time. Always doing stuff. Kind, too. To me, anyway. She was kind to me." He thought some more. "I really don't know what else to say except, well, I mean, she was very beautiful." *Yes, yes, I know about that, for God's sake. I want different information, not just what I can see with my own eyes.*

"Can you tell me what . . . kind of . . . mother she was, to Dani?"

"Oh, they were close. Yeah. Two peas in a pod, that kind of thing."

He was twisting his hands together. I could tell he wanted to leave, to end this inquiry, but his information was just hitting my veins and I wanted a bit more.

"Was Rebekah very hard on her? As a parent?"

He bristled, stepped away from me.

"I only ask because I am trying to figure out how . . . to be a friend to her, help her, you know?"

"She wanted the best for Dani, if that's what you're asking. Like all mothers do."

"And she and Max, were they happy?"

He looked shocked. "I'm sorry," he said, and opened the door to leave. "I really wouldn't know about that."

He shut the door behind him and left me alone next to *Winter's Girl*, looming above her slip, black water gently lapping below.

By the time Max met me a half hour later, the fire was fading and the boathouse was chillier, but I was no calmer. I had almost finished the first coat of paint on *Dani's Luck*, centering the stencil by eye. When he walked in he didn't say anything at first, and neither did I, still rattled by my dismissal in the kitchen and my awkward episode with Gus. Max crept over to where I was concentrating on making steady business out of the last letter.

"Mind if I watch?"

"Not at all."

He fetched two stools and placed them near me, sat on one, and propped a brown bag with my breakfast on the other. Those few minutes of silence were a palliative, reminding me of the afternoons and evenings we had spent in the Caymans on those rented boats, each our own little island, where we made the rules and no one lived there except for us. How naive I was to think that could be duplicated here.

"I don't like to be sent away like that. Makes me feel like a child," I said, bent over my work.

"I'm sorry."

"This isn't a gift for Dani, by the way. It's more of a gesture."

"It's a very nice one. She'll be pleased."

"What did you need to discuss with Louisa, without me?"

"Dani, mostly. Rebekah a little. My need to move on from the past."

I lowered the brush and faced him. "Have you?"

"Have I what?"

"Moved on from the past?"

"Yes."

"Because it feels to me every time I turn a corner here I get smacked in the face with things I never knew about you."

We looked at each other for a few moments. Dani's story was unhinging me and I couldn't keep it to myself any longer.

"If this is about the greenhouse, I—"

"I never meant to make a big deal about the greenhouse. I understand you have memories in there. But so does Dani, it turns out."

"What are you talking about?"

"She told me about the night Rebekah died. She remembers a lot more than she lets on, Max. She told me a woman came to Asherley, and that Rebekah was angry about her visit. There was a big fight in the greenhouse, and Rebekah took off in her car."

Max sunk his chin into his chest for a moment, thinking.

"Who was that woman, Max?"

He looked up at me. "When did she tell you this?"

His voice was soft but his temple twitched.

"Yesterday. Over dinner."

"I always suspected she was awake that night."

"So she's telling the truth? There was a woman?"

"Yes," he said, after some hesitation.

"Was she your girlfriend, Max? Were you cheating on Rebekah? Because that's what Dani thinks."

"*That's* what Dani thinks? *That's* who Dani thinks that was?"

His body now emptied of all tension, his relief palpable.

"No . . . *No*, that woman was not my girlfriend."

"Who was she, then?"

He looked at my face for what felt like a long time. "That woman . . . she was Dani's birth mother."

"You knew her mother? Who was she?"

"Just this messed-up girl from Bethpage. A drug addict. Painkillers and the like. Used to come around for money. I never wanted to give her any, but Rebekah would always panic and give her something just to make her go away. Dani doesn't know about her. She *can't* know. I think sub-consciously that's why I didn't tell you at first that Dani was adopted, to avoid any questions about her mother. "

"Right. Of course." I felt that satisfying click in my head, of puzzle pieces snugly fitting.

"She never came to see her daughter. We might have allowed it were she not so . . . . dangerous. She just wanted money. What else did Dani say about that night? Tell me everything." His face was etched with worry.

"Just that she came to the door. There was an argument in the greenhouse. Rebekah left the house. You told Dani she went to town to get a fan, and that's when she crashed her car. Dani thought she might have been driving fast because she was angry at you, at that woman."

"Well, that's partially true. I didn't want her to give her any money. In fact, I . . . I took the cash Rebekah was going to give her. A thousand times I wish I could relive that moment. Give it back."

He looked on the verge of tears. So was I.

"Rebekah grabbed the car keys, said she was going to an ATM. And they left. Together."

"But, Max, if they left together, where is she now, Dani's mother?"

"It's the craziest thing," Max said, shaking his head. "When they found Rebekah, I expected they'd find the mother's body, too, and for everything to come out. But there was no other body. There was no evidence that anyone else was in the car with Rebekah. So . . . I didn't say anything. I hired a detective to find out what happened to her. He eventually discovered she overdosed not long after the crash, near Tompkins Square Park. And I'm ashamed to say that all I felt was relief. So I made the decision to just . . . put it away. Selfish, I know, and quite illegal. But I was desperate to avoid a scandal, desperate to protect Dani. Losing one mother is bad enough. Two would kill her."

I took a deep breath. It felt like the first one I'd taken in an hour.

"I know," he said. "It's a lot to process. But I didn't want any kind of doubt to hang over your head, that I would have a lover, that I would cheat on you. By now you must know that I trust you with my life, and with Dani's life, too. Can I rely on you to keep this secret from her?"

"Of *course*," I said, taking him by the upper arms. I felt shock, yes, but also relief.

I stood up from my stool and wedged myself between his thighs and wrapped my arms around him until I could feel some of his awful burden shift over into my body. He must have felt it, too, because he began to return the embrace, most ardently, repeating, "Thank you. Thank you," over and over.

When I finally released him there were tears in both of our eyes.

"I came down here to tell you something," he said, wiping them away. "I have a past to contend with, one you now know all about. There are no more secrets between us. But I came to say my past is not located in any one place at Asherley, any one room. I brought you here because I love you and I want to marry you. My home is your home, and my stubbornness about the greenhouse was just born from stupid habit. Louisa helped me see that. And so did Dani."

"Dani?"

"Yes," he said, smiling. "She came back into the kitchen just after you left. The two of them really ganged up on me."

"Poor Max."

"I always thought Dani would be angrier than me if we reopened the greenhouse, because she grew up in there, at her mother's feet. Now I know that it also might have been where she last saw her mother. But she seems keen for us to have the reception there. And I think it's a good idea. That it's time for us to make new memories."

"I don't know what to say. I'm . . . amazed," I said. "At Dani, I mean."

"Me, too," he said. "She surprises me at every turn."

"I meant what I said, Max. I don't care where we hold the wedding, as long as it happens."

"I'll make you a deal." He reached over to grab my ring off the nearby shelf. "In exchange for being the lovely keeper of all my dark secrets, I'll open the greenhouse for your wedding."

I snatched the ring from his hand and put it back on my stained finger.

"Deal."

TWENTY-TWO

After Max told me the truth about Dani's mother, something inside me lifted. Fear, I think, of Dani in particular and our future in general. In return for helping change Max's mind about the greenhouse, I decided to let Dani assert herself in the last-minute wedding decisions. So it was white peonies for the centerpieces, a bow for Maggie, and a three-piece jazz band greeting guests in the foyer. I treated them all as genius ideas, each one perfect and welcome. As she walked through Asherley making her final checks, I found myself in the familiar position of running behind a bossy woman taking notes, this time with a smile on my face. We were forming some semblance of a team. It was a happy time.

"Flowers for these side tables. Posies."

"Check."

"White ribbons on the sconces."

"Lovely."

"Candles for the powder rooms."

"Great idea."

"Oh, get Gus to lay down the runners. And tell him to give the herringbone a coat of tung oil. It's about time."

When I told her I could do that job myself, being well schooled in wood preservation, she looked at me squarely.

"Why the fuck would you want to do that a week before your wedding? Go get a pedicure or something normal."

That was Dani, one minute angrily scolding me, the next, on the phone with the bakers, amiably telling them we wanted vanilla so I wouldn't get chocolate crumbs on my pretty dress. She couldn't have alleviated my wedding stress more thoroughly were she to have slapped on gloves and surgically removed it. And Katya followed her lead, dealing with the caterers herself, and I grew accustomed to starting my days with her yelling on the phone at them, usually about the cost of an ingredient for a dish she could find cheaper elsewhere.

Asherley, too, seemed to cooperate, its grounds beginning to green up a bit, the skeletons of wintering ivy unfurling pale buds across the cold gray stones, coating the meaner-looking garden gargoyles with a warm, leafy blanket. I began to note the position of the house. Once spring arrived, the morning sun was calibrated to slash through all its east-facing windows just so, lending a dramatic light to each room. The greenhouse also became hotter as the sun cut higher across the sky, the glass positioned like perfect magnifiers, creating bright pockets along certain walls and dark ones elsewhere. This place wasn't just for show. Once the rickety tables and broken shelves had been removed and the ground was leveled for the new floor, the greenhouse felt like a living and breathing entity that wanted to be put to work again.

Before we did any major repairs, Max brought out an engineer who assured him the structure was sound. Nothing was wrong, he said, that couldn't be addressed in time for the wedding. A few glass panels needed to be cut and installed, a new belt for the fan, the hinges on the upper vents oiled. Other than that, it was a lovely place for a wedding. And, he added, once the temporary floor was removed, we could even grow things in here, the soil still viable.

"We're not reopening the greenhouse," Max told him. "This is just for a special occasion."

I didn't press the issue. I began to realize I could get my way in increments, not great leaps. Once the wedding guests gushed about how beautiful it was in there, how lucky we were to have this space, there was no way Max could lock it back up again.

One day, after the workers had cleared out for a break, Dani walked in on me standing alone in the center of the glass expanse, counting my blessings, which now included her.

"Why do rooms feel so much smaller when they're empty?" she asked, looking around. "It's weird."

We both stood bathing in the noonday sun, amplified through the dusty glass. I understood then what really drew me here. It was the way the heat, tropical and familiar, traveled through my skin and into my bones, warming up my joints and deeply relaxing me. It was the only place at Asherley where I was never cold, where it felt, to me, like home.

"Thank you, Dani."

"For what?"

"For knowing how much it means to me to have the wedding in here."

She shrugged. "I wanted to be in here, too. Plus I like pissing him off."

"He's not angry. He just needed a little prodding."

She walked over to the highest wall and tented her fingers on the glass. She looked to her left, took a few steps until she landed on a particular spot and looked over at the door. "Ever think you remember something that you thought was from a dream, but it might have been real?"

"I don't know. Maybe."

She took a few steps to the right, murmuring to invisible actors on an imaginary stage. She seemed to have entered the same fugue state she was in when she told me what she remembered about Rebekah's last night in the greenhouse, and the other woman, a story I once resented, but now cherished, because I knew the truth, and it grounded me. It tied me to Asherley and to Max in a profoundly new way.

Just then Louisa walked in, wearing chic overalls and carrying a takeout coffee.

"Katya makes an excellent pot," I said.

"And it shouldn't be wasted on me when this swill will do," she replied. "So, where are we thinking for the head table?"

"Right . . . over here," I said, walking to where Dani was standing by the high spire. "After the ceremony, the chairs will be moved over to the round tables for the reception."

Louisa became wistful. "There used to be rosebushes up to the ceiling here. God-awful color but such long stems, heads as big as apples."

Dani, her head now down in her phone, excused herself.

"She all right?" Louisa asked.

"I think so." She did seem off. But she also had a lot to keep on top of these past busy days.

Louisa was still looking around. "You know, maybe I've been a bit too hard on this place. It really is something."

Max came in to say goodbye before heading to the office. He glanced about with a stern eye, noting what had been done, what still needed to be done. It was heartening, his interest in the wedding planning.

"It looks different with all that junk cleared out. Have you seen Dani? Adele's here."

"She just left," I said.

"I keep missing her."

Louisa asked him what he was wearing to the wedding, something I hadn't thought to ask myself.

"Not a monkey suit this time, thank Christ. I will wear shorts and a baseball cap if I feel like it. And thankfully I'm marrying someone who wouldn't give a damn." He turned to me. "Sweetheart, I have a late dinner in New York, so I might crash there."

"That's all right," I said, trying to sound more disappointed than angry. I knew I was marrying a busy politician, but this would be the third time in two weeks he'd spent the night in New York instead of coming home late. Albany I understood; it was farther.

"Next time I'll get Broadway tickets and we'll make a night of it," he said, as if reading my mind.

"Feel free to stay at the flat," Louisa said.

"I prefer the hotel," he said, putting his arm around me and kissing the side of my head. "I've been a shitty fiancé. But unlike you, these Wall Street types seem to need a ridiculously long courtship before they'll donate a dime to my campaign."

"Go. Really. I'm in good hands here," I said, indicating Louisa.

"I won't let her out of my sight," she told him.

What a difference the truth makes. How violently my confidence would have ebbed had Max left again and I still thought him capable of cheating. I would have been scouring for telltale signs: averted eyes, a fixation with the phone, fidgeting, constant excuses. Finding nothing, I would have assumed he was particularly adept at hiding it. I would have driven us both insane. As for Dani, considering how lovely and generous she was behaving towards me now, I let go of the idea that she had deliberately tried to plant doubts about Max in my mind. Sadly, she believed this about her father, and if, for her sake, Max was willing to let her, I had to as well.

Max not only stayed the night in New York, he was summoned to Albany for an emergency vote the next morning, which kept him away two more nights. But now it was Dani's absences that preoccupied me. She had skipped her lessons the day she'd drifted off in the greenhouse and ended them early the day after, leaving her room only to get a snack or to warm up some kitten food. There was a time I'd have been grateful for the reprieve, but she'd been so helpful, such good company, that now I missed her.

On day three I found Adele in the den, her feet propped up on Max's desk, video-chatting on her phone. When she saw me, she swept her feet off the desk and slapped her phone down on the mahogany.

"It's okay, Adele, I'm looking for Dani."

"She's not here yet. I texted her. I'll wait around a bit longer, but then I don't know . . ."

"She's been a bit distracted lately, I know. My fault, with the wedding and everything."

Adele stood, lowering her voice a little. "She's more than just normal distracted, though. Yesterday she couldn't stop checking her phone, then she got all anxious and said she wasn't feeling well and left early. I asked her what was wrong, she said nothing. I've been meaning to talk to you guys."

"Okay. That's good to know, thanks. I'll see if I can get to the bottom of it."

I headed straight to Dani's bedroom. I knocked and waited, then knocked again. I put my ear to the door. Nothing. I tried the handle and the door opened. The room was neat, her bed made. The cleaning staff wasn't due until noon, which meant she likely hadn't slept in her bed, since she never made it herself. And there was that smell. On the dresser by the door was an enormous stand of those red-black roses, this one with a card: *For my only girl, always.* There was no name, but it was from Max, clearly. Of course this warmed me, knowing how much these flowers meant to Dani. But I also felt that buckle of envy. That he had never sent me flowers, not even after I almost left him, wasn't what irked me. It was that he sent *these* flowers, Rebekah's roses, which I had come to loathe. They felt obvious, garish, their scent smothering and ubiquitous.

I shut the door behind me. The only other place she'd be was the turret, which had been locked, forbidden to her for the last couple of weeks. Max had planned to wait until after the wedding to let her back up there, with instructions to finally sort through Rebekah's things, choose what to keep, and get rid of the rest.

On the third floor, the gallery walls were still pocked with the shadows of the pictures that had once hung there. I wondered if the workers could paint this week, white for the wedding, anything but this lurid red. As I suspected, the turret door was still locked. But when I pressed my ear against the dense oak, I heard her, faint at first and then louder, her voice guttural with upset.

"Don't lie to me, Claire. It's not funny!"

I hesitated, afraid of wading into a volatile mood, or a fight between two teenage girls I was already afraid of. When I didn't hear Claire reply, I realized Dani was on her phone.

"Well then, who *is* doing it, *bitch*?"

I waited for a bout of silence before I bucked up and knocked. *This is what it is to parent.* Nothing. I called her name, once, twice. Still nothing. Too afraid to press any further, I headed to our bedroom, where my phone was charging next to the bed. I could call her, I thought, or text. Instead, my fingers unwittingly routed me to her Instagram.

I'd been checking it less and less since our relationship seemed to have found better footing. But I thought it might give me some insight into her whereabouts these past few days. There were new posts, mostly of her and Claire wearing their customary seductive pouts, sometimes cartoon ears and noses, always their breasts out, their backs arched, lips puckered. Some were taken in her bedroom, some in what I assumed was Claire's—more evidence of Max's ineffectual grounding. She'd posted a lovely shot of Isabel pasturing out near the barn, and a stylish one of Asherley crowned by a stormy sky, a filter lending the house a terrific ominousness. There was a jarring selfie out at the shooting range behind the stone ruins of the old barn, Dani provocatively blowing on the end of a gun, Gus miserable in the background with his rifle pointed down. Her most recent post was a moody black-and-white, taken in front of the Eiffel Tower. She was holding a cigarette, hair blurring across her face. How many takes had there been, how many filters applied, before this one was deemed perfect enough to post? The caption read, "miss u #Paris #tbt." Below that a few comments from friends, including Claire, who wrote "my reine" next to a crown emoji. The second-last comment stood out. It was right below Claire's and it read, "And I miss you, my darling daughter," below which Dani replied, "WHO THE FUCK ARE YOU?!! FUCKING STOP DOING THIS!" It came from an account called @rwinterforever.

I tapped the handle. It was a private account. There were dozens of posts and the account was following only one person. Though I was unable to see any of the pictures, just the name, @rwinterforever, gave me chills. I flicked back to the comments in Dani's other recent posts, the one of the horse, of the house, the gun range, and found more comments from this account, a compliment here ("Gorgeous shot!"), an endearment there ("Our lovely Asherley"), always followed with a reply from an alarmed Dani: "WHO ARE YOU? WHO IS DOING THIS? PLEASE STOP DOING THIS."

I dropped my phone as though it were hot, feeling winded by this particular bout of snooping. Was this the reason she was yelling at Claire? If so, it was an appalling prank. If this was just a random fan account, I couldn't think of a more malicious way to show appreciation for the late Rebekah Winter than to harass her daughter like this. I wanted to help. We were getting closer, weren't we? She might appreciate my concern. Or I might open myself up to more ridicule and a fresh bout of antagonism, so close to the wedding. *You're a lurker, so creepy!* Yet I was going to be her stepmother. I had to stop being afraid of her. Besides, I could broach the topic by asking gentle questions. *You seem down, Dani*, I could say. *You don't seem yourself. Is anything the matter? Anything you'd like to talk to me about? I'm here for you.*

I texted Max. He would know what to do.

Hey you, Dani skipped school again, Adele's worried. So am I. She's up in the turret, door locked. Seems to be fighting with Claire. Not sure what to do.

I stared at my screen for a few minutes, waiting for the pulsing ellipsis to alert me to an incoming text. When none came, I went downstairs to check on the progress in the greenhouse, constantly glancing at my phone while saying goodbye to the workers for the day. Alone at the island eating dinner, I kept my phone perched in front of me, the way Dani always did. Finally, while I was heading upstairs to bed, a message dinged in my pocket, and I realized I had passed an entire day waiting for a text from Max.

Sorry love, back-to-back meetings. Can we deal with Dani tomorrow night? Will be home by dinner. Mx

That's it? I thought, conjuring all sorts of angry responses to his reply. *Your daughter is distressed and I am not equipped to handle it, and I wait all day and THIS is your reply?*

Out of fear and inexperience, and yes, out of selfishness, I simply replied: *Ok. Safe flight back, x.* And then I went to bed.

Louisa invited herself to dinner the next night, since Jonah had come back with Max from Albany. By then Dani's mood was noticeable to everyone at the table. She was present, but her mind miles away, her food mostly untouched. She was even immune to the charms of Maggie, boxing the table-cloth's tassels by her ankles.

Finally, Max snapped his fingers in front of his daughter's blank face. "Hey. Hello. Hi. Remember us? The people you live with? What is up with you, sweetheart?"

She shook her head. "Sorry," she said, checking her phone again. Maggie jumped onto her lap. Dani's eyes remained dead as she robotically pet her.

Max stared at her, waiting for her to elaborate. She glared back at him.

"*What?* What is it, Daddy?"

"You tell me, doll. You're sitting there like a barely animated corpse. I'm worried about you."

"*We're* worried about you," I added.

"Oh my God, I'm fine," she said, turning to me as though her head were on a swivel. "The dress should arrive any day now. I'll keep it in my room. We don't want Dad peeking."

"That would be great," I said.

She carefully sliced off a section of her meat. Her teeth clanged against her fork. She chewed slowly, swallowed with some effort. I stole a look at Louisa, whose eyes had widened with bafflement.

"Oh and thank you for the flowers, Dad. You didn't have to do that."

"Of course I did."

"I think I'll go upstairs now. I'm tired."

"All right," Max said. "Feel better soon."

"I told you, Dad, I'm fine."

She left without kissing him, uncharacteristically leaving Maggie behind as well. I scooped her up.

"See what I mean?" I whispered.

Max shrugged. "She's allowed to be a little moody before the wedding."

"But she never speaks to you like that," I said. "Don't you think something's going on?"

"A lot of things are bound to be going through her mind. I wouldn't worry."

He continued to eat. I had barbecued steak that night, with some success.

"You're looking at me like you have a theory," he said.

The three of them blinked at me like owls.

"You think it's the greenhouse?" Louisa said.

"No, it's not that." I gathered Maggie and rose to shut the dining room door.

"Now you're worrying *me*," said Louisa, her eyes following me back to my chair.

I hesitated, having never faced such a rapt audience in my life. "This is embarrassing, but . . . for a while now I've— Well, there's no other way to put this. I've been snooping on Dani's Instagram. I only do it now and again, not every day. And I only do it to keep an eye on her." I winced, waiting for the response.

"I do that," Louisa said matter-of-factly. "Not since Paris. But I do."

"So do I," said Max.

"You do?" I looked at one, then the other.

"She's fifteen," he said. "Of course I do. Or I *should*."

Louisa smiled at me. "If I see something I don't like, I rat her out to her Luddite father."

"Yes, and then I tell her to take things down and she has a meltdown, switching to private mode so we can't see anything, after which I take her phone away, then she gets another one with a new number she won't give me, and on and on it goes. I need to do a better job of monitoring, for sure. Rebekah used to, but she was only twelve when she first got on there. It was all unicorns and best friends forever, but now . . ." He gave a shudder.

"You have to snoop," Louisa said. "That's what all the books say."

I could have cried. Of course they would monitor her social media.

"Now I'm doubly embarrassed. I was *supposed* to be doing this."

"Don't beat yourself up," Max said. "You're not a parent. At least you weren't until now. I, for one, am glad you're doing it. Has it been bad?"

"Well, it's not that her pictures are that bad, really. It's that there are these very odd comments, from one account in particular, a private one, and then her reaction to them."

Max rolled his eyes. "Here we go again."

Louisa took out her phone and reading glasses. "Let's take a look, shall we?" She tapped the app on her phone, instead of going through a browser, as I did.

"You have an account?" I was genuinely surprised; she didn't seem the type.

"Oh good God, no, I'm too old. It's just a dummy account for snooping. And not just on Dani, by the way. My friends are complete idiots. Grown women doing duck-face selfies. Using puppy-ear filters. Imagine. What am I looking for?" she asked, peering down her nose through her tiny glasses.

I puffed up like an expert. "Here. I'll show you." I took Louisa's phone from her and scanned through Dani's last few postings. "See? Here. The greenhouse one. Just below. Read that comment."

Louisa took her phone back. Her lips moving as she read the words. Then she honed in on the account's name. "At R . . . Winter forever. R Winter. That's . . . Is someone commenting *as* Rebekah?"

"I don't know. It's weird, though, isn't it?"

"What the—" Max snatched the phone, squinting to read the comments. Louisa handed him her glasses. "You talked to her about this?"

"No. I didn't have the courage," I admitted. "I'd never hear the end of it from her. But when the comments started popping up, that's when she started acting strange, disappearing, turning sullen, wandering the greenhouse in a daze. You know how she's been, Max. I tried to tell you about this yesterday."

He poked through her other posts.

"Who would do this?" I asked, looking at all three of them.

"Let's see." Max put down the phone. "Her friends, or rather her *ex*-friends. They're all little shits."

"Claire especially," Louisa said.

"Yes, she's a particular piece of work," Jonah said. "From a whole family of assholes, to be honest. Wasn't the father nabbed for insider trading or something?"

"Embezzlement," Max said.

"Right."

"Well, the girls are fighting right now," I said. "I overheard Dani yelling at Claire on the phone, accusing her, I think, of doing this." I left out the part where I had my ear pressed to the door.

"Dani's been a very talented bully over the years. Especially online," Max said ruefully. "It could be Claire, or someone else she's pissed off giving her a taste of her own medicine."

Louisa took her phone back and continued to scan the posts. "I hate to say this, but . . . this . . . this might also be Dani," she said. She placed her phone down on the table as if she had solved the mystery, case closed.

I looked towards the door, suddenly worried Dani would walk in on four grown-ups analyzing her social media. I lowered my voice. "You think she did this *and* she's faking anxiety over it? To what end?"

"Does she know you snoop?" Jonah asked.

"No. Yes, maybe." I remembered how she had laughed at me at the restaurant, said that she'd made a bet with Claire.

"This is classic Dani," Louisa said, tapping her phone with an index finger to punctuate her point. "Dramatic. Weird. Puts her at the center of attention."

"Look at us all talking about her right now," Jonah added, with a laugh.

"*And* she likes to rub Rebekah in your face," Louisa said to me. "You know it's true. Plus, she knows how to play a long game."

There was a collective groan. Louisa continued.

"Remember, Max, when she wanted everyone to hate the Waterston girl for some mysterious reason? She planted a few of her belongings at their house and then *later* accused the kid of stealing them. She was *eight*. When she finally told Rebekah the truth, what did Rebekah do? She laughed. She thought Dani was so clever."

"I can't believe she'd do this on the off chance that I'd see it. We've been getting along so well. She's been such a help." I turned to Max. "What if one of her friends *is* taunting her? What if it *is* Claire? We have to do something. We have to help her."

"Are you always like this?" Jonah asked.

"Like what?"

"Kind and lovely and perfectly sane?"

"Oh, look, Joe's got a crush on the second Mrs. Winter, too," Louisa said. Jonah shot her a look and shifted in his seat.

Max covered my hand, ignoring them. "I'll talk to her," he said. "I promise."

My shoulders dropped, relieved he was going to take it on and not me. "Thank you, Max."

"No. Thank *you*. For your big, good heart. For caring about Dani. It's having an effect on her. Or maybe it's that damn kitten." He reached over and scratched Maggie's ruff.

"You mean this sweet little thing that you told me to get rid of?"

He smiled. "This kitten was your wedding gift. But that's *all* you're getting," he said, touching my cheek, confirming he could no more get rid of Maggie than he could Dani or me.

TWENTY-THREE

There wasn't much left to do for the wedding, so Dani mostly stayed in her room those last few days, watching endless amounts of TV and playing with Maggie, only dragging herself out of her hole to help Gus load the horses heading to their new stables in Montauk. I watched her from the kitchen window, laughing with Gus as they made several attempts to back the trailer up to the barn. She calmly walked each horse up the plank and into a long trailer, Isabel and then Dorian, stopping to whisper into their flickering ears. She seemed happy, comfortable, like her old self. Max came up behind me and wrapped his arms around my shoulders, and we watched them for a moment.

"I talked to Dani this morning," he said, kissing the side of my head.

I turned around to face him. "And? Did she mention the account?"

"No. But she was flinty and defensive when I asked about Claire. They *are* fighting, so I think we have our culprit."

"Did you ask her about those weird messages?"

"Not outright. I just opened a channel of communication, as they say. Good God, teenage girls terrify me. They hate each other today, but they'll be best friends tomorrow. Besides, the pranking seems to have stopped."

"You checked?"

"Nothing in the past couple days. Let's let it go for now. Okay?"

I turned back around just as Dani climbed into the truck beside Gus.

"Jesus Christ, she's not supposed to go with him," Max said, taking out his phone.

I covered it with my hand. "Max, just . . . let her."

I was trying to keep what I felt was a precarious peace. The wedding was only days away. I still had the naive belief that afterwards I'd be imbued with powers I lacked before marrying Max, making me better equipped to tackle any demons that might arise, hers, mine, or ours.

I was down in the boathouse, laying the last coat of varnish over the stencil, when Dani texted me to say the dress had finally arrived from the seamstress, and not a day to spare. Without replying, I threw my brush down and sprinted to the house, completely forgetting the force field Dani had erected around her. I ran past the party-rental people rolling tables and carting chairs out of their truck, skidded across the foyer, and raced up the stairs. I entered Dani's room without knocking, without waiting for an invitation, just as she was hanging the long white garment bag in her closet, the dress still zipped inside.

"Um, hello," she said.

"Let's have a look!" I said, lunging for the bag.

Dani yelped, slapping at my hands. "Whoa! What have you been doing with those?"

I looked down at my fingers. Brown varnish coated my nail beds and settled deep into the creases of my knuckles.

"Go and soak those gross paws and don't come near me until they're absolutely fucking clean."

I stuck my hands into my pockets. "Sorry. I got so excited. The seamstress really cut it close."

"No, *we* were cutting it close. *She* went above and beyond. My mother would suggest that we send her something nice in appreciation."

"Yes, of course. Let's do that."

My mother. I suddenly felt grubby and uncouth. Of course Rebekah would suggest that. Dani gently punched the puffy bag into the closet, then almost shut the door on Maggie. She was batting around a dried rose petal fallen from the bouquet Max had bought for her, now resting stems-up in her garbage pail.

I brought up Claire in hopes she might talk to me about her recent troubles.

"So . . . what time is Claire coming tomorrow?"

"She's not."

"But wasn't she going to help you with hair and makeup?"

"We had a fight or whatever. It doesn't matter. Tomorrow's not my special day."

"I thought maybe you'd enjoy yourself more if you could bring someone. Are there other friends you can ask?"

She turned to me, her eyes liquid with sadness. "Haven't you figured it out by now? He doesn't want me to have any friends. Not Claire, not Maggie, not Gus, not even you."

I took a step back. "Who are you talking about?"

"Who do you think? My beloved father, Senator Winter."

Her voice was laden with conviction, her face set for battle, lips pursed, chin quivering, a statue of lovely defiance. Were my hands not so dirty I would have grabbed her face to drive home my full-throated rebuttal.

"Dani. *Dani.* What are you talking about? I don't know a father on earth who loves his daughter as much as Max loves you. And I . . . I feel quite a lot of love for you, too," I said, choking up, because it felt true. I might just love this torturous and tortured little brat.

"That's nice to hear," she said. "I wish I believed it."

"Oh, Dani. You *can* believe it. I know this wedding has been hard for you—"

"He fired Gus."

"He didn't fire him. It's more like a transfer. And you'll still get to see him when you visit the horses."

"Ha! You'll believe anything he tells you. He fired him because of me. Daddy said he didn't like how Gus acted around me, but I told him Gus never did anything wrong. He was my friend. He protected me. He taught me horses. He taught me to shoot and fish. He was teaching me how to drive. He was my only friend here."

"I'm your friend here, too."

She studied my face for a moment. "Can you please leave me alone right now?"

I looked over at the closet door. "Dani, I'm quite worried about you. I think I know what's been—"

"Please go. I'll be all right. I'm just tired all of a sudden."

I stood there.

"I mean it. I'm all right. I say crazy things sometimes. Just go."

"Okay. But I want you to know that I'm here for you. I care about you. Your father cares about you. *We* care very much."

She gave me the slightest of smiles. When I stole one more look as I shut the door behind me, she seemed so small. Dani wasn't "coming around." She was descending a well of dark thoughts that threatened to consume her, and us.

I looked for Max. I searched all over Asherley, going from room to room. Each was a locus of activity. Florists all around the house were positioning small sprays of tulips, daisies, lilacs on the side tables, country flowers, no roses. Caterers swarmed the kitchen and the outdoor barbecue area. In the great hall, Katya was shooing the cleaning staff into the corners of the house, charging them to leave no spot undusted, no window smudged. I found Louisa in the greenhouse, the place unrecognizable now with dozens of stands of white gladiolas, peonies, and lilies all around the perimeter, the round tables skirted with white tablecloths, silver place settings sparkling in the afternoon sun. She crossed the room towards me, her steps echoing on the raised floor.

"There you are. I know it's very hot in here but don't worry, we're going to crank open those—"

"Have you seen Max?"

"Yes, they're putting up the smoking canopy near the garage. What's the matter?"

Without replying, I headed out the back door, ran across the gray-green lawn. Damp heat rose up from the grass; tomorrow called for rain, but it would be warm for April.

From a distance I could see Elias awkwardly manning the portable backhoe, Max hovering over the hole, two men doing a job Gus could have done alone. Max's dark T-shirt was sticky with sweat, his jeans covered in dirt. I don't know that I had ever seen him look as attractive.

"Hello!" he yelled over the motor.

"How's it going?"

"Not well. At the fourth stake we hit a root, I think."

Elias shut the machine off. "Try again."

Max took his shovel and stabbed the earth. There was a great clang, a sound that reverberated through my chest.

"Pipe," Max yelled, scanning the ground as though he could see through the dirt. "The drain for the troughs, I bet. Should we relocate?"

Elias threw his head back in frustration.

Max noticed my filthy hands. "How's that going? Almost done?"

"Yes. Top coat's drying. Max, I need to talk to you about Dani."

"Can it wait?"

"I don't think so. I—"

Max looked over my shoulder and gave an enthusiastic wave. It was Jonah, carrying a shovel and wearing big black boots.

"There he is, the second person I call when I'm knee-deep in my own shit. I'm sorry, sweetie, what were you saying about Dani?"

"Max, I'm worried—"

Jonah gave me a sturdy pat on my back as he passed. "Excited about tomorrow?"

"Yes. Very much," I said.

Max swept Jonah into a complicated discussion about where the old plumbing crossed the new, and whether the fourth stake could be sunk farther away or whether that would compromise the tent or whether they'd need to up and move the whole contraption. I saw no way to draw him away from what was clearly an important job they were all intent on tackling.

"Max, I'll just go," I said. I turned back to the house.

"Hold on, guys, I'm sorry," he said, and jogged to catch up to me. "What's going on?"

"It's Dani." Max rolled his eyes. "No, listen. She's very emotional. She told me she doesn't think you love her. That you don't want her to have any friends."

His shoulders caved forward. "Okay, right now, I *don't* love her," he said, sounding weary rather than angry. "I mean, I *love* her. Of *course* I love her. I'd jump in front of a goddamn train for her because she's my daughter. I've sent her flowers. I've texted her. I told her she could keep the kitten! But I'm *tired* of our whole life revolving around her every fucking mood. Besides, teenagers all think their parents hate them. They *all* feel unloved. I did—though I actually *was* unloved," he added with a chuckle.

"But, Max, this is different from her regular poutiness. There's something really off about her. And she's really sad about Gus. Maybe we shouldn't have let him go."

"I didn't have a choice." He lowered his voice. "I've been meaning to tell you. In his quarters I found a picture of Dani pinned to the wall next to his bed."

"What kind of picture?"

"Not a *bad* picture. One from when she was a toddler. But it gave me pause. So, yeah, I did have to fire him, because I love her and I don't want Gus around my fifteen-year-old daughter. And I can't tell her about the photo because it'd make her even more upset."

He took me by the wrists. "Sweetheart, I'm grateful that you're concerned about Dani. I really am. It might be the single most important reason why I am marrying you. You understand how troubled she is, and why I've kept so much from her, especially"—he looked over his shoulder—"about her mother. But Dani Winter does not suffer from a shortage of love. Quite the opposite. I love her too

241

much. I've let her get away with a lot of things that have made your life here miserable. And she's done this before, retreated from family life, lashed out. I promise you she knows exactly how much I love her. So she's not testing me with this. She's testing *you*. And the way to pass this test is to try to enjoy *your* big day. Okay?" He glanced over at Eli and Jonah trying to maneuver the tent rope and pole. "I really have to—"

"Yes. Go."

"You know I love that brat," he said. "I mean, I love her more than you. But you're catching up really fucking fast!"

I gave him a half-hearted laugh, and he ran back to join the men.

It was a slow walk up the hill to Asherley. The rentals truck, now emptied of its chairs and tables, beeped a warning and backed out of the side drive. I could see the workers testing candles in the greenhouse, their long shadows dancing across the now-sparkling glass. How different the greenhouse looked spruced up and populated, like a breathing organ that felt vital to the house, not a useless, decorative appendage. I cursed the chill that dusk brought, soothing my anxiety by running through a litany of the good fortune that was hurtling towards me. In twenty-four hours, I would marry inside Rebekah's greenhouse, making Asherley my home, then one day my children's home. When I was old, I'd rest on that porch chair and put my feet up on that wicker ottoman. Max would grumble about the ancient ivy threatening to blot out our view of the bay, while I pulled my shawl tighter around my shoulders. I would traipse every acre of this island with my children in their little red raincoats. We'd drift down inlets in a boat, spying on nesting ospreys and the swans raising their cygnets in the rushes. While we ate on the warm rocks, I'd tell them about their ancestors from the paintings, the bad ones who owned people and sheltered pirates and the good ones who fought for the Union and worked to protect one of the largest stands of white oak on the entire Atlantic Seaboard. These things were finally at hand, but not if my happiness remained inversely proportionate to Dani's sadness.

I looked up, aware she was watching me before my eyes confirmed it: Dani, in the turret, defiant as ever. No lock could keep her out of there. We looked at each other. When she did not return my wave, I took Max's advice and left her alone, heading to the boathouse to scrub my dirty hands clean.

TWENTY-FOUR

Over these past few months, I've come to understand more about what trauma, both emotional and physical, does to the brain. It's remarkable how the mind's censors can work over a conveyor belt of madness, discarding the rotten bits so we consume only the parts that are acceptable. I don't recall waking up next to Max on the morning of our wedding or whether we had breakfast together. I do remember being in the boathouse that morning, in my bathrobe, where Dani found me checking to see if the stencil was finally dry. It wasn't how I had planned to unveil her gift. I'd hoped to wait until after the ceremony. But when Dani poked her head inside the door, my heart leapt at the sight of her scrubbed face, her hair wet down her back.

"Dani, I'm so glad to see you. I have—"

She walked over to me and gently clasped my wrist. "Come with me," she said, tugging. "Right now."

"What is it?"

"Just . . . come," she said. "Everything's going to be okay."

There was no anger in her voice, or worry, just instruction.

"Wait. I have something I want to show you."

"I know. You refinished Grandpa's boat. Nice job."

I freed my hand from her grip and pulled the tarp back. "Look at the back."

After her eyes scanned the hull, she walked around the boat, stopping to read the words across the transom. "Dani's . . . luck."

"For Daneluk," I said.

A slight smile cracked her stern expression. She looked at me then at the boat. "Why did you do this?"

"I wanted to give you something of your own on our wedding day."

She kept looking at the name. She seemed sad.

"We can take it for a spin around the lake later if you—"

"Daddy let you do this for me?"

"What do you mean? Of course he *let* me," I said, skipping the part where he strictly said not to get the spoiled girl who has everything a wedding gift.

Before I knew what was happening, she made a tiny leap into my arms, and I wished for Max to see this, our détente turning into what I hoped was a lasting peace. He was so wrong about this and I was so right and I couldn't wait to tell him.

"Thank you," she said. "You're not very cool, but you're a nice person. Now it's my turn to show *you* something. But you're not going to like it at all. Please promise me you won't freak out."

"Okay, but . . ."

She grabbed my hand and dragged me across the lawn, past Louisa ordering florists around in the greenhouse, past a frantic Katya shooing caterers to the second fridge down the hall, then across the foyer where we could hear Max and Jonah laughing in the den, and all the way up to her room, the whole way me repeating, "Where are we going? You're worrying me, Dani. What's going on?" and her saying, "I don't want you to worry, everything's going to be okay," our roles strangely reversed.

She flung me into her room and shut the door behind her, marched over to her closet, pulled out the garment bag, and threw it across her bed. "Okay. It's a *problem*, for sure. But I don't think it's a total *disaster*."

She bent to unzip it, freed the wedding dress from its plastic cocoon, and carefully laid it on her bed.

We both looked at it, fists on waists.

"That is . . . *not* my dress."

"I know."

I repeated my observation while the room seemed to take a loopy turn. This dress was nothing like the simple one we'd chosen. This one was lacy, sexy, with a Spanish cut to the square bodice, its three-quarter-length sleeves flaring out at the elbow. The waist was cinched with a deep red sash, and its lace, layer upon layer of it, was a mesmerizing circular design, like a million mandalas sewn together, the material hanging a bit longer in the back than the front. It was strikingly beautiful, but it was not my dress.

"I already called the store. They're closed. Good fucking Friday."

Heat spread up my neck to my face. When I finally spoke, it sounded like I was being strangled.

"You said this is not a disaster. How is this not a disaster? Not just for me but for the woman who's got *my* dress?"

"Oh my God," Dani replied, nearly laughing. "That never occurred to me."

Tears sprang from my eyes.

"No, no, no," Dani said, tugging my hand. "No. Don't cry. Listen to me. Here is why this is *not* a disaster. A disaster would be if they sent us an *ugly* dress. But this dress is not ugly. It's actually pretty, and I bet, I just *bet*, it'll fit you and that you'll look very pretty in it and no one will know the difference and it'll just be a funny story we'll tell everyone after the ceremony. No one knows you didn't pick out this dress, right? See? It's okay. Try it on."

How could I say no to her, to this version of Dani, my crisis manager, my expert soother? Here she was, the object of my worry, being sane, supportive, tossing out her troubles and making mine hers. She slid off my bathrobe and helped me step into the center of the lacy circle she made out of this stranger's lovely dress. She inched it up my skin, to let my body acclimate slowly to this new shape and material. And Dani was right. It not only fit me, it *was* pretty—stunning, even—far more stylish than the one I'd chosen for myself.

"*So* not a disaster," she said, smiling at me in her mirror.

"No. Not a disaster," I said. "Except for the fact that your father won't recognize me in this."

"Why not?"

"It's too beautiful for me. It wears *me*."

Dani rolled her eyes. "When are you going to drop that shit? *Look at me, I'm such a nobody. Why is Max Winter marrying little old me?*" she whined. "I want you to walk down those stairs like you meant to wear this dress. That's what my mother would do. That's what she'd tell you to do."

How odd, to be getting secondhand advice from Rebekah Winter through her daughter on the day of my marriage to Max. The dissonance was vertigo-inducing, but once it passed, I stepped out of the dress and laid it carefully across her bed.

"And anyway, we don't have time for disasters," Dani said, handing me my bathrobe. "Right?"

"Right. Thank you, Dani."

I pulled her in for our second hug, one to which I committed slightly more effort than she. It was all I could have asked for that morning.

★

The final hours flew by. The smell of pork roasting outside permeated the halls, mingling with the sickly sweet lilies and Katya's hot cross buns. She was meant to be a guest, but there was no keeping her out of her kitchen. Louisa, God bless, brought a bottle of champagne to my room and offered to be my benevolent greeter. I watched from our window as she sweetly chatted with each arrival, opening an arm to usher them inside. There was no groom's and bride's side of the aisle; they were all Max's guests, a fact that bothered me less and less as the hour ticked closer. To amuse myself I imagined Laureen Ennis holding court at the back of the greenhouse, her face turning as I entered, her smug expression melting into deep admiration as I walked down the aisle wearing a dress that probably cost more than her smallest yacht.

Dani wore a short black baby-doll dress with a white Peter Pan collar, made of a delicate satin that shimmered when she moved, and patent leather kitten heels with big silver buckles. Her hair was up in a tight bun. She looked lovely. But when she insisted on doing my makeup, I balked.

"The last time I let you near me with a lipstick, we both ended up in tears."

"Um, I was wasted?"

Still I hesitated. "I can't wear a lot with my features," I warned.

"I know. Just let me. I'm really good at it."

I slumped forward, eyes closed, chin turned up, surrendering to her ministrations. The brushes tickled now and again, but her hand was confident. Perhaps it was her proximity, or the fact that I could feel her breath on my skin, but I felt emboldened.

"You seem more like yourself."

"Hold still. This lash is a bitch."

"Sorry." I adjusted my body. "Did you and Claire make up?"

She stopped what she was doing. I opened my eyes, a fake lash dangling perilously off my left lid.

"Why is everyone so concerned about me and Claire? No, we did not make up. Claire did a cunty thing and I never want to speak to her again. Now close your eyes. I don't want to talk about anything negative right now. Let's focus on the positive."

"Is she the one who's been posting those weird comments on your Instagram?"

This time she took a step back, her arms crossed. She wasn't angry. She seemed impressed that I had the courage to just blurt that out, to admit I knew.

"Well, now. You *do* lurk."

"I couldn't help it. I was worried about you. Adele said your mood dipped whenever you checked your phone, so I . . . I poked around."

"You talked to Adele, too? Did you, like, pick up a book about being super stepmom or something?"

"I just care."

"Well, I *don't* care. It stopped anyway."

"So it was Claire?"

"No. It was my dead mother," she said. "Now close your eyes. I'm almost done."

While I shut them, I heard the fizz of a glass of champagne being poured.

"Dani."

"Come on. It's a special occasion. I can handle a mouthful."

She drank more than a mouthful, then tipped the glass to my mouth, offering me a careful, fortifying gulp.

"Mm. Thank you." Our eyes met. "Thank you for everything. Especially today."

She shrugged.

"I couldn't have done this without you. I would have had a
meltdown over this dress. I wouldn't have recovered."

"Crazy how well it fits."

I peeked at the mantel clock. A wave of nausea washed
over me.

"Don't move," said Dani, still fidgeting with a lash. "Almost
there. And . . . done."

She held up a mirror, and I blinked a couple of times to get
used to the weight on my lids. My face looked like my face,
but dramatically alive.

"You *are* good at this. I mean it. This might be your calling."
She beamed.

"Tell Daddy that and he'll have a heart attack. If I don't go
to an Ivy League college, he'll be even more disappointed in
me than he already is."

I slapped the mirror down on the dressing table. "Listen to
me. I'll tell you this until you believe it. You are loved exactly
as you are. By your father, by your whole family. And by me."

She smiled, then yanked me to my feet. "Let's get that dress
on and get you married. I'm sick of you two living in sin. It's
fucking disgusting."

Zipped back up into the dress, sash secured, matching lipstick dabbed on my mouth, I waited in the room while Dani
checked on everyone downstairs.

I looked at myself in her full-length mirror. Before Asherley
I didn't covet beauty, not this kind, heightened and illusory.
But today of all days I wanted to look exactly like this, to be
thought of as beautiful, and if not as beautiful as Rebekah,

then at least worthy of Max's attentions, his love, this home, Dani's esteem, this dress.

She ran back into the room, flush with excitement. "It's time."

I fetched my bouquet from the bathroom, where it rested on the cool marble vanity, a simple bundle of white wild-flowers, the first to bloom at Asherley. At the top of the stairs I could hear the guests now gathered in the greenhouse. The small band cued up the "Wedding March."

"See you on the other side," Dani said, and headed down.

"Wait. Walk with me."

"What?"

"Be my maid of honor," I said. "I can't do this alone."

She hesitated.

"Please? Nothing would make me happier."

She climbed back up the stairs and lifted her elbow to me. I slid my arm through hers.

"Let's do this," she said.

Now I was overcome.

"Oh God. Don't cry now, dummy. You'll fuck up my makeup job."

She led the way, my legs useless. We inched down the stairs, past the painted eyes of ancestors unrelated to both of us, whose stories we'd inherit and pass down to our own children. As we crossed the foyer, I could hear the train of this stranger's dress swishing across the marble tiles. The greenhouse chatter stopped as we reached the kitchen. Then the musicians landed on the part of the tune that indicated the march begins. *Won't Max be so happy to see us like this*, I thought, *former enemies and now possibly friends?* Maybe not enemies. Perhaps we'd been rivals, but over what had we been fighting? For Max's attention? For primacy at Asherley? A kitten? How stupid it all seemed now, the petty spats, my fear of her. She was just an angry teenage girl resisting her father's new love. It was natural, an age-old story. Yet ours would have a happy ending. I squeezed her arm again and we kept marching through the kitchen and down the pantry hall, lit on either side by a hundred dancing tea candles, the luminous greenhouse waiting for us at the end.

The music got louder. The flowers stuffing the greenhouse came into view, then the backs of the chairs, each festooned with white ribbons, the tables arranged behind the bridal arch. We kept marching. At the threshold Dani gave me one last squeeze and went to break for her seat. I tugged her closer.

"Take me all the way down."

I wanted her to bring me up to my spot where Max stood, the smile on his face clear from the back of the bright white room. I wanted to run to him, but I also wanted him to really take this in, the two us, a team. At the reception, when he would gush at how beautiful I looked, I couldn't wait to tell him it was Dani, it was all Dani's doing. She averted disaster, buoyed my spirits, gave me the courage to put on this accident of a dress.

One by one, faces turned to look at me, at us, their oohs and aahs drowning out the sound of the *Times* photographer's clicking as he discreetly orbited us with his camera. But then a strange chill seemed to ripple through the room, starting at the back and undulating over the small crowd to the front, where Louisa slowly, oddly, rose to her feet. I'd felt this before, in the middle of the Caribbean, when a beautiful sky darkens in an instant and it's time to race the boat back to the marina. Dani felt it, too. Time slowed. Our bodies tensed. We pulled each other in a little closer. My eyes darted around the room, noting how familiar smiles seemed to melt into horror, Jonah's then Elias's, their mouths dropping open. I looked at Dani, followed her gaze to Max's face, where his initial joy had been replaced by something dead-eyed and angry, aimed directly at Dani. What was happening?

"Why?" he asked Dani, his voice raspy.

Louisa's hand was now over her heart, taking in the whole of my dress, from top to bottom.

"What a thing to do," she whispered, sounding almost impressed.

I let go of Dani's arm and rushed to Max, shook him to jar the frightening expression from his face. "Max, what is it?" I said, afraid to look around.

He wouldn't stop glaring at Dani.

Finally, thankfully, Louisa spoke to the confused guests, a stiff smile on her face. "Everybody, I'm so sorry, but would you all please meet us in the great hall? We're just going to be a little bit delayed." She signaled a throat cut to the photographer.

Guests, complete strangers to me, shot pained expressions in my direction before fleeing. Dani looked cornered by a pack of wolves. Then, over her face came the strangest of expressions, the kind you get when you slowly, finally come to a deep realization.

"Oh," she said. "I think I know what's happening here."

Max looked at me. "I believe you've been the victim of a vile prank," he said.

"I don't understand."

"That dress you are wearing," he said, spitting out each word, "that is . . . Rebekah's wedding dress."

I remember the feeling of my knees giving way, of other people's hands guiding me down to a chair. I heard Jonah say, "Max, calm down," and Louisa add, "Let me take her upstairs and put something else on her," their voices thick, mingling under dark water. I saw Max pacing, driving his hands through his hair, just like that hot day he'd pulled up in front of my shabby townhouse, desperately trying to come up with a plan that could keep us together. This was his plan. *Come to Asherley with me*, he said. *You'll be happy here.*

My eyes sought Dani's. "Did you do this to me?"

She gave me the slightest of shrugs. "Would you even believe me if I said no?"

Max spoke with a ferocious calm. "Dani, go upstairs. To *your* room. Shut *your* bedroom door. And stay there until the guests leave. Then I will decide what to do with you."

"Why? What did I do, Daddy?" she asked. "I want you to tell me what I did. Say it out loud."

"Don't play with me right now."

"You think I did this? You think *I* put her in Mum's wedding dress?"

"I can't even look at you," he said.

She turned to me. "Don't you see what's happening? *They're* doing this!" She looked at Louisa, the corners of her mouth turning down. "Even you."

Louisa was so stricken by this accusation, Jonah had to steady her down to a chair next to me.

"Dani!" Max yelled. "I'm telling you—"

"They're trying to make me seem crazy so they can put me away again—"

"Dani!"

"—this time for good, so he can take charge of the money and start a family with you, the pure and innocent new wife who'll obey him like a good little Winter girl."

"Dani, upstairs!"

"You're just jealous of me. You've always resented me because she only loved *me*, not you."

I leapt up and grabbed Max's arm, afraid he might lunge at Dani, who stood there clutching at her own dress, leaving sweaty, star-shaped handprints on the black satin.

"Please believe me. I told you he's never loved me. Only *she* loved me." She burst into tears, throwing her head back like an anguished toddler, sinking to her knees in front of me, a human being coming apart at my feet. "Please believe me," she wailed, lurching towards the hem of my dress, Rebekah's dress. When I flinched from her, her expression was that of a puppy that had just taken a rolled-up newspaper to the nose.

Louisa rushed to lift her off the ground, and Dani shoved her violently.

"Get away from me, you bitch!"

Louisa turned to stone.

"Dani, leave," Max seethed.

She stood up, smoothed down her dress, and used both hands to flick the tears off her cheeks. "Oh, don't worry, *Daddy*, I'll leave. And when I do, I'll tell everyone what you did. I might be crazy but I'm not stupid. I remember what happened in here that night!" she yelled on her way out of the greenhouse. "I saw!"

I'll never forget Max's face in that moment. He looked defeated, like a king watching the slaughter of his army from a high hill. My skin suddenly flushed, my whole body in mutiny against this horror of a dress. It was suffocating me, squeezing the air out of me. I wanted to rip it off and run screaming into the cold bay. Now I, too, fled from the room in tears, not caring who saw me in the kitchen, an obstacle course of caterers and milling guests, eyes widening as I passed. By then the dress felt as though it would burst into flames were I in it a second longer. Louisa called after me as I took to the stairs in twos, but I kept running. I didn't want anyone to touch me or even look at me.

I went one flight up and then another, carried by a wave of anger so potent I understood how murder can be a crime of passion. I slapped open the door at the top of the turret, then locked it behind me. I knew I'd find her there, against her father's orders, standing with her back to me, blowing smoke out an open window, and yes, it crossed my mind to push her. It was at least five stories high with only concrete below. *Do it*, I heard myself say. *Why don't you? Tell Max she jumped before you could save her. Who would dispute her instability? Think how happy you'd be if she were gone from here forever.* What stopped me wasn't my moral code, I'm ashamed to say, but rather fear that the fall wouldn't kill her, and that I'd be the one leaving Asherley in handcuffs.

Dani turned around, holding her cigarette aloft, acting like a bored actress. But it was a facade; her face, like mine, was stained with tears. "I guess they really have you where they want you, don't they?"

Louisa knocked, tried the handle. She called our names. We both ignored her.

"Why would you do this to me?" I cried, holding a fistful of lace. "Why? Answer me."

"Yup. You've been turned."

"I don't know what you're talking about, Dani. All I know is you tricked me into wearing this . . . *her* dress, for some insane reason. Why would you humiliate me like this? To get back at your father? For what? For falling in love with someone so disappointing to you? For trying to move on with his life? We were getting along so well. What is *wrong* with you?"

"Oh, there's a *lot* wrong with me, I know that. But I didn't do *this*." She blew out a long stretch of smoke and took a step closer. "Mr. Winter is a bad man. My mother didn't make it out alive. I don't think you will, either."

"How can you say that about a man who saved you from—"

"Saved me from what?"

She came closer still, studying my face, sensing a secret lodge inside like a dog at a foxhole. I scrambled to change the subject. "Nothing, I was going to say . . . that I'm only trying to find my place here."

"Well, you did, didn't you? In my father's bed. So congratulations. From lowly boat girl to the mistress of Asherley in a few months. Damn. The sex *must* be good because frankly I'm not seeing it here," she said, circling my face with her cigarette. "And you were right about the dress. It looks like shit on you."

Suddenly I felt very tired of her, of her childishness, her threats and dramas. Even my tears had evaporated by then. Rebekah's dress felt like nothing against my skin; I forgot I was wearing it. And if Dani was a product of Rebekah's mothering, even Rebekah ceased to be my antagonist. They may not have been related by blood, but fifteen-year-old girls don't learn this particular brand of toxicity, the insults, the shaming, the trickery, from men. They learn it from other women.

I was reminded in that moment of every superhero movie I'd ever seen, when the cartoon idols acquire their particular power, usually while staring defeat in the face, or death. I felt flooded now with something new. It didn't come from outside of me; it wasn't otherworldly. It felt familiar, always there, radiating from within and now coating me like a protective shield. I could only describe it as a warm sense of myself, something that had been placed there by people who loved me. Dani could never win because she had no idea what this feeling was or even what this fight was really about.

"Dani, I know you think I'm an awful little gold digger, an evil stepmonster who's only marrying your father for his money. But you don't know anything about me, or my life, or the things I've had to endure up until now. You've never been left alone to fend for yourself, treated like a dog, ordered around, used, disrespected, all day, every day. You've never been poor or hungry or worried about where you'd live if you left a job that was killing you, after it killed your last remaining parent. You've never worked twelve hours a day under a hot sun, then six more serving drunk men who might or might not make a move on you just for the fun of it. And you have to let them because you need the job so you can eat. You wouldn't last a minute in my old life. Your first callus would send you crying to your daddy. So don't talk to me about who you *think* I am, or what I did before I met your father, who, by the way, was the first man since my own father died to show me some respect and decency and kindness. When I laid eyes on Asherley I didn't think that I'd hit some jackpot. I just . . . I felt *safe* for the first time in a long time. You know nothing about why I'm here or how I love. Because I bet in your brief, trite little life you've never done

one goddamn thing for another human being if there wasn't something in it for you."

She just stood there, no rebuttal percolating, her triumphant sneer gone, makeup cried off, hair a wilted mess, cigarette ash freckling the carpet. I reached around the back of Rebekah's wedding dress, unzipped it, and let it fall in a pile around my ankles. Then I gathered it up in my fist and threw it at Dani before turning to walk back to my room wearing only my bra, stockings, and heels.

TWENTY-FIVE

That rainy April afternoon, I married Max Winter in the great hall at Asherley, wearing a forgettable dress Louisa had brought to wear to the reception. The *Times* photographer was sent home with apologies, agreeing with Max that the ceremony had turned too dark to document, going so far as to erase the photos so they'd never resurface to embarrass us, especially Dani. It began to thunder just as we were told by the officiant to kiss, punctuating the day so perfectly that there was nothing left to do but laugh.

The way Max looked at me that night, the admiration I felt, his pride, his deep amity, sustained me through the worst of it. I did my best to move from couple to couple, all of whom I was meeting for the first time, under the worst and best circumstances of my life. But towards the end of the evening, when the first of the guests announced they were leaving, it opened up a floodgate of departures. Valets brought a dozen big black SUVs around. One by one the guests fled down the drive like a high-speed funeral procession, tires spinning up great walls of puddle water. Katya cleaned up, having never really ceded the job to the caterers anyway. Max sent her home with slabs of food to drop at a local shelter and instructions not to come in for a few days, a reprieve for which she was grateful.

All the while Dani remained out of our sight. But I could sense her above us, pacing, smoking, hatching plans, our little mad girl in the attic.

Most parties die in the kitchen, and there we found ourselves gathered around the island, Max, Jonah, and I, tired yet vibrating from the residual energy that had abruptly drained from Asherley. Louisa volunteered to check on Dani, Max being too angry still, and I too afraid.

Max reached to touch my face as though to see if a fever had broken. "How are you holding up, Mrs. Winter?"

"I'm okay," I said, smiling. I meant it. Hours earlier I had stood mortified in front of a crowd of strangers in the greenhouse. But now I was among family, my new family, and I felt buoyed by their sympathy.

"You married a remarkable woman, Max," Jonah said, pouring scotch into his coffee. "Most would have crumbled after that terrible incident. Louisa told me you really gave it to Dani."

Just then Louisa returned holding an empty bottle of champagne. "That's what you get when you lock me out of a room." She carefully placed the bottle on the counter. "Dani's out like a light, all tucked in with her little kitten. She'll be very hungover tomorrow, but much more reasonable, I suspect. Maybe this time she'll volunteer for rehab."

"I've already put in a call to intake," Max said, his hands around a mug of coffee. "And Dr. Sherman's been notified."

Louisa slapped the marble. "Listen, why don't you two go on a honeymoon after all? I know you wanted to take Dani, but if she's going to rehab . . . We can check in on her while you're away, can't we?"

Jonah looked alarmed. "What I saw tonight put the fear of God and of teenage girls in me, this one in particular," he said. "Almost made me glad we had shit luck in the baby department. No offense, Max. But you two have your hands full."

The notion of no longer delaying our honeymoon did appeal. Maybe that's all we needed, space between Dani and us. Not Paris. Somewhere neither of us had any history.

"Let's talk about it tomorrow," Max said, letting out a yawn. "All this teenage subterfuge has knocked my lights out. We need our rest to deal with the little beast in the morning." He put his arm around me and kissed the side of my head.

"Well, we can take a hint," Louisa said. "Husband, fetch my coat and bag, will you?"

"Oh. Wait," I said. "Let me change out of your dress."

"Return it another time. We'll leave you two alone now. It is your wedding night, after all. And I hope not everything is ruined."

Louisa gave me a long embrace at the front door. Max walked them under an umbrella to their car. I stood there alone until their taillights disappeared down the drive, inhaling the musty forest smell the rain unleashed. Max joined me back on the porch, scooping me up into his arms so abruptly I let out a yelp.

"May I carry you over the threshold of your home, Mrs. Winter?" He stepped inside and gently placed my bare feet back down on the cold marble. "Welcome to Asherley. What a horribly lovely day we've had."

Despite the earlier drama and the late hour, I was no shy bride that night. I seemed to be using his body to blot out the memory of myself in Rebekah's cursed dress. I took his hands and placed them where I wanted to erase her: my breasts, where her strange lace had touched me; my waist, where her red sash had cut me in half; and my face, where tiny brushstrokes had painted me into a darker version of myself.

Afterwards Max fell fast asleep, but I drifted in and out for hours. I kept coming up against the two obstacles in the way of my complete happiness. One I could do nothing about. Rebekah's memory would always permeate our lives, stoked in large part by Dani, who was the second, more complicated obstacle. I felt guilty about my earlier rage, but I still allowed myself the fantasy of a blissful life without her lurking around every corner, sabotaging my happiness, undermining my relationship with Max. Perhaps there was a school she could attend far from here. Maybe Paris for a year. I couldn't go back to living under the same roof as someone who could pull that kind of stunt, who could career from generosity to humiliation, from good to evil, from sweet to mean in minutes. It was destabilizing. I thought I'd seen glimmers of something resembling reason, but I was wrong. She needed the kind of help I was not equipped to provide. I was done. The day had sapped me of my last reserves of kindness.

Sleep had finally begun to pull me under when a horrible scream cut through the still, dark house, one so high-pitched and mournful it didn't sound real at first, or even human.

Max shot upright in bed. "What was *that*?"

His feet had barely touched the floor before another scream came. This time we knew it was Dani. Max bolted ahead of me downstairs. I needed to hold the balustrade, terror turning my legs to liquid. I caught up to him in the kitchen, where he already had Dani pinned to the floor, her arms and legs flailing beneath him, her eyes horror-stricken.

"Dani, Dani, shh," Max said, using what seemed to be all his strength to contain her. "It's all right, it's all right, you're all right."

Her nightgown was filthy at the knees, the collar pulling at her neck as she tried to break free of Max. I fell on the floor beside them, reaching for her hands, her nails black with dirt.

"Dani, what happened?"

She pointed down the hall that led to the greenhouse, opening and shutting her mouth like a fish fighting for air on the deck of a boat. No words came out. I smelled the wine on her breath.

"I s-s-s-saw her. In there," she stammered, her body still convulsing with terror. "I saw her!"

"Who?" She crawled towards me, clutching at me. I pushed the hair out of her sweaty face. "Tell me what happened."

She looked at Max, her face panic-stricken. "*Why?*"

"Stay here with her. Do not move," he hissed. "Do *not* let go of her."

I nodded, Dani's terror mingling with my own. Max headed to the greenhouse.

Dani began clawing my upper arms, her voice a desperate rasp. "Listen to me. I saw her. She's in there."

"Who, Dani?"

"*My mother.*"

She was drunk, but she believed this madness. By then I could hear Max in the greenhouse, throwing stuff about, a bang, a shuffle, overturning tables or chairs.

"Dani, you're not well."

"You have to believe me. She's in there. I saw her," she said, slumping back onto the floor. "I'm gonna be sick."

I left her to retch on the floor while I ran to grab a bowl and to wet a tea towel, which I brought to Dani's forehead. Then the noise in the greenhouse abruptly stopped.

"Dani, stay here. I'll be right back," I said over her retching.

I stood. Slowly I made my way down the dim hallway to see what had unsettled her, what had Max in a frenzy. It was quiet. Too quiet. Just as I reached the greenhouse door, Max swiftly exited, his body blocking my view. He looked shattered.

"Sweetheart, please don't go in there."

Over his shoulder, I caught a glimpse of what looked to be a dirty wig on the ground next to a deep hole.

"What *is* that?"

"That's . . . the kitten."

"Oh God. *Maggie!*"

He spun me around and forcefully walked me back to the kitchen, where we found Dani tripping over her own vomit, trying to stand up.

I ran to her.

"We need to get out of here," she slurred, tumbling to the floor, taking me back down with her. Max crouched in front of us, trying to secure eye contact with Dani, but she was lolling drunk.

"Dani, honey, look at me. Look at me."

"*No.* Stay *away* from me." She burrowed herself deeper into my arms like a terrified animal, shaking her head at him.

Max made a "phone call" gesture. "Do not move from her this time," he whispered. "Stay. Right. Here."

Dani kept her eyes trained on him. As soon as he rounded the corner to the den, she turned to me. "Did you see?"

"See what?" *Oh, Maggie. Poor Maggie.*

"My *mother.*"

"No one's in there, sweetheart."

"I'll show you."

She made another feeble attempt to stand. I restrained her, pinning her back down with me on the floor. Moments later Max returned, cradling the phone to his ear, listening, pacing the hall to the greenhouse like a goalie guarding a net.

"Yes . . . yes, but worse this time," he murmured. "Delusions again, but now . . . violence, maybe. I don't know . . . Yeah, I found some from the last time . . . Okay . . . We'll wait right here. Thank you. Thank you so much."

He hung up and handed me a small white pill.

"Here," he said. "Under her tongue, if you can. Dr. Sherman's coming, Dani."

I hesitated to put my fingers near her mouth, but when Dani saw the pill, she opened up like a hungry bird. Max brought her a glass of water but she would only take it from my hand. She took a gulp, then handed the glass back to me. She tapped her head with her index finger.

"Guess what, Daddy?" she hissed. "I remembered all about that night, what happened in the greenhouse." Her filthy hands suddenly distracted her. "*Wow*. Look how gross my nails are. They're like yours," she said, laughing up at me.

"Dani, rest," Max said.

She continued to ignore him, turning again to me. "I'm sorry I threw up. I'm sorry for everything."

"That's okay, sweetheart," I said, patting her sweaty head. "I forgive you. Just rest now, okay?"

"I know I did some bad stuff, but I didn't do the dress. I don't hate you. But *he* hates me," she said, going a bit limp in my arms. The pill started to kick in and soon she was staring blankly at the floor, not awake but not asleep.

Twenty minutes we stayed like that on the floor, in our pitiful Pietà, while Max ran upstairs to pack Dani a bag and

some toiletries. Then he cleaned up the vomit and straightened the kitchen. When the doorbell finally rang, Dani
didn't hear it. She barely noticed Max returning with two
ambulance attendants pulling a quiet gurney behind them.
But at the sight of a tiny older woman, white-haired and
calm, she threw open her arms like a toddler wanting to be
picked up.

"Dr. Sherman!" she exclaimed.

The doctor gathered Dani in her arms and they fell into a
familiar routine, the doctor asking her gentle questions, Dani
murmuring answers.

"It was very good champagne, Dr. Sherman."

"I bet it was. How much of it did you have, love?"

"Maybe like half a bottle. No, a whole one."

"What else?"

She shrugged.

I looked at Max, who closed his eyes. He looked helpless,
ashamed.

"Dani, I have to know for your own good."

"One teensy Valium. Three at the most."

"And?"

"She gave me a little white one," she said, lifting her limp
hand in my general direction. The doctor gave a brisk nod to
the attendants, who gently pried Dani from the doctor's arms
and placed her across the gurney, strapping her down.

When they started to roll her away, I grabbed a rail. "Wait.
Where are you taking her? Max, we have to go with her."

Max and the doctor exchanged a look. They'd done this
before.

"She needs to be detoxed first," the doctor said. "Until
then there's nothing for you to do."

267

"The rehab's not far from here," Max told me. "One of the best in the country. We can visit in a couple days. Dani, honey, we'll come see you as soon as you're out of detox."

Dani found the last reserve of clarity not blotted out by the champagne, or the pills. She twisted her body around the side of the gurney and addressed me as though we were alone.

"You have to believe me. I need you to believe me."

"Oh, Dani." I reached for her again. She seemed so lost and alone.

Max came to my side. "Dr. Sherman is going to help you, Dani," he said, walking beside the gurney to the front door. "You're a good girl, Dani. We know it was an accident."

"Noooo!" she wailed, squirming under the straps. "Don't *say* that! I know I'm good. It's you that's bad!"

Once she was rolled out of earshot, Dr. Sherman turned to Max. "I'll call you once we check her in. How did the kitten . . . ?"

"Broken neck, I think," Max said quietly. "She seemed to be in the process of burying it. It might be what set this off. My hope is that she found the kitten that way."

"I've never known her to be violent," said the doctor. "But anyway, we can talk about a plan in a couple of days, once I've assessed her." She turned to me. "It was nice to meet you. Sorry it's under such distressing circumstances."

The wheels of the gurney had a tricky time on the wet driveway, pocked with little puddles from the rain. I thought of the last time I had seen my father alive, how frightened I was navigating the boat around those bloated cruise ships, racing him to the dock and the waiting ambulance. I remembered the white sun glinting off the hot chrome of his gurney and the doomed sense that my entire life had just changed in an instant, and none of it required my permission. That happened to Dani that morning. Her gurney was swallowed into the ambulance like a tongue rolling back into a large steel mouth. She would never live at Asherley again.

TWENTY-SIX

Max closed the front door and gathered me into his arms. We stayed like that for a long time, Asherley thrumming hollowly around us. Even on the days I hadn't seen Dani's face I always knew she was somewhere in the house, watchful and coiled. Now the house felt dead inside, the only sounds coming from the morning crows that had a habit of screaming at their own reflections in the east windows. Everything hurt. It hurt to think, to talk, to breathe, to hold on to him, and to finally release him.

"I'm sorry," Max said.

"For what?"

"I'm sorry about Dani. What she did to you. What she's going through. I knew she was off, I just didn't realize how badly she was spiraling."

"I wish I could have done more, too," I said.

"Listen, we have plenty of time to admonish ourselves for the mistakes we made, mistakes *I* made. But you." He stopped to carefully tug something from my hair. "You need a shower."

I looked down at my vomit-spattered robe.

"Not how you hoped to spend the morning after your wedding. Listen, I'll join you in a minute, after I bury that poor kitten."

"Let me help you. I'm not squeamish. I'd like to see how she died."

"*No.* No. I don't want you to go in there, or see that," he said. "You've already been through enough grief. I mean it."

"You think it was an accident?"

"I don't know. I hope so. Go. You're starting to turn," he said, scrunching his nose and nudging me towards the stairs.

I didn't go straight to our room. I went up to the third floor, looking for something that would explain Dani's state of mind. Her room had been left in shambles, clothes everywhere, empty wine bottles scattered about, an overflowing ashtray on the windowsill—evidence of substance abuse on her part, neglect on ours.

I headed to the turret and was surprised to find the door unlocked. All these months I'd wanted to come up here alone, to lay across Rebekah's bed, to try on her jewelry, her perfumes, not the way it was with Dani, manipulative, under duress, but leisurely, sensually. I wanted to savor my discoveries, like a girl left in a department store overnight. But now I hated these rooms. Where I once envied the majestic gilt mirrors, the circle of windows bracketed by creamy drapes hanging like long hair, the closet full of beautiful clothes, now everything felt ludicrous and unnecessary. In fact it was here where Rebekah's memories were stored, in these rooms, not the greenhouse. And it was here where Dani incubated her anxieties and cultivated her delusions, especially the ones about her father and what had really happened that night. Perhaps she needed to hear the truth, needed to know everything there was to know about both of her mothers. Maybe after she healed and got some help, we'd tell her everything, so she could put it all behind her and start anew.

This room, too, was in total disarray, clothes piled on the marbled island, some flung on the backs of chairs and over doors. When I opened the closet door, I was hit by the smell of Maggie's litter box. My heart sunk again. Poor little thing, a victim of my misplaced trust in Dani. Hangers hung crooked in the closet, clothes barely holding on. I could still detect Rebekah's perfume hovering in the air, musky and expensive.

Stepping over Maggie's crusty food bowls, I spotted it, the cursed dress, the red sash like stray guts down its side, the hanger poking from the lace bodice like a broken collarbone. I knew what I needed to do while Dani was away; I would remove everything that had been coming between Max and me, and Dani and me, starting with that goddamned dress. Every curtain in the house needed to be flung open to the light, every side table emptied of her pictures and mementos, all the walls painted white, blank slates for new stories, *our* stories, every room purged of ghosts.

I went to the window overlooking the brown bay. Dawn was breaking over a sickly gray sky, yet from here it was clear enough to see all the way to Orient Point. A night of rain had begun to turn the lawns green and brought out the pink in the hydrangea bushes that edged them. I must learn the names of everything that lives and grows here, I thought, and of all people in the paintings and all the flowers in the gardens. We could open the pool soon, have parties. There should be so much more life here. A dog or two. Children, of course; I was ready. That would be my focus, that and caring for Dani, helping her get well again, in order for Asherley to thrive under her eventual watch. I no longer felt afraid of Dani, just *for* her. She was a damaged, angry child. She was the exile, not me. I was the one standing in the turret, overlooking the expanse of grounds, surveying the land, making plans.

Everything must go, I thought. I'm Mrs. Winter now.

★

I took a hot shower, threw on jeans and a T-shirt. As I headed downstairs, I could hear chatter in the foyer. There I found Max, who'd also changed into jeans and a T-shirt, a hand propped against the open door. He was speaking to two police officers, a man and a woman. He seemed relaxed. But when he turned to me, I saw that his eyes were bloodshot, his face drawn, his jaw tense. He had aged overnight. Even his hair seemed whiter, the lines on his forehead more pronounced. I wondered if the officers could tell that his affable voice did not match his dour expression.

"Ah, here is my wife now," he said, extending his arm and draping it around my shoulders. *My wife.*

"I understand you got married yesterday. Congratulations," the female officer said, handing me her business card.

"Thank you. Is this about Dani? Is she all right?"

"They're explaining to me that apparently before they took her phone away at the detox, Dani managed to call the police to tell them what she told us, that she'd seen a dead body in the greenhouse. And they take these things seriously around here, no matter how ludicrous the claim or how young and drunk the claimant."

"We do take that seriously," said the female officer.

"Did you tell them what she might have seen?" I asked Max.

The male officer jumped in. "The doctor mentioned a dead kitten. But Dani said that's not what she saw. She said the kitten was alive when she last saw it."

"Well, you know Dani's got quite an imagination. I think you've dealt with her before, haven't you?" Max said to the female officer. "Was it shoplifting, or the fire she started on the Wolitzers' dock?"

"Underage drinking."

"Right," Max said. "She keeps us all very busy."

"We could take a quick look around," she offered, like a favor. "Reassure her there's nothing to worry about."

I looked at Max. Why wasn't he inviting the police inside? *Let them go see for themselves*, I wanted to say. Even if he'd buried the kitten while I showered, it wouldn't be too difficult to dig her back up again and show them. Then we could close the chapter on this grim story.

But the way he gripped my shoulder, the tension I felt in his ribs, his lower back—somehow I sensed it was best to say nothing.

"I don't want you to think I'm rude," Max said, his voice low and stern. I gathered the back of his T-shirt in my hand to steady him. "And I do very much appreciate the job you do, and the fact that you take these things seriously. It's reassuring to me as a citizen, and as your senator. But, for the sake of my very sick and very young daughter, if you want to step foot inside Asherley, you'll need to return with a warrant, and assurances from you and your direct supervisor that you will not leak this sad incident to the press. Dani already had an embarrassing meltdown in front of some important people yesterday. This would send her over the edge before she even has a chance to recover."

"Of course, Mr. Winter," the male officer said. "We're not implying—"

"Yes, you are. You're implying that there might be some veracity to my daughter's claims that she saw a *dead body* in the greenhouse—her late mother, if we're going by what she said just before she was strapped onto a gurney and wheeled out of here ranting and raving and covered in her own vomit."

"Max, it's all right," I whispered.

"Mr. Winter, we're very sorry—"

"But I'll say this, without the benefit of a lawyer present. My lovely, *ill* daughter did not see her dead mother. My daughter saw a dead kitten. How it died, we don't know. But I do know she did not kill it. She doesn't have that in her. She loved the little thing. But she was wasted and upset. Our wedding was a happy day for us, but it was not a happy one for her. What I suspect is that she found the kitten dead—a lot of cars came and went from here yesterday, and it was raining heavily. And she wanted to bury it somewhere dry. But if you insist on indulging her sad and drunken delusions, then come back with a warrant. And I will get my lawyers involved so at least *I* can protect her, since you two officers don't seem to be doing that."

They stood there blinking at Max, each waiting for the other to say something. I was speechless, too.

"Well," the male officer said finally, "we'll be on our way, then. We're very sorry to have bothered you."

"Will you be around later today, Mr. Winter?" the female officer said, as if she hadn't heard a word he'd said.

Max inhaled deeply. I tightened my grip on the back of his shirt.

"Yes, I'm sorry," he said, much more calmly. "Forgive me. It's been a long night. But we'll be here. Until my daughter gets better, we're not going anywhere."

They said their goodbyes and he closed the door. Then he bent forward, his hands on his knees.

"Fuck," he hissed. "*Fuck.*"

"It's okay, Max." I peered through the peephole, watching as the detectives got back in their car. "They're leaving."

He straightened his back and looked at me, letting out a strangled sort of cry, as if it had been stuck in his throat and now it was safe to let it out.

"You're worrying me."

He capped his head with his hands and squeezed his eyes shut.

"What is it?"

"I need you to do something for me."

"Anything," I said, placing a hand on his flushed face.

"Leave Asherley for the day. Don't ask why. I'll call Louisa and tell her to expect you."

"I'm not going to do that, Max. Tell me what's going on."

He walked towards the kitchen. I trailed after him as he spoke.

"Go there now. Stay there until you hear from me. I'll meet up with you tonight. We can have dinner somewhere, the four of us."

"Slow down. What's wrong? I don't think the police are going to come back, if that's what you're worried about. Besides, even if they get a warrant, all they'll find is a little dead cat!"

"Ha. God, you *are* naive," he spat.

This felt like a slap. The man who said those words to me wasn't my kind, caring husband, understandably distraught at his daughter's breakdown. This man was a stranger to me. Reluctantly, I followed him into the kitchen, where he began to throw open drawers, lift and toss lids, kick out the stools.

"Where's my phone?" he grumbled, stalking about. "I have to call Eli."

I joined the search, waiting for normal Max to resurface. But he was gone, replaced by someone frantic, cornered. He kept pacing, muttering unintelligibly, pinching the skin between his brows as if to dig out a solution from inside his own skull. Finally, he patted himself down, finding his phone in his front pocket, something we might have laughed about any other morning.

"Max, tell me how to help."

"I told you what you can do," he said, scrolling his contacts. "Leave. Right now."

We had only been married one day and he was throwing me out of his home.

"Talk to me. I love you. I want to help."

"You *think* you love me. But you don't. You won't."

I didn't know how to respond to this. I'd spent days, weeks, worrying whether he might wake up and realize the mistake he was making in marrying me, but for me to stop loving him? Impossible.

He tapped the screen and held the phone to his ear, avoiding my eyes, which were now brimming with tears. When he began to speak, the sane, reasonable Max surfaced.

"Eli. Max . . . To be honest not a wink." He recounted the events of the night before, wincing at the part about Maggie, ending with the visit from the police. "Look, I don't know if they're going to make a big deal about it. I fucking hope not . . . Well, I wasn't *nice*. But Dani's so fragile right now . . . No threats. Just your usual pressure. I just don't want this to get out, not after yesterday . . . No. Just need a day or two, long enough to figure out what happened . . . Yeah. She's okay. She's going to Louisa's. She's had a rough couple days . . . Yes, a trouper. No, no, no, don't come out. We're fine."

He sounded so loving on the phone with Elias. But when he hung up, he sunk down onto a stool, exhaling as though he'd just spent the last vestiges of his energy on that call.

"Okay. Where were we? Yes, you're going to pack a bag and drive to Louisa's. I'll meet you tonight."

"I told you. I'm not going anywhere until you tell me what's going on."

"We're not fighting about this."

"I know that."

He looked at me plainly. "Do you love me?"

"Yes, very much."

"Then you'll do as I ask."

"That's not how it works. I want to know what's going on. And you have to tell me."

"I can't."

"Why? Max, you *know* you can tell me anything."

"If I told you this, you would leave and never come back here."

"Then you don't know me."

I placed a stool directly in front of him and sat. I was now his benevolent interrogator, our knees touching. I watched his face go through a remarkable series of emotions, from stubborn coldness to pity for me to reluctant surrender.

"I'm very tired," he said. "Of all of it. Of everything."

"We had a long night."

"No, I'm tired of the lies. If you hadn't been here when the police came just now, I would have happily raised my wrists for the handcuffs. I would have told them to take me to the station. Because I have nothing left in me. No fight left."

My blood cooled. Hairs on the back of my neck lifted.

"She was right," he continued, his eyes welling up. "She said she'd win everything in the end. She was right."

"Who?"

He said nothing for a moment. Then he let out a laugh. "God, Dani's *smart*, isn't she." He sounded like a proud father. "She's *so* smart. Rebekah always focused on her looks, trying to get her hair just right, sending her off to dance lessons and manicures. But that girl's got a *hell* of a brain. I always said she could be anything she wanted to be, if she could just develop some character. Did I ever tell you how beautiful her mother was?"

"You didn't need to. There's evidence of that all over this house."

He smiled at me. "You think I'm talking about Rebekah. No, she was all makeup and filters and some very good work. I'm talking about Dani's birth mother. Before the drugs took over. When she was young, she had this natural beauty. She was completely unaware of it. Like you. Too bad she had none of your goodness. *She* said she'd win everything in the end. And she just might be right."

"But . . . she's dead."

"I know. I was there."

"Where?"

"About a mile from here."

"Wait, who are you talking about?"

"Dani's mother. She died about a mile from here. Right after she smashed the car into a tree." He sounded blithe, matter-of-fact. "She was alive. Briefly. She looked right at me. And then . . . the car exploded. The fire spread so quickly. I couldn't . . ."

No. That's not right. Now I was angry. What he was saying was very wrong. These were not the correct facts, not the ones he'd given me, that I had memorized, had turned over and over again like worry stones in my pocket. I took him by the shoulders.

"Max, no. That's how *Rebekah* died. You told me *Rebekah* smashed her car into a tree and *that* started a fire. And Dani's mother died later. In the city. Are you now telling me that Dani's mother was driving the car?"

"Yes."

"But I don't understand. Then where was Rebekah? How did Rebekah die?"

His answer came swiftly and unadorned.

"She was murdered. In the greenhouse," he said, "a couple of feet from where I buried her."

TWENTY-SEVEN

I felt myself pulled backwards, the walls expanding around us, curving as if time itself were slowing down so I could take in this madhouse version of events. My senses heightened like an animal's, tuning in and out of every sound and sensation: the hum of the fan above the stove, the angry crows outside, my heart banging against my rib cage. I looked towards the hallway that led to the greenhouse, fully expecting Rebekah to be standing there, summoned by the confession, a gray specter in a bloody dress.

"Max."

His gaze was on the floor. I clapped loudly. He blinked at me a few times, until he recognized my face.

"Before the police come back with a warrant, you have to tell me. Is Rebekah still buried in the greenhouse?"

"Yes."

I reeled. *Poor Dani. She was telling the truth.*

"Did you . . . did *you* kill Rebekah?"

He got up from the stool and paced, stopping to tent his fingers on the island to steady himself, like a lawyer prepping an opening statement.

"No. I didn't kill Rebekah. You have to believe that before I tell you anything else."

I didn't know what to look for on his face; I was not a trained expert on lying. All I knew was that in that moment, and much to my relief, he looked and sounded like Max again, the man I loved, who I had always taken at his word.

"Do you believe me?"

"I do. Yes. But if you didn't kill her, who did?"

"Dani's mother."

I closed my eyes. The story Dani told me about that night collided with Max's, forming something new, and so much darker.

"It was self-defense. I think."

"You think?"

"I—I left the greenhouse. For *one* fucking minute. To make sure Dani didn't see . . . *oh God*." Again his eyes drifted to the hallway, the anxiety creeping back in around his eyes and forehead.

I guided him back down onto a stool.

"Max, focus. Tell me everything. From the beginning, please."

"Yes . . . yes."

I filled two glasses with water and placed them in front of us, marveling at how my arms and legs moved, seemingly without my command.

"Everything starts with her. It always does." He took a sip of water, whipping the rest back like a scotch. "Louisa met her first, at some silly fundraiser. She said, Max, I found her. The one. She's beautiful *and* she has a fortune. Rebekah knew about our name, our history, the land, the dilemma of an heir. She came from new money, Russian, very questionable, very considerable. You see, I married her for Asherley. We desperately needed an influx of cash, a lot of cash, to pay back taxes and to update the house in critical ways. Especially the causeway. We couldn't keep boating back and forth. The channel needed constant dredging. Louisa and I have a trust, but it was drying up, our credit in the toilet. We'd reached the outer limits of what we could borrow. But to release Rebekah's fortune, I had to sign Asherley over to her as a guarantee. All of it. Under the condition it would all pass down to our heir.

"Louisa and Jonah had given up on having a baby, so it was up to me, otherwise we'd be the last Winters and the land would revert back to local jurisdiction. That was the deal the original Lord Winter made with King Charles. It's partly why I ran for office. Figure out a way to change this law without drawing attention to how I'd benefit. It's been tricky. I mean, I never used to care about the place. I wasted my youth on pretty girls from modest backgrounds to piss off my father. But you get older and these things start to matter, too much, I'm ashamed to say. And I didn't want to be the loser, the one who shamefully brings the whole thing crashing down."

So much was running through my mind while he spoke, but what stuck out most was this: if Max married Rebekah for money, then he must have married me for love. What other reason could there be?

"So we married. Suddenly I wasn't rich in name only. We were debt-free, taxes paid, causeway construction under way. Scaffolding appeared around Asherley for the first time in generations, and a trust was secured for future upkeep.

"Rebekah was thirty-six, so we didn't wait to try for a baby. After a year, and nothing, we got tested. We both checked out. She did hormone shots. IVF. We tried surrogacy, but our embryos weren't viable. Rebekah tried distracting herself, thinking a pregnancy would sneak up on her as it had her friends. She threw herself into renovating Asherley, built that detestable greenhouse. Her tastes were bold, showy, nothing like mine. Time passed. I thought we'd grow to love each other. But we drifted instead. The failure to have a baby created so much resentment and anxiety, it felt like a third person in our marriage. I resigned myself to letting all this go. But the more she threw herself into making over Asherley, the more obsessed she became with keeping it and in passing it on to our children, *her* children."

I thought back to those endless articles I'd scrolled through about Asherley's renaissance, Rebekah's glowing competency in every frame. Rebekah pointing and delegating, smelling roses, posing in front of beautiful tableaus of her creation. All of it a mask for what she really wanted: a baby.

"Then, at another one of Louisa's fundraisers, this one for low-income mothers, Rebekah met Dani's birth mother, who was six months pregnant. She still wasn't sure whether she wanted to keep the baby or give it up for adoption. She was also a younger replica of Rebekah. I mean, at certain angles the resemblance was uncanny. Of course this appealed to Rebekah's epic vanity, the possibility of having a child who looked like her. Apparently the father was some feckless punk from Bay Shore who had already fled the scene. I told you everything we knew about her, which wasn't much. Rebekah had this misguided notion that she would mentor her throughout the rest of the pregnancy, keep her away from bad influences, and then convince her to give up the child, privately, to us, of course. Rebekah began to spoil her. Something in me held back. I didn't trust her, or the situation.

"Rebekah insisted we put her up in a little place in Sag, to get away from *those* people. Louisa could check up on her, too, since the rental was close to the ferry. She became their little project. The baby was born early, small, but she was healthy.

"But then Dani's mother delayed the adoption. She'd do it after she was weaned, she said, after winter. Meanwhile, Rebekah fell hard for the baby, slept at the hospital, shopped for organic groceries. God, she was such an easy mark. I saw it happening. I *knew* it. I warned her. I said you've gotten way too close to that girl, Rebekah. She's going to hit us up hard, you watch. She's manipulating you. And sure enough, a few weeks later she tells Rebekah, if you want to see the baby again, you have to pay me, otherwise I have to leave Long Island because I can't afford to live here once you cut me off.

"So Rebekah *paid* to see the child, a few hundred here, a few thousand there. Then one day, she goes to the apartment and the girl says, Guess what? I got an offer. For a job? No, she said, for the baby. And it's a lot of money. I'm going to take it. I *need* to take it. Now. Rebekah begged her not to. She said whatever they're paying, we'll double it. So that's how we came to *buy* a baby."

"Why didn't Rebekah just go to the police? Or child services? Surely there'd be a way for you to keep her legally."

"Because she'd already broken the law when she gave Dani's mother all that money even *before* handing her a hundred thousand dollars. Behind my back, I might add. What could I do? She controlled our money." He gave a snort. "I mean *her* money. I was enraged. This was beyond my comprehension. But Rebekah lived above the law. It was Rebekah's money that bought the place in the Caymans, the boats, the trips to Paris. She set Louisa up nicely, too. She had already convinced me to run for office, but I postponed my

285

political plans. No way I could make our lives more public at that point.

"And then, big surprise, a couple years later, Dani's mother came back, broke, face hollowed out, teeth gray, hair the color of something you might find washed up on a beach. It was meth, painkillers. Both. I don't know. She walked across the causeway and around the gate through the forest. She was soaking wet. Rebekah gave her more money. But this time I got her to sign something that said she would never bother us again, but really it was adoption papers Jonah drew up and backdated. Totally illegal. He could lose his license to practice law, go to jail. But we couldn't mess around anymore. I really thought, I *hoped*, that this last windfall meant Dani's mother could indulge all of her addictions, surround herself with the dregs of the earth, and maybe, with any luck, overdose somewhere quickly and quietly to leave us in peace with our child. This was my wish for a troubled young woman. For her to die. And that's the story I've told you about her, and Jonah and Louisa, a story born of the darkest kind of wishful thinking. That's why all of this is happening now. My horrible thoughts brought a curse upon Asherley, on us."

"People do desperate things when they're afraid, Max," I said. "Dani was better off with you, regardless of the circumstances of her adoption. Can you imagine the life she'd have had with her mother?"

"We told ourselves that. And I wish I could say she had an idyllic childhood. As the years passed, Dani went from being a colicky baby to an enraged toddler to a difficult child. She did not play well with others. She couldn't keep a friend, sit through a class, behave with nannies. But damn it if

286

Rebekah wasn't determined to fix what was wrong with her. She took her everywhere, to every expert, tried every cocktail of medication, acupuncture, horse therapy, a dozen different camps. She'd last two days, wet the bed, pick a fight, and come home. She absolutely clung to Rebekah."

"She sounds like a devoted mother," I said. "No wonder Dani misses her so much."

"Ha. *That's* what you think? *That's* your takeaway? No. Despite how badly she wanted a baby, Rebekah didn't know what to do with a child, especially a needy, angry one. You've been a far better mother to that kid in four months than Rebekah was in thirteen years. Oh, don't get me wrong. She *wanted* to be a good mother. She said to me before Dani came, I'll be the best mother ever, Max. I'll make every mother in the Hamptons jealous. What she meant was she wanted to be *seen* as a good mother. That's all she knew how to do. The pictures she took, the magazine profiles, that cursed social media, every picture told the story of the perfect mother, Rebekah Winter."

He was right, that was the undisputed narrative. I'd seen the images, visited them over and over for clues on how to be a good mother myself. There she was cuddling the baby in soft focus, the two of them holding hands on the seashore, Rebekah spinning Dani around, throwing her in the air, hosting extravagant birthday parties with ponies and clowns, cheering her from the sidelines with the other perfect mothers. Max continued shattering these images, one by one, his hammer hitting the glass surfaces, the shards piling up around my feet. *Their marriage was a financial arrangement. Rebekah was craven and imperious. She broke the law. Her beauty was fake. She was a terrible mother.*

"Rebekah became increasingly depressed, frustrated, full of regrets. She would have these anxiety attacks. She wasn't consumed with guilt so much as buyer's remorse. Motherhood was harder than she thought it would be. Draining, unfulfilling, one-sided, boring, constant. I wish I could say I made up for it, that I was a good father. My own father was an asshole, distant, distracted, and I carried on that proud family tradition. I became like him, always away somewhere, always busy. Rebekah started drinking more. She snuck cigarettes. Went on lavish vacations, often leaving Dani behind to be cared for by a succession of nannies, none sticking around once she returned. Turns out Dani wasn't what was missing in our marriage. She was the bomb that destroyed it. And I will never forgive myself for not filling in the gaps Rebekah's disinterest created, for not being a better father, for letting Rebekah ruin that child. For not trying to be the father she deserved, until it was too late."

I reached for his hand, but he recoiled.

"Louisa tried. She's been a good aunt. She took her to New York, to Paris. She's invested in Dani's success, at least for Asherley's sake. But Louisa wasn't her mother. Dani wanted her mother. She wanted Rebekah. And the more Rebekah pulled away from her, the more clingy and desperate Dani became. She can be like that with me now. You've seen it."

"But Dani doesn't remember Rebekah this way at all. She idolizes her. Still. To this day."

"I know. It's a crazy thing. Kids are remarkably selective in what they want to believe. But a neglected baby monkey will love a fork covered in duct tape if that's all they're given to hold. And as Dani got older, she committed the ultimate sin by resembling Rebekah less and less. She was darker, swarthier, bonier, taking after the father, maybe. She tried desperately to win Rebekah's approval, to gain her attention, even demanded, at eleven, that we let her dye her hair the exact same color as Rebekah's. I'm ashamed that I ever said yes. But I couldn't say no to anything that pacified Dani, no one could, least of all Rebekah.

"When she turned twelve, she shot up, got those legs, her real mother's looks before the drugs ravaged her. And suddenly Rebekah had competition. She resented the attention Dani received, from anyone, especially me. So I pulled away even more, just to keep the peace.

"Then she came back again. Dani's mother. She showed up at the door that hot summer night almost two years ago. You know a part of the story. The air-conditioning was broken. The house was an oven. We sent Dani to bed. There was a knock at the door. But I left out the part about how Dani's mother . . . she looked different. She said she hitchhiked to East Hampton from Florida, where she'd been living after getting out of prison for some minor drug charge. That's where she got clean. I mean, I don't know if she was clean, but she looked healthy, almost pretty again. I asked if anyone saw her come out here or knew she was coming back to Long Island. She said no. She had no home, no friends, no family would talk to her anymore. This time, she said, she came for Dani. She wanted to get to know her daughter, and for Dani to know her. She'd changed, she said. She'd seen her on the local news campaigning with me and was so proud of her. We were months away from the election and I was doing well in the polls. Now *I* was the one offering her money to go away. But she said she didn't want money. Rebekah said, You promised this would stop, that this was over. I offered two hundred thousand, three, five, name your price, I said. I couldn't imagine this woman in our lives. She was clean now maybe, but for how long? I slapped car keys into her hand and said, Take the Jaguar. She threw the keys on the floor. I want to see Dani, she said. She's all I have left.

"That's when I said, Let's go into the greenhouse, so we don't wake Dani. I thought we'd reason with her. I thought we'd tell her about Dani's troubles, convince her how disruptive it would be to introduce them now, in the middle of the campaign. If we could just wait until later, we could introduce them the *right* way. I think I meant that. I really do.

"But once we were in the greenhouse she turned into her old threatening self again, saying, wouldn't everyone want to know that the future senator's wife was a shady criminal, that his Russian princess bought a baby from a desperate teenage drug addict? Isn't that illegal? Isn't that thirty years in prison? And guess what? I'd get custody of Dani, she said, your *heir*. Isn't that funny. I'd get the money *and* the baby. Maybe I'd even live here. I'd win in the end, she said, because the courts always side with the mother. The *real* mother.

"Then Rebekah laid into her, screaming at her, threatening her, telling her that our lawyers would annihilate her, unearth every rotten crime she'd ever committed these past thirteen years. I told her to keep it down. I ducked out quickly to check on Dani, in case she woke up. I couldn't have been gone more than two minutes, but when I returned . . . There'd been a struggle. I don't know who started it, but Dani's mother had . . . sunk gardening shears into Rebekah's neck. I'd never seen so much blood. I tried to stanch the flow with an old blanket, telling Dani's mother to call an ambulance, but she just stood there mumbling, I didn't mean to do that, I was defending myself, she came at me first.

"Rebekah just . . . bled out onto the dirt floor. She was dead in less than a minute."

Max clasped his hands in his lap, as if in surrender. A cold dread crept over me. The ghosts I'd felt were real. They'd been here all along.

"It finally dawned on Dani's mother what she'd done. She looked at me and . . . she ran. And all I could think was, I can't let her get away. What if she disappeared again? She was homeless, indigent. What if they think *I* killed Rebekah? Everything would come out. Buying a baby, faking an adoption, the payoffs. I threw a tarp across Rebekah's body and tipped a table in front of her, propping it up like a shield in case Dani came down looking for us. I shut off the lights. I locked the door behind me. Dani's mother had found the keys she'd thrown and taken off in the Jaguar. I ran to the garage to get my car. I remember Rebekah's blood on my hands.

"She was driving fast, reckless like Rebekah. I could see her taillights ahead of me, swerving to stay on the road. I knew the curves well. She didn't. I worried what I'd do if I caught up to her. What then? Would I kill her? I was afraid I would kill her. But sadly, she did me the favor."

He told me he heard the impact before he drove up to the scene of the crash, the front of the car accordioned into an old oak, Dani's mother slumped over the steering wheel, her hair a tangled curtain covering bone and blood where a pretty face used to be.

"She was almost dead," he said, "her body just crumpled. I couldn't get her out if I'd tried. And . . . I didn't try. I just . . .

left her there. I left her there, knowing she was almost dead, knowing the gates were closed and that no one would find her for hours."

His face was impassive.

"It all fell together, a plan. I had to create a scenario where there was just one dead body, just Rebekah's. And if Dani had to grieve the only mother she ever knew, she could not know her real mother had killed her. She'd never recover. There are things you do when you're desperate, things that would shock you. I raced back to the house. I had to make sure Dani stayed asleep. I had a lot to do. I washed my hands, put on a clean shirt, then I woke her, or so I thought. You see now what a terrifying thought it is, that she was awake that night after all. Anyway, I gave her some water with a crushed sleeping pill and rubbed her back until it knocked her out. Then I went downstairs, unlocked the greenhouse. I knelt by Rebekah's body. I said a prayer. I asked for her and for God's forgiveness for what I was about to do, but that it was the only way to put this all in the past for good. I removed her wedding rings. I wrapped her body in a large linen tablecloth, tied it with belts. Then I got out that portable backhoe and dug a hole. The whole time I comforted myself with the idea that were this legal, it's where she'd have wanted to be buried. I lowered her body down. I covered the hole with compost, clean dirt, and then a table."

I thought of how I had frolicked with Maggie in there, planted an imaginary garden, hosted a wedding of all things.

"It was two thirty in the morning by then. I drove back to the crash site with several cans of gasoline from the boathouse. She was dead. I checked to make sure. I placed Rebekah's rings on her finger and I doused the car and the

292

perimeter, and I watched it burn for a while. I didn't mean to light up six acres, but it was a small sacrifice, I suppose, to the gods, in exchange for a fire that rendered her body completely unidentifiable, except for three diamonds melted in a pool of gold."

He straightened up, relieved of some of the weight of the story. "I've done many awful, selfish things in my life," he continued. "But bringing you here, marrying you, lying to you, and now dumping all of this on you are among the worst. Sometimes I think I fell in love with you knowing that everything would come to light, that Dani's mother would win, that I'd go to jail and Dani would need looking after by someone good. Someone like you. Would you do that? Take care of Dani for me? I do love her, you know. She drives me crazy, but I do."

Throughout his confession, I passed through every emotion: fear, confusion, anger, resentment. But one rose above the rubble, a dissolute kind of joy. Max had said I was a better mother to Dani than Rebekah ever was. I could be a better wife, too, because now there were no secrets between us and I could help him. I could fix this. Max wasn't going to lose Dani or Asherley. Nor, for that matter, was I.

"Don't talk like that, Max," I said, standing up. "No one is going to jail. Dani's mother didn't win anything. You made a horrible mistake, but you didn't kill Rebekah. Everything you did was to protect Dani. You can't save Rebekah, but you *can* save Dani. She needs you here, not in jail. Let me help you. Who else knows about that night? Who else have you told?"

"Nobody. I mean, Jonah drew up the fake adoption papers, but I told them Dani's mother died of an overdose. Dani has

293

pieces of the truth, as you know. She thinks that woman was my girlfriend, something we can't disabuse her of. But last night she said she saw something in the greenhouse. And she knew to dig *right there*."

I shut my eyes. Rebekah was dead, her body a few feet from where we were sitting. This was a fact. But I was no longer afraid of her, or of his past with Rebekah, or of my future with Dani. Nothing could hurt us. I felt a rush of manic purpose. I took his hands in mine, tugging on them for emphasis.

"Listen to me very carefully. Surrendering to the police won't undo what happened, what Rebekah did, what Dani's mother did, what you did. These things are in the past. Right now, *today*, is what matters. We have each other, we love each other, Dani *will* get well. I'll do everything in my power to make sure she can put all of this behind her. But we have to do something about the . . . body. Today. Before the police *do* come back with a warrant and start poking around. Do you understand what I'm saying?"

"Yes, I do. I thought the same, but I was afraid to say it. Out loud. It's why I wanted you to go to Louisa's. I thought perhaps I could take her out past the barn—"

"No. She can't stay on the island." I had never felt more right. A plan was falling into place, *my* plan, one that would save Dani, Max, and Asherley. "No. I say we . . . we take her out on a boat, on the Aquarama. It's fast, small. It has that shallow aft."

"Yes," he said.

"It's still cold," I continued. "There won't be many boats out on the water. We'll head out past the bay—"

"No!" he said, throwing my hands off his. "Not 'we.' I've already implicated you with my confession. You will *not* be accomplice to anything worse."

"Max, you can't do it alone. You know that. You need my help. I'm strong. I'm not squeamish. I can drive. It's a fussy boat and I know how——"

"No. I can handle it. This is something I have to do alone. I can't involve you. I'd never forgive myself. I won't budge on this."

"I *want* to help."

"You want to help? Where's your phone?"

"Upstairs."

"Fine." He tapped in his password and gave me his. "Here's what you can do. Call the rental company. Tell them to come get the chairs and tables tomorrow afternoon, not today. Then call Louisa. Tell her we're coming to their house for dinner. This will stop her from checking in on us, plus if we take the boat to their house, it'll explain why I was spotted out on the water today. Then call Eli. Find out if there are any updates about the warrant or if they're just letting this go. Then call the rehab. See if Dani's okay. Find out when she's out of detox. Tell her doctor we're not mad at her for calling the police. Find out when we can visit. But before you do any of that, bring me a warm sweater and something to . . . transfer the body into. A thick blanket or something. And some belts. Nothing monogrammed. These are the things you can do for me."

While unburdening himself of these dark secrets made him seem lighter, more purposeful, I felt heavy. But it was a welcome weight, one that grounded me in my love for him, and for Dani and this place.

When I turned to leave, he grabbed my arm.

"Thank you," he said, and kissed me. "I will spend the rest of my life and the entirety of my fortune making sure you never regret loving me."

TWENTY-EIGHT

The rich have so much, but one of their most precious commodities is privacy. The gates to Asherley were closed. We were expecting no one. Max could move a body in broad daylight and not even God would be watching. We had the island to ourselves, and now, for the first time since I had arrived, I felt that I had Max to myself as well. I loved him, maybe even more so than before, because his life now depended on me and on my ability to keep all of his secrets.

With the sound of Max's shovel stabbing the dirt in the background—*tch, tch, tch*—I made the first call, postponing the table and chair pickup, citing a scheduling conflict. Then I went upstairs. I dug into Max's closet for his favorite nubby Irish sweater, smelling it. Max didn't wear cologne, but he used a velvety sandalwood soap from France that became something new on his clothes, something musky and male. I grabbed plain belts, a wool scarf. It would be cool on the water, colder still the farther out he went. The sound was about forty-five minutes from here at forty knots. I would suggest to him that he round the point at Montauk and head due southeast for another hour at least. The Aquarama could go fifty, maybe sixty knots in open water. The motor was newer. I'd tell him to drop the body in the Atlantic, not in the bay or the sound. And to watch the gas tank. I wasn't familiar with the boat so I didn't know how quickly it drained. I planned to rough out latitude and longitude points, just so I could keep track of where he was and how soon he'd return. I knew the waters around the Caymans, where to dump large fish carcasses so they didn't wash up near tourists, but I hadn't yet learned the local currents.

In lieu of a blanket for the body, I opted for the garment bag Rebekah's wedding dress had arrived in, now abandoned on a hook in my closet like a shed skin. I didn't intend irony or even poetry with this choice. The bag was sturdy and long. It had strong handles on each end and a good metal zipper. This was a practical decision. I was thinking of Max, not Rebekah.

As I lifted it off the hook, a small piece of paper wafted to the floor—a business card that must have been lodged in the clear plastic pocket. At first I thought it was the one the police officer had handed to me. But this was from a place called Hannah's Sew Fine, a seamstress with an address in Sagaponack. Ah. It must be where Dani had sent Rebekah's dress for the alterations. *I have someone good on Long Island.* I debated letting it go; there were more pressing concerns that morning. But I was also curious how she had pulled it off. Did they take my measurements from the first pinned dress? How does a fifteen-year-old girl send in a wedding dress for alterations, no questions asked of the bride herself? Surely they'd be open by now. I dialed the number.

A woman, presumably Hannah, picked up on the second ring. "Mr. Winter! So nice to see your name pop up on my screen. How did it go? Did the dress fit okay?" I went to speak but the air had completely left my lungs. "Hello? Mr. Winter? Are you there?"

"Yes. No, this is . . . this is *Mrs.* Winter," I said, my mouth dry. "I'm calling to . . . to *thank* you. For doing such good work on the dress."

"Oh, you're *so* very welcome, Mrs. Winter. You know, your husband didn't leave us a ton of time, so I couldn't do a really nice bound seam inside the bodice. I hope it wasn't too scratchy."

"No, no, it was fine," I said.

"And it fit okay?"

"Yes. It fit . . . perfectly. Thank you."

"You know, I never heard of a man surprising his wife with a wedding dress before. It was tricky to keep it from Dani, too, but it *was* the prettier dress, I must say. Man, people can be so creative nowadays. Were you surprised?"

"Yes, quite. Well, thank you again."

"Must have been so beautiful—"

I hung up. My hands were shaking.

My fear felt eviscerating, like it was turning my body inside out. Who did I marry? What else had he done? I scanned his phone in confusion, looking for something, anything strange, when I came across the Instagram app, hidden within a miscellaneous folder on his home screen. I touched the icon, and there it was, the open end of the locked @rwinterforever account, solely following Dani. Through new tears I scanned the dozens upon dozens of Rebekah pictures, and read the replies from Dani begging to know who ran this account, who was doing this to her, and why.

I dropped the phone on the floor and thought of Maggie, another crime Dani passionately denied. The bumping and crashing, the overturned tables—Max struggling to contain the kitten before he killed it. How fast he had to move knowing we were mere yards away. How easily he lied to me when he shoved me away from the door, telling the doctor that the source of Dani's distress was that gruesome discovery, telling the police the same thing this morning with such fatherly conviction he might have chased them away from Asherley for good. And how she begged me to believe her.

It was a lucky thing to find such a necessary prop at a critical moment, luckier still to have the stomach to pull it off. But a man that would kill a kitten and hang the deed on an unstable girl was nothing if not bloody-minded. He knew her mind was damaged and porous, had so little ability to discern between fantasy and reality, that she'd eventually own these crimes, too, filing them away like fresh pages of foolscap in a binder. He was tormenting his own daughter, a child. But why?

I looked around the bedroom we shared with growing revulsion, not just for Max but for myself. Everything he had told me so far had been beyond my comprehension, until it wasn't. He had justified his crimes with a story about the murderous lengths to which a father would go to protect his child, and I had joined him there, wanting to prove I was worthy of his trust, and of Dani's love. But his story was only true if Max actually loved Dani, something she denied. She *knew*. And yet how blind I was, how willfully, tragically naive. *There are things you do when you're desperate, things that would shock you.*

My awful complicity brought me to my knees. I grabbed the phone.

I had to call the police. And then what? Make a run for it? Call Dani? The police would tell me what to do. That female officer would tell me what to do. What was her name? My hands still shaking, I frantically patted my pockets for her card. It had to be somewhere. I couldn't have lost it.

I jumped when Max's phone rang in my hand, as loud and insistent as it had ever sounded. It was Elias. *I could tell him. He could call for help.*

Wait. *He's Max's "left- and right-hand man." He'd be his ally.*

I picked up on the third ring. "Elias. Hello."

"Hello there, *Mrs.* Winter. Max there?"

Could I trust him?

"He's out . . . he's out at the barns. What is it?"

"Well, listen, I have very good news. The police are not going to pursue a warrant. They're going to treat it as a private family matter this time. But I'm afraid Dani's on their radar now."

How happy this news would have made me five minutes ago.

"That's great, Elias."

"Any news on the poor kid?"

"Not yet, I'm just about to call Dr. Sherman. We're very worried about her," I said, my voice cracking. *Oh Dani.*

"She's in good hands. But I would like to talk to Max about the conservatorship when he gets back. I think, after yesterday, it might be a good idea to have a new plan in place."

"Yes, a plan. I think that's . . . a very good idea."

"I'm just being cautious. She fought it last time. But she's about to receive the first big payout from Rebekah's estate, and given yesterday, well, I can imagine how worried Max is about her having unfettered access to that fortune."

"Yes, he's very worried," I said. My mind spun at the word "conservatorship." I knew it. The pieces clicked into place and my purpose here was revealed. I was the catalyst brought in to tip his unstable daughter into madness, the most lucrative kind. I dropped the phone away from my ear, Elias's voice becoming tinny and small.

"She *knew*," I whispered.

"Who are you talking to, sweetheart?"

I whipped around. Max was standing over me in his T-shirt, now dirty, pushing the hair off his sweaty forehead.

"I came to see what was taking you so long." He looked at the detritus around me, the bag, the belts, the sweater, his phone in my hand. I could hear Elias calling my name, over and over. I opened my mouth to speak but nothing came out. Max snatched his phone back.

"Hi, Eli . . . I don't know what's wrong with her. She's in a bit of a daze. It's been a crazy twenty-four hours."

He made a funny face at me, a "what the hell?" face. As he listened to Elias, I nervously began to gather up the things he'd told me to fetch. The seamstress's card peeked out from under his sweater. I covered it with my hand, clawing up both as I stood. He kept his eyes on me as he spoke with Elias, studying my features, the way my hands shook, and the single hot tear that betrayed me as it snaked down my cheek.

"Well, thank God for that," he said. "Good, good. Listen, I'll stop by there next week and chat with the officers myself. Give them an update on Dani . . . Fair enough . . . Yes, yes, agreed, we *should* talk about that again, but not today. Thanks, buddy. Good work."

He hung up, then quickly scanned through his phone before putting it in the back pocket of his jeans. *Oh God, had I closed the Instagram app? Could he see I had made a call to the seamstress?*

His face belied nothing.

"Good news about the warrant," he said.

301

"Yes. Thank God."

"Still, we're not taking any chances. Right?"

"Right."

He looked around the room again as if someone might be hiding behind the curtains, under the bed. "Are you okay?" he asked. "You seem a little off."

"I don't know, Max. I do feel a little off," I said, my voice trembling, my eyes resisting contact with his. "Maybe everything's catching up to me."

I watched his eyes land on my own phone, charging by the nightstand. He looked back at me.

"Yes. You've taken a lot in," he said. "What did Elias tell you just now? When I walked in your face was white."

"Just about the warrant."

"And?"

Tell him what you found: the business card, the fake Rebekah account. Maybe there's a good explanation.

"He's just . . . worried about Dani, too."

He tilted his head, studying me. "You're lying to me. You're terrible at it, but you're doing it."

I glanced at my phone again. "What are you talking about?"

"My love, I don't have time to cross-examine you. Shall we head down?" He turned to leave.

My feet were stuck to the carpet.

"Max, you . . . you said you wanted to do this alone. That might be a good idea. I mean—"

"I did, didn't I? Well, it turns out it's a bigger job than I thought."

The woman I was when I'd offered to help him was gone, replaced with someone deeply aware of Max's ruthlessness.

"Well, then, I—I should grab a sweater," I said. "I'll meet you down there."

"I'll wait."

I headed to my dressing room, my heart racing so fast I thought I'd pass out. I pulled a fleece off a laundry pile and went back out to the bedroom, making a casual beeline for my phone. Max beat me to it, gently lifting it off its dock.

"I've got this. You have your hands full."

"Max, my phone." I put my hand out.

He looked at it, his eyes sad. He seemed unsure how to proceed, what to do next, how this would go. "I'll keep it safe," he said, and slid it into his other pocket. "I promise." He stood so close to me I could feel his breath on my forehead.

"Max."

"Yes, my love."

"Why?"

I already knew the answer.

He shrugged. "When you have something like this"—his arm took in the room, the house, the island itself—"you have to protect it from anyone who might destroy it. Even if it's family."

"Did you ever love me?"

He sighed deeply, then bopped me gently on the nose with the tip of his finger. "From the moment I laid eyes on you," he said. Then he glanced over my shoulder. "Oh, look at the time. Shall we?"

Without waiting for my reply he turned. I followed behind him, my vision blurring. He didn't take my hand. He stared straight ahead and walked, my jailer leading me to the gallows. We passed beneath the oily painted faces of

303

his ancestors and I finally saw these men for who they really were: pirates and criminals, men who kissed up to kings and did business in the shade. That one kept bound boys. This one fought arrows with cannons. And him, the original Lord Winter, he stole this island in exchange for blankets full of diseases he had survived. How many crimes did these men commit to keep this land? How high a price do you have to pay to earn a place on this wall? How close had I come to paying it?

Tears fell freely down my cheeks now. There was no hiding my terror. As we passed through the foyer, I eyed the gun cabinet. Were any of them loaded?

Max turned, catching the tail end of my longing gaze. The front door wasn't locked. I could make a run for it. How far could I get on foot? If I made it to the causeway, would he mow me down on that narrow road?

In the kitchen, hunger hit me hard. When had I last eaten? Was it the cold buffet? Our wedding cake? How apt.

When he opened the door of the greenhouse, the air smelled extra sweet, helped along by the flowers that still stuffed the space, clinging to life in their vases. It wasn't unpleasant, the smell, but still, I covered my nose and mouth.

Then I saw her, or what must have been her body, lying under a blue tarp. Max peeled it back.

"It's actually not that bad to look at," he said. "Turns out four feet was deep enough. And two years is plenty of time for a body to decompose. Mind you, the conditions in here were perfect. Helped to keep the door locked."

I hated how he sounded, cheerful, pleased with himself. I couldn't bear it. My legs gave way. I collapsed to my knees.

"I can't, Max. I can't look."

"Come on. An hour ago you were Lady Macbeth in there, all 'I'm not squeamish. Let's do this, we're a team.' And *now* you're choking? When I need you the *most*? You're my wife. What changed?"

"Dani!" I screamed. "Dani is what's changed! I know what you did to her, Max! The dress, that . . . that *account*. The kitten, Max. I know what you did. And I know why."

He bowed his head and closed his eyes for a moment. Then he looked at me. "Are you saying you're taking her side?"

"Side? She's your daughter! She's a kid!"

"A *kid* who has done nothing but make *our* life a living hell, don't forget! I may have set her off, but she *is* a danger to herself and others, and if I don't get a handle on that god-damn money, she'll bring it all down around her, just like her mother almost did. Christ, the both of them."

"She's a *kid*, Max," I said, still crying, pleading for him to wake up from this nightmare and become the man I knew.

He fussed with the zipper of the garment bag. "But here's the thing. She's not *my* kid. She was Rebekah's. And that was your only job, your one gift to me. That's all I wanted from you, a baby, an heir, a *real* one, so we could challenge Dani's inheritance. And in exchange, you'd get this wonderful fuck-ing life, which you're now throwing away."

His words doubled me over.

"Now what do you want from me?" I asked, terrified of the answer. I knew everything now. And he was right, I *was* on Dani's side. Which meant there was no one on mine.

He shook open the garment bag. "A little help would be nice. Oh, don't look at me like that. I didn't want to hurt Dani. I just wanted to prove she is in no way fit to inherit everything. I mean, my God, Rebekah left her *everything*. Or, rather, she left the heir to Asherley everything. And that should be *our* kid. I was hoping you'd understand that. Now let's get this done. It's not so bad, I promise you."

I sat up, wiping my nose with the back of my hand. "Are you going to kill me?"

He laughed. "I'm not a cold-blooded murderer," he said. "Everything I did, I did because I had to. And everything *we're* doing now is because *we* have to. You're in this now, too, babe. After all, the boat was your brilliant idea. Now give me a hand."

He threw back the tarp. There she lay, the woman I'd feared and loathed, her body still wrapped in its original shroud, filthy and eaten away in patches, beneath which was brown skin flaking off gray bone and tufts of her hair, dirty blond, a term I could never hear again without shuddering. Was that what Dani had seen last night? Her face was thankfully obscured by what remained of the tablecloth, the leather belts still intact. They were loose enough for us to slide our hands under and lift her into the garment bag, her bones collapsing only slightly. Max was right, she weighed very little. At the sound of the garment bag's zipper, I wanted to throw up, but there was nothing in my stomach. I closed my eyes to pray instead.

Max took the front handle of the bag, waiting for me to lift the back. "Let's go," he said. He'd already pulled the truck up to the greenhouse. We placed her on the flatbed. He escorted me to the passenger's side of the truck and we drove together to the boathouse. Max remained silent for those thirty seconds, and I sat next to him, thinking, trying not to panic.

Max's instructions were the only thing keeping my limbs from turning to silt. Winch the boat down onto the slip, he said, while I unload the body. I did. Pull back the aft cover, would you, love? I did so as he carefully lay her down across the back of the Aquarama. Get some kettlebells for me, please. I grabbed two from the gym on the riser. Where are those belts? I handed them over. He looped the new belts through the handles of the kettlebells and cinched them tight around the outside of the garment bag. As he pulled, the plastic crinkled and I could sense the gathering of her bones. He covered her body back up with the boat tarp, instructing me again to help him snap it down until she lay flat. When we finished, I placed my hand on the bump and said something to the effect of "please forgive me." Release the boat, he said, and with a turn of the winch, *Dani's Luck* slid elegantly into the water, barely making a splash.

He handed me the keys. "You drive. It'll be like the old days."

I slapped the keys away.

"Get in the boat."

"I'm not going with you, Max."

He stood seething, uncertain. I knew if I got on that boat, he would kill me, I would become another luckless casualty in Max Winter's storied life. His bride of one day, an experienced boater, no less, lost at sea, presumed dead.

"Get in."

"No. When you come back, I will be gone and you'll never hear from me again."

I turned to leave. He hooked his hand around the back of my head and yanked me close to his face. "Get. In. The. Fucking. Boat."

I stiffened, my feet welded to the dock. He grabbed a fistful of my hair and pulled me towards the Aquarama. I began to scream, a pathetic howl that bounced around inside the cavernous boathouse. I had done this to myself, I thought. I crossed a line with him, never thinking there'd be another line awaiting me, then this final one, barbed and vicious. But still I fought him hard, resisted him with all my youth and terror, twisting like a cat in his grip, kicking and spinning. Then a loud crack echoed through the boathouse, and my legs gave out beneath me.

I thought the sound had come from above us, that when I hit the back of my head on the dock, one of the beams had fallen on top of me. My ears rang with a high-pitched scream, not mine. I tried to lift my head but it felt weighted down by a sticky, dull ache. Craning my neck, I could make out Max in silhouette, coming at me. He stepped over my body, muttering, "Jesus Christ, Dani."

Dani? NO! Get out of here!

Then I found something in me, a drop of adrenaline, enough to roll myself onto an elbow. There stood Dani in sweats and a wrinkly shirt, hair a wicked fright. Her tiny arm shook as she pointed her too-big gun at her own father. I lifted my hand, a weak, useless stop sign.

She shot at him again—*crack*. This time he caught the bullet in his shoulder and he pivoted, like a fierce, awkward dance move that stilled him only for a moment. Then he wound himself up again, unwrapping the rope from the Aquarama. He limped aboard as a bloody star spread fast across his upper chest.

"I'm sorry, baby," he yelled, starting up the engine. "But I really have to go now."

Dani stepped closer to me, taking shaky aim over my body. Though my vision was blurred, I saw her wet cheeks, her quivering chin. I heard another crack. If she hit him, Max didn't flinch. He simply circled the steering wheel with a finger, sweeping an arch of water out of his way. Then he was off, *Dani's Luck* lifting like a swan about to go airborne, churning the black bay into a long white arrow in its wake.

TWENTY-NINE

For the longest time I could not cry, something I blamed on the concussion, along with the fact that I couldn't recall if I'd actually seen Dani leave the boathouse with the gasoline that she used to burn Asherley down to the ground. I wasn't lying by omission, or to protect Dani. She denied nothing, her reason for the fire particularly poignant.

"He killed my kitten. So I burned his fucking house down," she said, an alarmingly reasonable explanation that still landed her in a New York hospital for a month of psychiatric evaluations, to determine what, if any, charges should be laid.

Very little of the contents of Asherley was salvageable, beyond a couple of marble busts, some silver frames, and several pieces of heirloom jewelry locked away in a fireproof safe that Dani had no knowledge of until everything around it blackened and fell away. To this day it moves me that amidst her fiery rampage, Dani thought to bring me ice cradled in a tea towel for the back of my bleeding head. While the flames took hold, she sat next to me on the woodpile, lit a cigarette, and apologized for wanting to wait until the second floor caught fire before she called an ambulance.

"I want it all to come down, so we can never come back here again," she said.

We held hands and watched the flames take everything except for Rebekah's greenhouse. The glass panels directly attached to the house were stained with licks of smoke, but otherwise the structure remained undamaged.

We heard the sirens before we saw the lights. The two officers who had come earlier that morning got out of their car and separated us. (Thinking back now, those few hours, each of us telling them our own version of events, might have been the longest we spent away from each other for the better part of the year.)

At that point, I wasn't yet aware how Dani had arrived at Asherley that morning. She was always doing that, taking off, running to and from places. So I assumed she had just walked out of detox and got into a cab. Later, when they reunited us, she told me Gus had picked her up and taken her as far as the gate, unable to drive any farther because Max had changed the security code. Dani assured him she could walk from there, afraid to get Gus into more trouble than she already had. When she heard me screaming in the boathouse, she said she knew Max would kill me, and she took her target practice gun from the cabinet in the anteroom. I tried to imagine being a fifteen-year-old girl, running towards a murderous scream with a gun I intended to use, and I could not. Dani Winter became the bravest person I had ever known.

Dani hadn't come to Asherley that day to kill her father. She only intended to quit rehab, pack her stuff, and flee to Louisa's pied-à-terre until the first big chunk of her inheritance came through on her sixteenth birthday. She said an image had resurfaced, one so disturbing that even drugs could no longer blot it out. The image was of her father in the greenhouse, rolling a blanket into a shallow grave, a tuft of Rebekah's unmistakable blond hair jutting out from one end. She remembered it the way Max had told me it happened. So we concluded that Dani had stumbled downstairs before the tranquilizer Max had laced her water with had taken full effect. That image became buried in a watery dream she'd have for months after Rebekah's death, one that eventually dissolved, until the day they discovered me in the greenhouse with Maggie and everything flooded back to her: the heat, the other woman, the fight, the car speeding off, Max's visit to Dani's bedside, Dani creeping downstairs in a semi-drugged state in time to see her father bury Rebekah's body in a hole he'd dug in the ground. When I told her, in a quiet moment, who that other woman really was, that she was not a lover but her birth mother, a young, troubled woman who had come to Asherley looking for her, Dani wilted in my arms.

"My mother," she cried, inconsolably. "She came for me. She loved me."

"Yes, she did," I said, stroking her dirty hair. "She loved you very much."

"He killed everyone who ever loved me."

"No, he didn't," I said. "Not everyone."

There was one place where our stories didn't dovetail, didn't knit themselves into one cohesive narrative. I was certain Max had told me he had gone upstairs twice that night, the first time to check on Dani, giving Dani's mother the opportunity to lunge at Rebekah with the shears. The second time it was to drug Dani back to sleep so he could deal with the aftermath of Rebekah's murder and the fatal car accident. But Dani was certain he'd come upstairs only once, which, in her version of events, put Max in the greenhouse when Rebekah died, and who murdered her in doubt. He had, after all, more reason to kill Rebekah than Dani's mother did.

Rebekah's fatal error had been leaving the entirety of her fortune to Dani, and Max was running out of money, hence no prenup. He didn't want me to see there was really nothing to divvy up in the event of a divorce. His fake Instagram account primed the pump of Dani's instability. The dress swap provided a breakdown both public and indisputable. Dani couldn't damage Max's reputation by loudly contesting a conservatorship this time. Everyone who mattered, who might affect his reputation, or his reelection, saw plainly that Dani was unhinged, maybe even dangerous, and that poor Max, a loving, caring father, was just trying to get on with his life.

Though I believed Dani, there was no way to prove Max murdered Rebekah. So it remained a theory, but one to which Gus adhered because, he said, Dani's mother was not capable of violence. He knew this, he said, because she was his older sister. This news was both shocking and welcome. In fact, the picture Max had found on his wall was of his sister as a child, not Dani, though the resemblance was uncanny. Gus admitted that he only ever took the job at Asherley because he knew his sister had left Dani there. So for years he kept one eye on his niece and the other on the long driveway in case she returned, not believing, like his family in Bethpage, that she was dead. He told us her name and talked about her hopes and dreams, painting a picture of a complicated young woman who was much more than just the cartoonish junkie Max described. The biggest regret of his life, he said, was staying away that hot night, when Rebekah had insisted. She knew Dani's mother was coming by for what she thought would be another payout, one she was willing to make, even if Max was not.

Some of these things I learned firsthand, some through bits and pieces I read online, because ours was a story that had captured the world's attention, everyone being sick to death of politics that year. I learned new things, too, about Rebekah that were contrary to everything Max had said. She was, according to most reports, an excellent mother, and I began to believe this, because Dani believed it. Maybe children's memories are pliable, but their feelings aren't. Dani told me she felt loved by Rebekah, deeply, she said, so therefore she was.

After those first few days of questioning, when we were finally alone, surrounded by flowers and food left for us by Louisa, whom we did not wish to see, we looked at each other for a long time.

"Thank you," I finally said, kissing her hand. I was out of words. I had only feelings left, and the strongest one was of gratitude for this remarkable girl.

"I'm sorry about Daddy," she whispered. "I had to."

"Yes, you did," I said, nodding vigorously.

And then she cried and cried, and made me promise to never leave her alone. So when Dani wasn't talking to her doctor or spending time with Claire, to whom she had apologized, she was with me, reading, listening to music, watching TV, or walking around in a circle holding my arm until she was tired enough to fall asleep.

Six days passed before the coast guard found *Dani's Luck*, empty, capsized, out of gas, and gently turning in a natural whirlpool four hundred miles southeast of Montauk. By then I had been discharged and was staying at a hotel near Dani's hospital, selected because its underground garage allowed me to avoid the press gathered in the lobby. Having no social media profile, a good photo of "the second Mrs. Winter," as I would come to be known, fetched top dollar. Some even called down to the Caymans, offering a lot of money for my staff picture. Laureen Ennis told them to bugger off.

"I said, you got nothing better to do than harass a young widow after her husband tried to murder her, you fucking vultures? Go fuck yourselves, I said."

If you had told me four months after I slammed the door of her shabby office that Laureen Ennis would drop everything and fly to New York to help me, and that I would fall into her arms when I saw her, I'd have laughed and laughed. But she remained by my side the whole time I was admitted for the concussion, alternating from my room to Dani's until Dani was transferred.

The first thing Laureen said to me was, "Jesus Christ, I figured he'd be a difficult man, but I had no idea."

She was also in my room when a nurse, who had assumed Laureen was my mother, told me I was pregnant.

"Well," Laureen said, patting my hand, "you have options, you know. The fascists haven't taken that one away yet."

Laureen took a suite next to mine at the hotel. Every morning, during the weeks they kept Dani under observation, I could hear her yell at whomever she had left in charge of her boats, or anyone else trying to contact me for an exclusive interview. She brought me food and took away the papers. Elias wrote me to say he'd had no idea Max was so deranged; he truly thought a conservatorship was in Dani's best interests and was mortified to be implicated in the crime. Still, he lost his license to practice law, as did Jonah.

It took them twenty-one days to come to the conclusion that Dani Winter wasn't mentally ill, that she was guilty only of behavior endemic to any teenager insidiously gaslighted by her father, with access to too much money and unsupervised time. A judge determined that she was to be released under my supervision. I was made her legal conservator until she turned eighteen, after which they'd reevaluate. Dani agreed, teasing that this would make me her paid companion, despite the small fortune she insisted on bequeathing me once she decided to sell the island. Originally she had offered to split her half of the proceeds with me, the other half going to Louisa, a notion I found absurd. We compromised on a trust fund for the baby and enough money to open a boat-refurbishing business back in the Caymans, next to Laureen's marina.

Moving to the Caymans that coming winter, buying a house near Laureen's in time to have the baby, these were Dani's ideas. They had become surprisingly smitten with each other, Dani often typing Laureen's most memorable quotes into her phone to giggle over later with Claire. She wanted to learn everything there was to know about boats and fishing and running a business. But first we wanted to be on the move for a while, our travel plans unfolding organically.

Barcelona was the first stop in our beautiful exile, a place I loved the best. The food, the sea, the walking, all of it a necessary palliative. After a few weeks in the city we drove up the coast, rented a cliffside house with a red-tiled roof where we passed the rest of spring, which, we were told, was unseasonably cold for Spain.

After that we flew to Prague for a week of museums and music, then Italy for the rest of the summer and early fall. We shopped in Rome, loading up on summer clothes, bigger tops for me, bikinis and books for Dani. Then we hired a driver to take us along the Amalfi Coast, where another house and another season, this one hot and slow, awaited us. We read a lot, trying to avoid news from back home.

I remained anonymous, which made moving around easier for me than Dani, something she eventually came to envy. One day, while I waited for her at a café in Positano, a young woman with tanned skin and short brown hair plunked down next to me, chin in hand, grinning.

It took me a second to recognize her.

"Oh my God, Dani!" I said, touching her silky bangs. "Look at you."

"What do you think?" she asked, an uncertain hand pulling the baby hairs at the back of her neck. "I think it makes me look more like you."

"It's beautiful," I said, tearing up at her wide-open face. "But I think you look like you."

Louisa wrote us, asking to meet us. She was going through her own complicated grieving process; she loved her brother, after all, and, of course, Asherley. She'd lost much that day, too. Though the investigation cleared her of any wrongdoing, Dani remained skeptical, worried that if her father were alive somehow and on the run, Louisa would be the only one in touch with him. She agreed to see Louisa so long as we didn't divulge which hotel we were staying in and met in a public place.

When I saw her, however, I knew instantly that Louisa was our friend.

"My dear," she said, her warm eyes taking in my face, her hand on my growing belly. "I am beyond happy to see you."

By dinner Dani's doubts had disappeared, and she happily resumed gossiping with her aunt, showing her pictures of Spain and the road trip to Positano on her new—private—Instagram account. The next morning, side by side on beach chairs, swathed in sunblock and sunglasses, my growing belly under a towel, Louisa and I watched, with a mix of pride and trepidation, as Dani and a friend turned heads in the shallow waves, as sixteen-year-old girls in tiny bikinis do. Some invisible magnet would always pull Dani towards another easily bored princess type, a Brit or an American, with excellent manners and casual disdain for the adults who spoiled her. Sometimes, once they figured out who she was, what she'd done, and what had been done to her, they'd either retreat or get way too close, forcing Dani to eventually cut them loose. She navigated these relationships with the savvy granted to those who've gone through hell and come out the other end not giving a damn what anyone thinks.

That night, waiting for Dani to join us for dinner, I asked Louisa something to which I wasn't sure I wanted the answer.

"Do you think that he ever loved me?"

She squinted into the sunset. "He loved you as much as he was capable of loving anyone, I suppose."

"That's not very comforting."

"It's the truth."

"What about Dani? Did he love her?"

"I don't think so," she lamented. Then she pointed to my belly. "But he'd have been monstrously in love with this one."

"Old Dani might not have liked that," I said.

"True," Louisa said, tilting her glass towards me. "So here's to big and small mercies."

Before I became too pregnant to fly, or the weather turned cold, we returned to the Caymans. There was paperwork to do on the sale of the clubhouses, and bank transfers from the sale of the island, an inconceivable amount of money coming in from a numbered company out of Germany. Louisa posited the buyers were Russian or Chinese. Either way, they offered far above the asking price, making it impossible to turn their offer down.

Three weeks before the baby was due, I had an overwhelming desire to find my grandmother, who had sent my mother to live with her American father after the Cuban revolution left her with nothing. Dani, of course, came with me. We disembarked at the marina, where a car waited to take us to an apartment on the Malecón, one belonging to an old lover of Laureen's. We took a walk through Old Havana. Down a narrow alley, with Dani stopping every ten feet to take a picture, I swear I saw him, Max, ducking into a doorway. He was wearing a wide-brimmed hat and had that familiar set to his mouth. I had a sudden sense that the buildings were closing in on me, the deep-set windows above looking like the hooded eyes of Asherley. But when the man stepped back out into the street, I saw that he was just a man, a tourist like us, exploring the square on a beautiful day. No matter how often the coast guard assured us that Max couldn't have run out of gas that far out and survived, until there was a body, a part of me did not believe he was dead. I didn't alarm Dani with this vision, but she sensed a change in my energy and found me a place to sit and something cold to drink.

That evening I had the dream again, the one in which I watch with terror as Rebekah leaves Max's side to wade towards me in the bay. It's dusk. Asherley is lit from within by a hundred yellow lamps. Dani swims nearby, oblivious in the shallow waves. Rebekah inches her face towards mine, seemingly to kiss me before she kills me, like she always does. She plunges me beneath the wave, and I fight her, like I always do. But this time it's not Rebekah holding me down. It's Max. And I am no longer a boneless reed, helpless and flailing. Now my body feels young and angry. I push to the surface with all my strength and some of Rebekah's, too, for she is no longer my nemesis. She seems to form a part of me, has wrapped herself around my muscles and bones, Max no match for the two of us.

I woke up with that familiar catch in my throat, a longing, but not for the man who had almost killed me. Max had become two men to me, the one I met on my island, and the one who took me to live with him on his. That made it possible for me to mourn him, something that came easier than forgiveness, especially for myself. One day Dani would ask me why I'd been willing, at first, to keep Max's secret about who that woman was who came to Asherley, and to help him move her beloved mother's body. I only hoped they'd surface after Dani fell in love with someone who made her behave in ways she didn't recognize in herself, so that when I told her, *I would have done it for you, to keep your father out of jail*, she'd understand. And while this would be true, I would have also done it for myself. I had tried to leave once, but as time passed it had become impossible for me to imagine leaving Asherley again, or its lifelong comforts. I'd known poverty, the droning uncertainty of it all, and I could no longer go back to it. So I would have done anything to remain at Asherley, to be with Max, shuddering to think how close I had come to dying with his lies inside of me.

But these questions would come later. For now, I was happy to be sitting in Plaza de la Catedral with Dani, watching the sun pinken the sky, knowing my only job was to finish raising her not to be like that, like me. I didn't know what lay ahead for us, or that the next day I would find my grandmother, and that she would put her hand on my belly and she would tell me she was sure I was having a girl, and that I'd see my own mother's face in hers and I would finally be able to cry.

ACKNOWLEDGMENTS

Much thanks to Kristin Cochrane (that lunch!), Amy Black, Martha Leonard, Val Gow, Tonia Addison, Emma Ingram, Melanie Tutino, and everyone at Penguin Random House Canada, especially my smart, sensitive editors, Kiara Kent at Doubleday Canada and Sarah Stein at Viking, who helped bring this book over the finish line. Thank you also to Sara Leonard, Rebecca Marsh, Lindsay Prevette, Andrea Schulz, Kate Stark, Mary Stone, Brian Tart, Megan Gerrity, Allison Carney, Linda Friedner, Shannon Kelly, and everyone at Viking for believing in this book.

So grateful to Christy Fletcher, and everyone at Fletcher and Co., chiefly Grainne Fox and Veronica Goldstein, Melissa Chincillo, Erin McFadden, and Sarah Fuentes. Susan Gabriele, Sarah Durning, Meredith Oke, and Vanessa Campion read very early drafts and made me want to finish faster. Cathie James and Katrina Onstad offered valuable notes, as always, and Lisa Laborde helped me avoid legal plot holes.

Kathryn Meyers Emery, PhD in Mortuary Archeology, generously replied to my science-related queries about dead bodies and shallow graves. Suffolk County Historical Society Museum has a trove on the history of Gardiners Island off

Long Island. I borrowed some of that island's storied past and topography to inform my fictional one. Finally, my late mother, Joanne Gabriele, introduced me to the works of Daphne du Maurier, something for which I'll be forever grateful.

Lisa Gabriele is the author of several bestselling novels. Her writing has appeared in *Glamour, Vice, Elle*, the *New York Times Magazine* and *Salon* as well as various anthologies, including *The Best American Nonrequired Reading* series. An award-winning TV producer, she has lived in Washington, DC, and New York City, and now lives in Toronto.